the
WRONG KIND
of WEIRD

the WRONG KIND *of* WEIRD

JAMES RAMOS

inkyard PRESS

ISBN-13: 978-1-335-42858-5

The Wrong Kind of Weird

Copyright © 2023 by James Ramos

For questions and comments about the quality of this book, please contact us at CustomerService@Harlequin.com.

Inkyard Press
22 Adelaide St. West, 41st Floor
Toronto, Ontario M5H 4E3, Canada
www.InkyardPress.com

Printed in U.S.A.

For all the Geeks, all the Nerds, and all the Dorks.

CHAPTER ONE

"It's a simple, undeniable truth," Jocelyn said matter-of-factly, "if you watch dubbed anime instead of subbed anime, you are garbage."

She flicked her hot-pink hair as she leaned over the 3D printer, which was about two-thirds of the way through making the barrel of her buster rifle.

"Bullshit," D'Anthony fired back from the beanbag he was lounging in. He licked his lips and pushed his glasses back into place without looking up from his Game Boy Color, the one he'd borrowed (or perhaps stolen) from one of his older brothers. He'd been on this vintage game kick for the past few months; he was working his way through *Pokémon Yellow* now. "Watching subbed anime doesn't make you more sophisticated, it just makes you more pretentious."

I glanced at my phone for about the eighth time since Jocelyn and D'Anthony had started their argument five minutes ago. Those two were always bickering about something; their tastes were what you could call diametrically opposed, especially when it came to anime. Ordinarily it was my job to end the debate by choosing a side, but right now I was too preoccupied to keep up.

Still no messages.

I set my phone down on the table in front of me, screen down, and started thumbing through my worn copy of *Trigun*, a space Western about a legendary peace-loving sharpshooter set in a semi-dystopian future. It was one of my favorite manga, but right now I couldn't even concentrate enough to read the words.

From 1:15 in the afternoon until 2:10, the third-floor tech lab belonged to G.A.N.U.—Geeks and Nerds United, Hilltop High School's one and only nerd culture club. Jocelyn, D'Anthony, and I were its founding members. The room was a makerspace, the walls lined with workbenches, the interior dotted with hexagonal workstations and multicolored stools, chairs, and beanbags. There were a pair of 3D printing machines in the back, where Jocelyn had set up shop. The wall next to the door was a projection dry-erase board.

The text I was waiting for should have come by now, and I was only growing more anxious by the minute. I closed my book and checked my phone again.

"Hey, Cam, are you alright?" asked Jocelyn. "You look like you need to take a shit."

The pink hair was new for her. Up until last week it had been cotton candy blue. Her look lately was what she called "Kawaii Wednesday Addams"—today she wore black overall shorts and a floral print high-collared shirt. She was hardly five feet tall, but her chunky black boots gave her an extra four inches of height, not that she needed it. She had one of those personalities where she just seemed taller, somehow.

"You do seem a little keyed up," D'Anthony added, again, without looking up from his Game Boy. He was a firm believer in the fact that high school was not a fashion show and that he wasn't here to impress anyone, and so he usually opted for comfort, like rugby shirts and old skate shoes. Although, he always had a pick with him to maintain his immaculate afro.

"I'm fine," I said.

I hated lying to my friends, but this wasn't something they'd understand.

The PA system crackled, and Principal Standish's nasally voice rattled through the speakers. "Good afternoon, Hilltop Hawks!" he proclaimed. "I want to wish everyone a safe and happy Friday. Get out there and enjoy this beautiful weather before the snow hits. And now, just a quick message from our student council president, Karla Ortega."

I released my viselike grip on my phone. That explained that, at least.

"Hey, everyone," Karla said in her usual chipper voice, "just a few quick reminders. Yearbook Committee starts at the end of the month. Seniors, it's time to start thinking about your senior pictures." She paused between sentences, and you could feel the smile she punctuated them with. "Also, if you've got an idea for a superlative, be ready to turn it in to any member of the committee or student council. We love to hear from you." Another smile. "Lastly, this year's winter production is Jane Austen's classic, *Pride and Prejudice*. If you'd like to be considered for a role, auditions begin Monday after school in the auditorium and will be held until that Friday. Thanks, guys, and have a great weekend!"

"Ugh. *Karla*," Jocelyn muttered. "Could she be any more fake? And did you guys see what she was wearing today? Those tights, and that *skirt*? She's definitely appealing to a very specific demographic ever since she won the election."

"What, the every-allosexual-person-ever demographic?" D'Anthony laughed. "Yeah, of course I saw her. She's living, breathing fan-service, and that's *why* she won the election. Hell, I voted for her and I don't even like her. I may not care for sex, but I do understand sex appeal. Sometimes. I think."

"Guys, can we not?" I groaned. "Gross."

"Right, I forgot, Cam *hates* Karla," Jocelyn said teasingly.

"Remind me again what you have against art?" D'Anthony asked with a smirk.

If there was one thing those two could agree on, it was teasing me about Karla. They liked to do this bit anytime she came up in conversation or in real life, and seeing as she was Hilltop High School's premier golden girl, she came up a lot. "I don't hate her," I explained for about the thousandth time. "I just don't see the hype. Yeah, sure, she's good-looking—"

"Understatement," Jocelyn interjected.

"*But*, people act like she walks on water when she totally doesn't. Not to mention, she's super conceited. Every year she gets more and more selective about who she deigns to speak to."

"Maybe because everybody she speaks to is trying to jump her sexy bones," Jocelyn pointed out.

I scoffed, but before I could respond the door burst open, and Mackenzie Briggs sauntered in like a cowboy stepping into a saloon. "Sorry I'm late," she announced in a tone that made it clear she was not at all sorry. She dumped her back-pack on the ground, slumped into a chair at the workstation across from mine, and kicked her feet up. "What's up, dork?"

That part was directed specifically at me.

Mackenzie had transferred to Hilltop High from some art magnet in Minneapolis, which, if you asked me, was an egregious error on the part of her parents, her advisers, and who-ever else was involved in making that decision.

"Hello, Mackenzie," I said coolly. "I see you got dressed in the dark again."

It could very well have been true, that or she just threw on the first thing she yanked out of her closet. Today she had on high-top red Converse, green camo pants, a black hoodie, and a weathered jean jacket. She looked like a home-less hipster.

She sat up, curling her legs underneath her, and sniffed the air. "Hey, Cameron, did you know you're supposed to wear your deodorant, not eat it? It works better that way. Although, with all the shit you talk I guess you could do both."

I closed my book and set it down.

Here's the thing. I did not like Mackenzie. I didn't like her big curly hair or her pointy nose or the way the edges of her lips were always curled just enough that she looked like she was smiling at some secret joke and you were the punch line. I didn't like the languid, I'm-so-over-it way she walked, like she was so much cooler than everyone else, and even though she was sort of G.A.N.U.'s fourth ranger, floating in and out of our meetups whenever she felt like it, she made no secret of the fact that she didn't like me, either.

"Wait a second," I said. "*You* know what deodorant is? That's strange—do you put yours on before or after bathing in the blood of innocent virgins?"

"If I bathed in the blood of virgins, I would have killed you for yours a long time ago."

"Goddamn," Jocelyn said under her breath.

"Flawless victory," D'Anthony added.

My phone finally buzzed. I snatched it off the table faster than I should have.

Meet at our spot? XOXO

Fucking *finally*.

I was up before I'd finished reading the text. "We're still on for movie night tonight, aren't we?" I asked as I made for the door.

"I'm busy tonight," Mackenzie said.

"No one cares. You never show up anyway."

"Where are *you* going?" Jocelyn asked, eyeing me suspiciously.

"I, um, gotta take a shit."

"Gross," Mackenzie said, but I hardly heard her, because I was already halfway out the door.

The only two things you needed to know about Hilltop High School were:

1. The school was not, as its name implied, on a hill. If anything it was a knoll, and barely that.

2. From above (or on any campus map) the school, with
    its rectangular main building that connected to a pair
    of smaller, circular buildings, looked like a giant penis.
    It was common to hear someone say they had to get to
    their class in the shaft, or to meet up on the third floor
    of the southeast testicle—much to the consternation of
    our principal and the handful of teachers who didn't have
    a sense of humor.

The tech lab was near the base of the shaft, south of the
gymnasium. I headed south, through the enclosed breezeway
that connected the dick and the balls, then hit the stairwell
and descended to the basement level, where the lights were
dim and the air was always just a little dank, and it usually
smelled like cheese and old socks. I made my way deeper into
the bowels of the building. That's where the old library was.
It hadn't seen much use since the new media center had been
built; the stacks were covered in dust and the old reference
books on them were ratty and moth-ridden. But I couldn't
wait to get there. Each step I took sent a surge of electricity
coursing through me, and I was drawn like a magnet toward
my destination, and who was meeting me there.

I meant what I'd said about Karla. Thing is, Karla's crowd
and my crowd didn't exactly mix. Her friends were the over-
achievers. Student government types, theater snobs, the kids
who thought they were better than everyone else because
they could quote Shakespeare and had perfect 4.0 GPAs and
took AP courses. It was a very exclusive club, almost like a
cult, or a hive mind, where who your friends were, who you
dated, and who you were seen with were all dictated by the

group. Karla wasn't mean, per se, not like some of the others, but if you weren't part of the group she was happy to pretend you didn't exist.

Which was why I still had no idea why we had been hooking up since this summer.

CHAPTER TWO

A little bit about Karla.

When she was six years old she'd been voted cutest toddler at the Hennepin County Fair. At fourteen she'd been crowned Junior Ms. Robbinsdale at Whiz Bang Days. She was a varsity cheerleader, she ran cross-country track, and had set a state record in the pole vault last year. She had never had a bad hair day (it was a long-standing rumor that she woke up at three in the morning each and every day just to style it). It had once been rumored that a kiss from Karla was enough to induce a seizure, and that this was allegedly what had sent Scott Foreman, the guy she'd been dating up until the second week of freshman year, to the hospital after he'd had a grand mal seizure in the front foyer.

These were all things I'd heard about her before I'd ever even seen her.

I first met Karla in the ninth grade, when by sheer coincidence Ms. Lola assigned me to sit behind her in English class. After about ten minutes of staring at the back of her head she had suddenly turned around, flashed one of her ultrabright you're-going-to-remember-this-for-the-rest-of-your-life smiles, and said, "Hi, I'm Karla, what's your name?"

"Cameron," I'd said, completely and truly starstruck.

"Nice to meet you, Cameron."

Those eleven words were the first and only words Karla said to me that year. I still couldn't recall much else about that day, and she, being Karla Ortega, probably forgot about the whole exchange the second class let out. But I never did.

She was what one might call "sun-kissed." Like, if Kryptonians were real, and they drew their power and vitality from the sun, they would probably look like she did. She just had this glow, this indiscernible *something* that drew people to her. She was hot, as D'Anthony would and frequently did say, but there was a warmth to her, too. She really was the star around which the entire student body orbited, and she was a hypervelocity star, always moving faster than anyone else around her. Her campaign blitzkrieg had earned her the position of senior class president in what had to have been the most lopsided election in the history of democracy, and it was common now to see her flitting through the halls, smiling and waving at people as she blew past. It was a fitting role, since like most politicians she was ridiculously charismatic. When she spoke to you, she made you feel like you were the center of the universe, but just like she could crank the charm up to eleven, she could switch it off just as quickly, leaving you to fade back into obscurity. Many a poor soul had lost their way chasing her glow, but I liked to think I wasn't that stupid. If she was the star we all orbited, I might as well have been Pluto. A happy, contented Pluto who didn't mind his cold, lonely corner of the solar system.

The library was tucked away so that you could only get to it if you were looking for it, like a cursed temple, and making a trip to the library was like visiting a tomb, or some other ancient location that could be a set piece in an Indiana Jones movie. *Cameron Carson and the Cave of Relics*, a B movie made on a shoestring budget, premiering on the SYFY channel right after the latest *Sharknado* sequel. And just like a cursed temple or a tomb, very few people wanted to be there, which made it the perfect place to be when you didn't want to be seen.

Karla was already waiting for me next to a stack of outdated textbooks and dusty encyclopedias, casually flipping through a copy of Ursula K. Le Guin's *The Left Hand of Darkness*, and looking for all the world like the galaxy's sexiest librarian in her gray pencil skirt and dark nylons. That had become something of a uniform for her these days, now that she was president, instead of her usual rotation of assorted leggings and hoodie combo (on cheer practice days), her oversize sweaters and jeans (my personal favorite), or the time-tested flannel. Not that I paid attention to those sorts of things. At least, I hadn't used to. This past summer had changed all that.

I understood now what Jocelyn and D'Anthony had been talking about.

I still couldn't figure out why we did this, why it had happened that first time. Maybe she'd been bored. Maybe she lost a bet. Whatever the reason was, it didn't matter.

She marked her place and closed the book when she saw me, and wordlessly crashed into me like a rogue wave, like a force of nature, one who smelled like Victoria's most secret secret and tasted like cotton candy lip gloss. I may not have understood the why, but I very clearly understood that we weren't here to talk, we weren't here as friends, and we definitely weren't here for questions. To anyone else at this school, Karla and I were oil and water—we didn't mix. My friends couldn't stand her crowd, and her crowd pretended my friends and I didn't exist—but right here, right now, none of that mattered. This time was ours and ours alone, and there was no thought, only the heat of her breath and the taste of her tongue dancing with mine. The pinprick pressure of her fingers kneading my shoulder blades. The weight of her body as she rolled and rocked against me. Buttons coming undone, clasps unhooking, we found each other beneath our clothes. She trailed her fingers down my chest, and I felt the smile on her lips when I shuddered. My right hand slid beneath her bra and cupped the warm mound of her breast, and she sucked in a sharp breath and sighed with her lips at my ear.

"Wait."

I jerked both hands away, holding them up, palms out. "Sorry! Did I do something wrong?"

"No," she breathed. Her face was flushed, and the look in her eyes made me dizzy. She took a few more deep breaths and licked her lips. "I just…" She sighed and ran her hands through her messy hair. "I think it's time."

I shook my head. "Time for what?"

She smiled and bit her lip. "You know what."

I did. In the animal part of my brain. The logical part was having trouble accepting it.

"Wait, you *are* a virgin, aren't you?"

"Yeah. I mean, *no*," I blurted, too quickly. "I mean, yeah, totally a virgin. Are *you* a virgin?"

She laughed. "Does that surprise you? I think I might be offended."

"I didn't mean it like that. I just…" I stopped short of telling her how often her ex bragged about all the ridiculous sex they had when they were together. I should've known it was bullshit—a lot of what he described sounded like a play-by-play of some porno, and some of it wasn't even physically possible. I guess I just assumed they'd done it at some point along the way.

Here's the thing.

My mom was an RN, and a firm believer in health awareness, whether it was mental, physical, or sexual health. *Especially* sexual health. *I've met too many grown folks too timid to say the word penis or vagina*, she liked to remind my older sister and me. "Too many pregnant young women who didn't think they could get pregnant if they did it standing up, or on a full moon, or some other nonsense. That kind of ignorance is dangerous, and I won't abide by it in my home." Which was why she'd given me my first birds and bees talk when I was twelve—complete with photos and diagrams—and a refresher course just before I started high school. Those lessons held the top number one and two spots on my all-time most cringeworthy experiences list. But I knew how sex worked, probably better than a lot of people. How to properly put on a condom, the anatomy of a vagina, consent… Mom was very thorough. And my family wasn't religious, so I didn't have any moral compunctions about having sex before marriage. I just never in a million years would have thought that my first time would be with Karla of all people. That had to be the dream of at least 80 percent of the population at this school, and yet...

"Can I get back to you on that?" I asked.

A look of surprise flashed across her face, but she smoothed it over with a grin. "I'm not used to being told no. Not that I want to pressure you, or anything. I just figured..."

"Figured what?" That I'd jump on this one-in-a-million chance like some sort of horny kangaroo? "I mean, what are we doing? This whole thing? Where is this going?"

"Come on, Cameron," she said quietly. "You know how it is. You know how this works."

Yeah. I did. There were rules, after all. And we were breaking them.

We stood there, at the impasse, until her phone went off, *conveniently*, the chorus of Billie Eilish's "You Should See Me in a Crown" reverberating through the tomb-like silence that had enveloped us.

"Shit! Thought I put that on vibrate." She snatched her purse off the ground and rummaged through it until she found and silenced her phone. She stared at the screen, brows puckered in a cute little frown.

"Everything okay?" I asked carefully, cautiously, as if my words might ruin the fragile magic we'd woven here. But that spell had already been broken.

"I have to go—we have a pre-production meeting tonight."

I forgot Karla was involved with the play. She was the assistant director, "putting out the fires Mrs. Vernon doesn't have time to address," as she put it. She shook her forty-dollar lip gloss from her purse. I only knew it cost forty dollars because Jocelyn had gone on a ten-minute rant about it. "That shit's Yves Saint Laurent! Who the fuck needs Yves Saint Laurent *lip gloss*? And it's *nude*! Gratuitous, is what that is." I still didn't quite grasp the significance of any of that, but I knew enough to know that Karla was low-key extra.

She used the mirror on her phone to apply the gloss, rearrange her hair, and button up her blouse. Somehow, in seconds she'd done away with the hookup hair and was back to the prim and proper librarian aesthetic. "Look," she said as she slung her purse over her shoulder. "I'll… We'll… I'll see you." She paused just long enough to smooth out her skirt one last time, and then she was gone.

"No, you won't," I said to no one in particular. She never saw me. Not out there.

"These violent delights have violent ends." Shakespeare wrote that. *Romeo and Juliet*. Not a huge fan. I only knew that because we'd spent an entire semester of English lit analyzing that stupid play. He had a point, though.

Whatever this thing was between Karla and me, it was weird. And it was wrong, probably, on at least three different levels. I shouldn't have gone along with it, but it was Karla Ortega, and no sane person would turn down something like this. Someone like her. And she knew it.

At first the secrecy of it had been part of the rush, but that had ended right around the first time we'd crossed paths in the hallway, her surrounded by the entire Caravan, me with the G.A.N.U. crew, and she'd straight up blown right past me without so much as a sidelong glance my way. After that it just felt dirty. What we did was a secret, true enough, but it was one she was obviously ashamed of, and if I was honest, I was, too, just a little.

Stray far from timid, only make moves when your heart's in it.

That was the Notorious B.I.G. He had a point, too.

I needed to end this. I wasn't sure my heart was in it, and I was definitely sure Karla's wasn't, and besides, sooner or later it was going to blow up in our faces, and I had the feeling I was the only one who would end up covered in shit when it hit the fan.

I pulled my Jansport out of my locker and swung it over my shoulder before slamming my locker with finality. I'd made up my mind. I had to end it, if not for both our sakes, for mine at the very least. But even as the decision solidi-fied in my mind, my head was awash with fantasies of a very sexy, very naked Karla, and all the things we could do. All the things she might *want* to do.

And then an all-too-familiar voice barked my name, and it struck me like a thunderclap, turning all those thoughts to ash. I wheeled around to face Lucas Briggs, Karla's sometime-boyfriend and Mackenzie's twin brother. I groaned. I disliked Lucas even more than I did his sister, and I didn't really feel like dealing with any more of the Briggs brand of bullshit, especially when I almost definitely smelled like his now-ex-girlfriend's perfume, and I couldn't shake the sinking suspicion that he knew something I really didn't want him to know.

"What's up?" I asked innocently, planting my feet and squaring my shoulders in case this got real.

He crossed his arms, but he didn't swing, which was promising. "We need to talk. Now."

That part was not promising at all.

Violent delights. Violent ends.

Fuck.

CHAPTER THREE

They say you should keep your friends close and your enemies closer, which probably went a long way toward explaining why no matter where I went I was always running into one of the Briggs siblings. It was like their parents had birthed them for the express purpose of making my life miserable. Maybe I was cursed, like, one of my ancestors had pissed off one of their ancestors who happened to be some sort of witch, and this was all some sort of generations-spanning vengeance.

I first met Lucas—or, first encountered him—on the second day of the second semester in the ninth grade, in third period Physical Science. I'd fumbled my way through an entire semester, and I was finally beginning to feel like I was getting the hang of this whole high school thing. By the time Lucas had come sauntering through the door, twenty minutes late, we were already into our lesson, talking about the earth's layers. "Got lost," was the only explanation he offered our teacher, Mrs. Clark, as to his tardiness. I'd heard of him, seen him in the hallways, usually with the other meatheads, but the only real thought I had as he made his way down my aisle and slid into the desk behind was, "He's tall."

"As I was saying," Mrs. Clark said exasperatedly, "we have the inner core, the outer core, and what's next? The…"

"Lower mantle," we all mumbled in unison, like we were at a concert and this was the worst call-and-response in the history of live performance.

"Good. Next we have the…"

"Upper mantle," we chanted, somehow even less enthusiastically than the first time.

"Great, and the uppermost layer is called the—"

"Crust!" Lucas shouted from behind me. "Like what this guy's head is covered in."

The entire class turned around to see who the dandruffy dingus was, and when I shifted in my desk to look upon the poor soul who was about to become the laughingstock of the class, I found myself staring into a pointed finger, and I realized to my horror that the dingus was me.

That's when the laughing started.

Lucas lived like he was aggressively trying to tick every box in the "stupid jock" checklist, and he was doing a beautiful job of it until last year, because ironically enough, getting into fights, not giving a shit about grades, chronic delinquency— all staples in the Lucas repertoire—were the exact things that would get you kicked off the football team, which meant he wasn't a stupid jock anymore, he was just stupid.

And now all six feet three inches of that stupid was staring at me with a look that was somewhere between agitation and constipation. For a lot of guys, being cut from the team would've meant a steady sink into the chasm of social irrelevance and obscurity, but Lucas had remained just as popular as ever, a reminder of how unfair the world was when people thought you were gorgeous, and how fickle puberty could be. I had to admit that the planes of his face, like those of his sister's, were remarkably, annoyingly chiseled. Jawlines that could cut glass and flawless, sandy-brown skin obviously ran in the family. Even now, with his neatly trimmed goatee and his immaculately tapered fade and impeccable wave pattern, I was a little jealous.

"Look, man," he said grimly, "I've been thinking—"

"How'd that feel?"

Lucas may have been built like a football player and still carried himself like he'd just scored a winning touchdown, but I was older now. Wiser. I didn't take his shit lying down anymore. I knew that the best way to head off Lucas's idiocy was to get the jump on him, fight fire with fire, snark with snark.

"Come on, man," he groaned, "I'm being for real. I've been thinking, and…" He frowned and made a face like he was trying to speak a different, unfamiliar language. "I know we've had our differences."

"That's an understatement."

He drew in a sharp breath through his teeth. "Alright. Fine. Yes, I've been kind of a dick to you. I realize that. I admit it. I just think it's time we called it quits. You know. Put down the hatchet."

"Bury."

"What?"

"It's 'bury' the hatchet, and what are you doing, like, seriously? Is this your version of a senior prank, because you can't
play those on another senior."

"No, Cameron! I mean it. Goddamn. It's just…" He scrunched
his face up, then relaxed it. "Look, I've been a jackass to a lot
of people for a long time, but there's only so far that can carry a
person. It gets old. I think I'm better than that now. I *know* I'm
better than that."

I shouldered my backpack again, shifting on my feet and re-
laxing my posture. This obviously wasn't going to be a fight.
"That was almost a Star Wars quote. You know, after Ana-
kin killed the sand people and he confessed it to Padmé and
he went all emo…"

"You're a fucking nerd."

"There's the charm."

"Am I wrong? I'm sorry. My bad. There's nothing wrong
with being a nerd, I guess."

I had to give him props. This was a train wreck of a conversation, but by god was he powering through it. I looked
at him, scrutinizing his face for any of that pre-I'm-about-
to-do-something-stupid twinkle in his eyes. It wasn't there.
I pursed my lips. "You're for real?"

"That's what I've been saying."

"No bullshit?"

He groaned. "*No.* No bullshit. I'm having a party tomorrow night. You should come through."

I crossed my arms. This felt like a trap. Like a setup. I didn't
like it. "This is because of your breakup with Karla, isn't it?"
Shit. That was probably saying too much. I could only hope
Lucas wasn't smart enough to read into it.

His eyes lit up. "*No*. Of course not. What's this got to do with her?"

I narrowed my eyes. He was a horrible liar, and the timing was incriminating. They break up and all of a sudden he was Mr. Nice Guy? Yeah, this was her doing. I knew all too well how the power of Karla could change a person.

"I might make an appearance," I said, even though I had precisely no intention of showing up to a party where the guest list could probably double as the list of people I hated most in this world.

"Cool," Lucas said. He sounded relieved. "Hit me up on Facebook for the location."

"We're not friends on Facebook."

He scrunched up his nose. "Take my number."

"Now?"

"No, tomorrow. Come on, man."

"Oh okay." I still wasn't convinced he was for real until he'd rattled off his number and I'd saved it in my phone under "Numb Nuts."

I couldn't wait to tell Jocelyn and D'Anthony.

I didn't have long to wait. Friday nights were G.A.N.U.'s unofficial movie nights. For the past few weeks we'd been working our way through the collected works of Studio Ghibli, starting with *Nausicaä of the Valley of the Wind*, which had caused something of a disagreement between D'Anthony, who felt that since the film was released in Japan in 1984, a year before Ghibli was founded, it shouldn't technically be included in the studio's works, and Jocelyn, who maintained that since the success of the film led directly to the founding of the studio it definitely belonged. I'd ended the debate by siding with Jocelyn, mostly because I loved the movie.

Since then we'd watched *Castle in the Sky*, another of my favorites, and *Grave of the Fireflies*, which made us all cry, as always. Tonight we were watching *My Neighbor Totoro*, which was not just one of the greatest Japanese animated films of all time, but one of the greatest films ever made, period.

The three of us didn't live far from each other, so we took turns hosting movie night. Tonight it was Jocelyn's turn, and D'Anthony and I had gathered at her place, assorted snacks in hand, and descended to the basement, where I immediately cracked my head on a carved wooden loon that was dangling from the ceiling.

Jocelyn shoved past me and steadied it. "Come on, man! This thing is delicate."

"And my head isn't?"

"Nobody told you to smack your head into my duck."

"My bad."

"I know."

"Loons aren't ducks," D'Anthony so helpfully pointed out.

"Yeah, because you're an ornithologist," Jocelyn replied.

To be fair, I knew better than to let my guard down here. We called Jocelyn's basement the cosplay dungeon because it was what you'd get if Willy Wonka had been a cosplayer instead of a candymaker. Bolts of multicolored fabric, plastic tubs full of god knows what, and at least a dozen bare wig heads were strewn across the basement. Scattered amid the chaos, like it had crashed through the roof and exploded on impact, were pieces of what would be her magnum opus: a Gundam suit, a giant, weaponized mecha that looked like a futuristic samurai. MangaMinneapolis, Minnesota's biggest anime convention, was "only" three months away, and Jocelyn had made it her life's pursuit to place at this year's costume contest.

D'Anthony and I stepped gingerly into the clear space between the TV and entertainment center against the far wall and the IKEA futon in front of it. We settled on opposite ends of the futon, the only safe place to sit because the love seat beside it was occupied by a pair of massive arms.

Jocelyn cradled the gun she'd printed earlier like an infant and propped it delicately against the workbench behind the futon. It was actually two workbenches pushed together, and even then there was barely enough space to hold the piles of craft foam, PVC pipe, and corrugated plastic that were amassed around the giant helmet. On either side of the bench stood two dress forms (which, despite the fact that they looked exactly like headless, limbless mannequins, apparently were not, in fact, mannequins), one of which held the Gundam's body, the other its winged shoulders.

I told them about Lucas's invite while Jocelyn set up the DVD and D'Anthony started in on a bag of Cool Ranch Doritos. I was still shook by the whole thing; for once it was me who needed their advice.

"It's a trap," Jocelyn announced from behind the workbench, where she was loading a stick of glue into one of her glue guns. "An obvious one, too."

"For once, I agree with Jocelyn," said D'Anthony. "Lucas just stops being a dick just because he broke up with Karla for the millionth time? I call bullshit. Leopards can't change their spots."

"Actually, they can and do," said Jocelyn. "He's right, though, Cam. It's sketch as hell."

"It's just a party."

"Until they're drawing and quartering you."

I couldn't fault them for their pessimism. The summer of sophomore year, right before school started, my barber fucked up my hairline (he claimed I moved my head, I contended that he had tried to hold in a sneeze and lost control of the clippers). I was faced with the horrible choice of either starting the school year looking like I'd lost a fight to a pair of gardening shears or going bald and starting over. I chose the latter, assuming it would lead to less grief. No one could tease you about your hairline if it was gone, right? Lucas, of course, proved that theory to be incredibly flawed when, during PE, in the middle of the gym and with the eyes of god and both of the combined fourth period classes watching us, he'd pointed at me and shouted, "Bro, why does your head look like a giant penis?"

That was the day I found out what it was like to be laughed at by fifty-eight people at once, and later on that same day, when he'd rushed up behind me, yanked my hood over my head and shouted, "Wrap it up, Condom-Head!" I'd also found out what it was like to have at least a hundred people laughing at me at once. To add insult to injury, the nickname—Condom-Head Cameron—stuck with me until nearly the end of the semester, long after my hair had grown back. Jocelyn and D'Anthony were only looking out for me. They didn't understand the power Karla had, or what it was like to dance at the end of her strings.

Because that's who this was about. It wasn't like I was super into parties, and I couldn't care less about Lucas or his friends. But for some reason, Lucas and a few of his core group of bozos had found favor with the Caravan. Lucas existed in the overlap part of the Venn diagram of meatheads and theater snobs, and if I could find my way into his group, maybe I could find my way into that overlap, and from there, maybe, just maybe, I could find my way to Karla.

"I'm going," I said definitively. "It's just a party. Besides, it's what Goku would do."

D'Anthony shook his head, chuckling. "Here we go again."

Goku was one of the most recognizable anime characters of all time, and my personal hero. He was the protagonist of the Dragon Ball franchise, one of the most successful Shonen anime series of all time. *Dragon Ball* was, essentially, the story of Goku, a boy with a monkey tail and extraordinary powers, who had no memory of who he was or where he came from. He soon met Bulma Briefs, a brilliant inventor and heir to the Capsule Corporation, who was on a quest for the seven mythical Dragon Balls that, when collected together, summoned the great dragon Shenron, who would grant a single wish. As Goku grew older, he encountered dozens of enemies, each more powerful than the last, in his quest to become the strongest fighter on the planet. The next entry in the series, *Dragon Ball Z*, followed Goku's adult adventures, beginning when he learned that he was one of the last of the Saiyans, a ruthless warrior race that sent him to Earth in order to wipe out the population. *Dragon Ball Z* was *Dragon Ball* on steroids. The stakes were higher, the enemies were more powerful, and the battles were more epic.

I'd loved the series since I was eight.

Jocelyn looked up and dramatically rolled her eyes again. "Why Goku? He's not even a real hero."

"He's the best," I stated simply.

"In what way? Piccolo is a better father, Krillin is a better friend, Vegeta is a better Saiyan *and* husband. What is Goku actually good for?"

"He's saved the planet multiple times." She had fair points, true enough, but Goku was my hero, and I would go to the grave defending him and his actions.

Jocelyn huffed. "How many villains has he actually defeated? Raditz? No. Frieza? Nope. Cell? Hell, no. He almost died fighting fucking *Androids*, for god's sake."

"Regardless, Goku never backs down. Neither will I."

"Not true, but whatever," Jocelyn muttered.

"I'm down to go with you," D'Anthony said with a shrug. "Gotta explore the whole map if you want to beat the game. I've never been to one of these infamous house parties, so at the very least I'll get some wild stories out of it."

That was reassuring. And he was right. The three of us historically didn't do parties or dances, even the ones hosted by the school. The one dance we'd gone to was last year's homecoming, which we'd only done out of boredom, and even then we'd gone as a group.

"You in, Jocelyn?" I asked hopefully.

"Hell, no," she said resolutely. She waved her hands around the basement. "Do you not see this shit? Con-crunch is in full effect. It's all hands on deck. Now can we please watch this damn movie?"

I couldn't argue with that. "Fair enough."

Two of us wasn't as good as three, but it sure as hell was better than one.

★ ★ ★

D'Anthony agreeing to come with me didn't mean I was out of the woods yet. I'd made up my mind about going to the party, but I still had one more hurdle to cross, and in retrospect I should've crossed this one first.

"Do you know who all is going to be there?" Mom asked. She was in her purple scrubs, feeding carrots, apples, and celery into her juicer at the sink. It was one of those fancy, stainless steel ones with adjustable pressure settings and an automatic pulp ejection system. My sister, Cassie, and I had saved up for a whole month to surprise her with it on Mother's Day last year.

"Not too many people. D'Anthony would come with me," I added. My mom loved D'Anthony.

"Who's the girl you're chasing after?" Cassie asked with a snicker as she slathered mayonnaise on a ham sandwich at the table. "She better be cute."

"Shouldn't you be focusing on finals instead of my business?" I clapped back at her. Cassie was five years older than me, but I swear sometimes she acted like she was five years younger. "For the record, I'm not going to chase girls."

"Oh, of course not, because there are *so* many other reasons for someone as aggressively introverted as you are to want to go to a party all of a sudden."

"I won't be out too late," I told Mom, ignoring Cassie's remark. I couldn't do this now, not when the stakes were this high. I *was* being honest, in a matter of speaking. I was supremely certain that Karla would not be making an appearance at her ex-boyfriend's house party, so there really wouldn't be any girls there I was interested in.

Mom took a second to fix me with one of her scrutinizing looks. "Have you talked to your father?"

I scowled. She did this sometimes. It had nothing to do with getting his permission. She used times like these as leverage to get me to keep in contact with Dad because she knew I wouldn't otherwise.

"I'll call him."

She narrowed her eyes, but she accepted my answer. She quickly poured her juice into a bottle and screwed on the lid. "How are your grades? Thank you, sweetie." She planted a quick kiss on Cassie's head before shoving the sandwiches she'd made into her lunch bag along with her juice.

"As and Bs, as always."

"How are you getting there and back?" She threw on her coat and slipped into her shoes at the back door.

"D'Anthony's borrowing his brother's minivan."

"Hmm." Mom deliberated for a few seconds. My mom was not one to suffer fools lightly. Straight talk and straight answers, that was her rule. None of us had the time for anything else, she liked to say. It didn't help that she was headed to a twelve-hour shift tonight. I wouldn't ordinarily have dumped this on her as she was on her way out, but if I didn't ask now I wouldn't have another chance until it was too late.

"Go ahead, sweetie," she said as she snatched her keys off the hook. "Have fun. Don't do anything you wouldn't want me to know about."

"I won't."

"There are leftovers in the fridge." She flashed us a quick smile before rushing out the door. Cassie and I lingered, listening for the familiar sounds of the garage door creaking open, the car door shutting, the engine starting, and the tires crunching as Mom backed out. I hit the button to close the door when she'd gone.

"Hold up," said Cassie. "Was Mom wearing makeup?"

I frowned at her. "I dunno. Maybe. So what?"

"*So what?*" She looked at me like I'd asked the silliest question in the history of silly questions. "Mom never wears makeup to work, or her hair in anything other than a ponytail."

"I still don't see your point."

Cassie rolled her eyes. "You're so oblivious. Girls love that," she said sarcastically.

"Kick rocks," I said as I made my retreat to the refuge of my room, pausing in the kitchen doorway just long enough to flip her the bird.

CHAPTER FOUR

The Briggs residence was a five–thousand-square-foot home in West Calhoun, a neighborhood where the average household income was over a hundred grand a year and you would never see a car that was more than two years old. Except for D'Anthony's 2003 Chrysler Voyager we rode into town in.

West Calhoun was ten miles and a world away from Robbinsdale, where I lived. Robbinsdale was a nice enough suburb, where the only exciting thing to ever happen was when new neighbors moved in or old neighbors moved out, and I couldn't remember the last time that had happened. Quietness aside, I liked it there. Robbinsdale wasn't far from Minneapolis, the younger, hipper of the Twin Cities. I'd spent half my life in Saint Paul, the capitol, where the culture was much more conservative, and it wasn't until we moved that I'd met people who shared my interests, people I could be myself around.

West Calhoun was quiet, too, and the homes were set among manicured evergreen trees and hilly lawns covered in leaves that somehow seemed more crisp and vibrant than they did back home. Lucas's house was at the end of a cul-de-sac that was already lined with cars on either side. D'Anthony edged the minivan into a narrow space at the end of the block after spending five minutes trying to parallel park it. "I'm normally good at that," he said sheepishly as we climbed out.

"Sure you are."

I could see flashing lights and hear music and voices coming out of the house as we approached, and I felt an unsettling blend of trepidation and anticipation stirring in my guts. This was either going to go really well or really, *really* horribly, and I had no idea which way the pendulum would swing. A sidelong glance at D'Anthony told me he was thinking the same thing.

"You good, man?" I asked.

His walk had stiffened and his steps had slowed, but he nodded. "Took my meds before we left."

"Cool." I made a note to keep an eye on him tonight. It had been a while since he'd had a bad anxiety attack, but I didn't want to press our luck. And I didn't want him to think I was wearing kid gloves with him, either, the way some people did. If he said he was good, he was good.

On the other hand, I could feel my heart beating faster and faster as we got closer to the house. I could see silhouettes in the windows, and it looked like a packed house. I hesitated on the brick steps with my sneaker hovering just outside the glow of the porch light. This was it. There was no going back anymore, and there was no middle ground, either. I could feel the energy of the party pulsing from inside like a heart-beat. D'Anthony was at my side, waiting for my next move. I'd convinced him to come here tonight. I couldn't let him down. But my resolve was quickly eroding. Maybe it wasn't too late to turn around. No one had seen us. It would be like we'd never been here at all.

And then the door flew open, and Lucas framed the door-way with his arms wide, backlit by bright light like some Greek god in a V-neck and joggers.

"Cameron?" he bellowed in a hoarse voice. "You showed up!"

He reached out, unsteady on his feet, and pulled me into one of those bro hugs I could never quite get the hang of. One thing I never understood was the bro hug. It was like an actual hug that had been strained through the filter of fragile masculinity. That was one of the cool things about having a woke mother and an older sister who was (sometimes) ma-joring in women's studies—you learned about shit like that, shit that was so deeply ingrained in us that we didn't realize it was rooted in a fear of being perceived as feminine. I hated the bro hug, but right now was probably not the time to give my dissertation on the subject, so I brought it in, bumped shoulders and slapped backs with him, then stepped back so D'Anthony could do the same.

I felt like such a tool.

Lucas straightened up, clearing his throat. He smelled like weed and liquor. "Good you made it, man. And you brought…this guy."

"D'Anthony," he said meekly.

"That's right! I know you. Get in here."

We stepped into what turned out to be a wide, circular foyer, where a marble staircase curved above a tall fireplace. A delicate chandelier sparkled from above, suspended in the center of the rounded ceiling. The floors were polished marble with a large round rug that didn't look like it was meant to be stepped on. These warm, tasteful surroundings were in harsh contrast to the debauchery taking place. A smoke circle five strong lounged at the foot of the stairs, passing a blunt back and forth. People posted along the walls and on either side of the fireplace, all holding red Solo cups. People raced back and forth with their phones held high, documenting the insanity for their Snapchat and Instagram stories, spilling beer, and trampling the poor rug the same way the wildebeests did to Mufasa. The chandelier trembled from the noise of the music that growled from somewhere deeper in the house, and a heavy cloud of smoke hung just above our heads, thick enough to make me cough. So, this was what a Lucas party was like. And we hadn't even made it six feet past the front door.

Lucas shoved between D'Anthony and me and draped a heavy arm around each of our necks. "Let's get you fuckers faded!" he shouted, and before either of us could protest he was steering us left, down a hallway, past a nice-looking mantelpiece holding a mirror and a set of vases that probably wouldn't make it through the night. I caught a quick peek at my reflection, and I looked like I was being herded to my execution. I took a deep breath, tried to relax my shoulders, straighten my back, and act like I was supposed to fucking be here. But then we entered the kitchen, all gleaming titanium appliances and granite countertops that were absolutely

lousy with so many kinds of alcohol that it looked like someone had raided every liquor store in town, and the ounce of
bravado I'd just started to squeeze out of myself evaporated.

Leaning against the center island, under the range lights
over her head, looking like an angel haloed in the warm glow,
was Karla Fucking Ortega.

"Holy shit!" I jumped back like I'd stepped on a Lego, and
both Lucas and D'Anthony jerked their heads and stared at me.

I was eight years old the first time Mom and Dad let me
ride the Wild Thing, the biggest roller coaster at Valleyfair,
Minnesota's answer to Six Flags. The first hill of the Wild
Thing was two hundred and seven feet tall with a pants-
shitting sixty-degree drop. The scariest part of the ride wasn't
the drop, it was the breathless, timeless moment between the
slow, clattering climb and the sheer free fall, when you were
suspended weightlessly, helplessly, with the maw of the void
staring back at you.

That's exactly what I felt like right now. I held my breath,
knowing she'd see me. And then she did, and her eyes nearly
bugged out of their sockets.

"You good, bro?" Lucas shouted. I barely heard him. I
could barely hear anything, except for the blood pumping
behind my ears and the sound of my own heart threatening
to beat itself right out of my rib cage. Karla was huddled between Lydia and Naomi, cupping a Dos Equis in both hands
and very purposely avoiding making eye contact with me
like the other two were. In fact, she was staring so intently
at the center island between us now that she looked like she
was doing complex calculus in her head.

Why on earth was she here?

In a lot of ways Lydia and Karla were a study in contrasts, aesthetically and personality-wise. While Karla typically opted for a warmer palette, Lydia dressed almost exclusively in subdued jewel tones. Tonight it was a sapphire blue cable-knit sweater that matched the color of her fingernails. Her hair was straight black and fell halfway down her back, and her flat bangs covered most of her forehead. And while Karla was always smiling, even if there was no reason, Lydia's default facial expression was somewhere between bored and annoyed, so I couldn't tell if that's what she was actually feeling now.

Lucas either didn't notice any of this or didn't care, because he sauntered to the fridge, took out two cans of Budweiser, and offered one to D'Anthony, one to me. "Let's get you sorted, yeah?" he said with a grin.

"I'm good," D'Anthony said. "I'm the designated driver."

"I respect it," Lucas said.

What the hell? I took the can he offered me and cracked it open and guzzled until I couldn't stand the taste anymore. I hadn't planned on drinking tonight, but I hadn't counted on Karla being here, either, and that changed everything. A drink or two might be just what I needed.

"You ladies need anything?" Lucas asked, shouting above the music and waving a can their way.

"We're good," Karla said flatly.

This was what Jocelyn would call a "second-generation clusterfuck," that is, "a clusterfuck born of two smaller clusterfucks who fucked each other." I was going to have to un-fuck myself, and do it fast.

I inched my way farther into the kitchen, posting up beside the fridge. Lydia and Naomi shook their heads. They regarded D'Anthony and me like we were aliens.

"Do you speak Japanese?" Lydia asked.

Random. "I wish, but no."

"Then why do you have it all over your shirt?"

I looked down. "Oh. This is…from a TV show?"

"Which one?"

I hesitated. *"Dragon Ball Z,"* I mumbled unwillingly.

"My brother watches that show, I think," said Naomi.

"Really?"

"Yeah, he's twelve."

"Oh."

Karla whispered something to the others, and they stood up in unison and marched across the kitchen, rounding the center island with Lydia and Naomi trailing behind her like fledgling geese. D'Anthony and I flattened ourselves against the threshold to let them by. Naomi scoffed, Lydia rolled her eyes and muttered something, but Karla didn't slow down, didn't look at me, didn't acknowledge I was there at all. Lucas stared longingly at her as she passed, but she very pointedly ignored him, too.

"Girls, right?" he said with paper-thin bravado. I didn't know how to respond, so I just shrugged and chugged more beer. I was white water rafting right now, struggling to navigate the twists and turns while fighting to keep myself upright and above water. They weren't back together. That much was obvious. It didn't seem like their relationship was on the mend, either. That was encouraging, and I might have appreciated it more had my head not been swimming while flop sweat pooled under my arms and trickled down my spine. What other surprises was I going to encounter tonight?

"I gotta piss," Lucas announced. "You two do…whatever it is you do."

With that he left for parts unknown, leaving D'Anthony and me in what was now hostile territory. This party sure as hell did not feel like a party. People squeezed past and shoved around us, spilling beer and liquor all over the place. The music rattled my skull. My mouth tasted like I'd just kissed a fresh corpse, and I was definitely hovering somewhere between throwing up and shitting myself. I looked at D'Anthony, and he looked back at me wearing a panic-stricken expression, and a silent understanding passed between us: we had no business at this party. We didn't belong here, catching contact high from all the weed in the air, glazed with the damp, sticky sheen of booze, in a place where if I were to draw a Venn diagram of all the people who hated me versus all the people at this party, it would be a circle. This whole thing may not have been a prank like Jocelyn said, but the joke was still on us.

I set my half-empty can down, ready to bail, when my pocket vibrated. The pendulum swung toward vomit rather than shit when I saw the text alert from Karla.

Meet me in the bathroom. Upstairs. Two minutes.

My anxiety ratcheted up to eleven out of ten. This was a red shirt, all-hands-brace-for-impact level scenario. The rapids were about to end in a sheer drop.

"I'll, uh, I'll be right back," I shouted at D'Anthony as I

shoved my phone back into my pocket, nearly dropping it in the process. "Gotta take a shit."

"TMI, dude," he said with a grimace. "Gross."

"Sorry." I was already moving back through the hallway. The foyer was more crowded now. I spotted Lamont, Gerald, and Todd, the musketeers of moron kingdom and three of Lucas's best friends, and ducked before any of them could see me. Once I was sure the coast was clear, I ninja-ran up the stairs.

I paused on the landing, letting my eyes adjust to the darkness. The bathroom, or what I assumed to be the bathroom, was just to my right. It was the only door with a thin bar of light shining from underneath it. I took a deep breath, hoping to god there weren't two bathrooms up here, and that I wasn't about to walk in on someone shitting, throwing up, or fucking, and cracked the door open.

"Took you long enough," Karla hissed, waving me inside. "Hurry up! Get in here."

CHAPTER FIVE

Summer

It was early June of last summer when I found out that Karla had been hired at Pair-O'-Moose Coffee—*my* Pair-O'-Moose Coffee—and I was, in a word, unnerved. And when the store manager, Rebecca, assigned me the task of training her, I went from unnerved to full-on terrified.

Pair-O'-Moose Coffee, or just The Moose, for short—was the Midwestern answer to Starbucks. It was founded in the late '90s by this young entrepreneur who, after a few failed endeavors, went hiking in Gooseberry Falls State Park in search of inspiration. Just when her canteen ran dry and she'd tasted her last drop of caffeinated anything, the clouds parted, the birds sang, and she came across—you guessed it—a pair of moose grazing in a clearing, a moment which somehow inspired her to open up a coffeehouse, which quickly spawned a chain of them.

I couldn't say whether any part of that heartwarming story

was true or just a really good branding gimmick, but honestly, it didn't matter, because everyone who worked here knew it by heart, and nearly everything here was moose-themed, from the little embroidered antlers on our aprons to the drinks—no, really, our dark roast was called the Buck Blend, and our light roast was the Bambi Brew—you cannot make this stuff up. Having a part-time job was part of the deal between my mom and me: if I wanted to get my driver's license, I had to contribute to the car insurance bill, because, apparently, adding a teenager to her policy sent her rates up through the roof, and if I wanted a phone that wasn't laughably outdated and with a decent data plan, I had to pay my portion of that bill, too. Not that I minded. Most of the time I made enough just in tips to cover most of my expenses and have spending money left over, and all things considered, Pair-O'-Moose was a cool place to work.

A sentiment I was seriously rethinking now that I knew Karla would be working here, too.

"Why me?" I demanded the moment I could. "Oscar's the shift manager. Shouldn't he be training her?"

"Oscar's got his hands full as it is," Rebecca said as she hefted commercial-sized boxes of sugar packets.

"What about Stella? Stella's such a better barista than I am." And she would never let me forget saying that if she heard me.

"If I didn't know any better," Rebecca said in her Texas drawl as she stacked the boxes, "I'd say you were afraid of that girl." She straightened, dusted sugar off her hands and placed them on her hips. "I figured the two of you'd get on fine, what with you going to the same school and all. A little camaraderie and all that."

"Wait, she told you we go to the same school?"

"Do you not?"

"I mean, yeah, we do."

Rebecca nodded. "Way she tells it, you're a nice young man with a good head on his shoulders. Now, if you really just can't stand that poor girl, alright—I'll have Stella train her."

I chewed the inside of my lip. I couldn't recall the last actual conversation I'd had with Karla. I was curious, I had to admit, as to how she'd come to her assessment of my character.

"No, it's fine. I'll do it."

Rebecca smiled as if she'd known all along I'd agree. "That's my boy. You two'll do just fine."

Yeah. Just fine. *Sure.*

Two hours into our shift we were standing behind the bar, before the massive espresso machine. But this was just an espresso machine the way the Batmobile was just a car. This was the La Pavoni Bar BT-2, a chrome-plated solid brass monstrosity with two built-in steam wands and a fourteen-liter boiler capacity that was capable of brewing up to six hundred cups a day. The thing cost more than a used car. If Thor were a barista, the La Pavoni was what you'd get if Mjolnir had been forged to make espresso, and just like Mjolnir, only few were worthy of wielding it.

Today I was to train Karla to be one of those few.

"Brunhilda the Bean Butcher?" Karla asked dryly. "Did you come up with that?"

"That would be Rebecca's doing, actually," I told her. I regretted mentioning it.

Before she'd left, Rebecca told me she'd written my schedule to match Karla's, and she'd be doing so until she felt Karla was ready to be on her own. "Gotta get those training wheels off," she'd gleefully said. It occurred to me that she probably thought she was doing me a favor. Pairing me with a pretty girl like Karla, the two of us working in close quarters; she probably thought this was a fucking love connection waiting to happen.

Little did she know.

There was no love lost between Karla and me, and I was looking forward to working with her the same way people looked forward to having a root canal—I wasn't. Not one bit. This place was my sanctum. I was the barista superstar here, coffee-ground god, caffeine kingpin. I knew my regulars and what they drank by heart. I was the adorable brown kid the old ladies loved to question about his ethnicity and whether I was born on an island—they always tipped big; for that I could deal with a little casual racism. I could whip up a latte in less than a minute. I had an encyclopedic knowledge of our mixed drinks menu. I could describe the characteristics of our light or dark roast of the day so eloquently you'd feel like you'd already drank it. And here she was, desecrating the sanctity of this place with her big brown eyes and her impossibly too-flawless-for-an-adolescent skin. It was bullshit. I didn't care how many passengers were on the Karla hype train, I wasn't about to climb aboard.

So far she'd been perfectly pleasant.

We'd gone over using the nitrous oxide chargers to make whipped cream with the dispensers. I'd shown her how to use the register. She knew how to brew the coffee, how to prep the bagels and the oatmeal we served during the breakfast hours, and the sandwiches and rolls during lunch and dinner. I had to admit, she was a quick study. But working the espresso machine was the litmus test of a true barista.

I handed her the bucket and handle. "Whosoever holds these tools, if they be worthy, shall possess the power of the barista."

I said it more out of habit than anything. I wasn't expecting her to laugh, but she did. "You're weird, you know that?" she said with a grin.

"I did, actually."

I waited. The other shoe would drop, I knew it. It was only a matter of time.

"Basically the machine works by forcing pressurized water through the puck," I told her, "which is in here." I held up the basket, which looked like an ice cream scoop. "You want to tamp the grounds down so they don't spill, even if you turn the basket upside down."

I demonstrated, flipping the basket over. She nodded. "Like they do with the Blizzards at Dairy Queen. Got it."

I watched carefully as she tried it herself.

"Now you take that and slide it into the machine here. Make sure the handle locks, or it'll explode."

Her head snapped in my direction. "Seriously?"

"No. At least I don't think so."

She bumped me with her hip. "Don't scare me like that! I don't wanna be the girl who blew up the coffee shop on her first day."

"You won't be. You're doing great."

"Really?" She looked at me, eyes sparkling.

I shook myself. "I mean, yeah."

She smiled proudly. "Thanks. You're a good teacher."

I felt my cheeks burning, and ducked to check the milk in the cooler beneath the bar. I'd checked it ten minutes ago, but I needed to gather myself. I didn't cross paths with Karla much at school. She was usually at the nucleus of the Caravan, an exclusive and closed clique that typically consisted of Lydia Vang, student council vice president and probably the scariest girl ever to walk the halls of Hilltop High, Naomi Long, who was voted "most likely to be famous" two years in a row, and Jackie Freeman, who somehow knew everyone and everything that ever happened in school despite taking a full IB course load and hardly ever being seen by the general populace. The hanger-ons made up the bulk of the Caravan's mass on any given day, some of them athletes, a couple of music nerds—the cool kind, who acted like rock stars and played in shitty punk rock/rap bands—and the entire homecoming court, who apparently didn't know that they weren't actual royalty. It was a bygone conclusion that members of G.A.N.U. hated the Caravan and everything they stood for. That's what Jocelyn insisted. According to her, I was supposed to hate Karla, and Karla was supposed to hate me, or at the very least strongly dislike me. But we seemed to be getting along well.

I took a deep breath and came up. The other shoe would drop, eventually. It had to.

"Right. So. A small cup gets one shot of espresso, medium and large get two."

She frowned. "Wait, large and medium drinks have the same amount of espresso in them?"

"Yep."

She looked horrified. "My life is a lie."

"The real world is a cold and unforgiving place."

"Tell me about it," she said. I nodded, still waiting for the other shoe to drop.

By the end of our shift she was making mixed drinks like a pro.

"Can I ask you something?" she said as we finished cleaning Brunhilda.

I patted my hands dry. "Sure."

"What made you decide to work here? Was it your passion for coffee? Or because you look good in an apron?"

I grinned. "Partly, yeah. The coffee part, not the apron. Although, thanks. I do really like coffee. I've been drinking it since I was eight. My mom—she's a nurse, so she used to work nights a lot—she was always drinking it to keep herself awake, so I started, too. I thought it made me more of a grown-up."

"I didn't think you were supposed to let kids that young drink coffee," she said. "Doesn't it stunt your growth or something?"

I shrugged. "Who knows. Guess I got lucky."

She cocked her head to one side and looked up at me. "You are a lot taller than I remember you being."

"Or maybe you're just short."

"Hey!" She swatted me with her towel. "I'll have you know that I am perfectly average height for a girl."

"Uh-huh."

"I'm serious! I'll prove it."

She snagged her phone from her back pocket and started typing. "See! The average height for a woman in the US is five feet four inches. I'm exactly five feet three and a half inches. Suck it."

I bowed. "Google has spoken."

"Damn right."

Once we'd closed shop we took off our aprons and hung them on the rack. The coffee aroma still clung to our clothes. That never got old.

"Hey," she said as she brushed coffee ground dust from her shirt. "Thanks for teaching me all this stuff. You're good at it."

She smiled at me. A real smile. A megawatt you're-going-to-remember-this-forever smile. I'd never seen anything like it. It was like looking into the face of God.

It didn't matter when the other shoe would drop, or if it ever would. I stared blankly, knees weak, head full of marbles, and my stomach so full of my own words I could shit my autobiography, titled: *I'm a Fucking Idiot: The Cameron Carson Story.*

That was the beginning of the end.

CHAPTER SIX

It was hard to believe that first shift working with Karla had been almost four months ago.

I had something of an idea why we were meeting like this, in the Briggs residence's upstairs bathroom, and when she crossed her arms and glared at me I knew I could confirm my suspicions about this not being another make-out session.

"Did anyone see you come up here?" she demanded in a strained whisper.

"No, I was very stealthy."

"Good." She took a sharp breath. "What the hell are you doing?"

I figured she'd feel some type of way about seeing me here, but something in her tone pissed me off, and it was my turn to cross my arms. "As a matter of fact, I was invited."

"Obviously. You wouldn't be here if you weren't invited, and that wasn't my question. What are you *doing*, full stop."

"What I'm *doing* is trying to have fun at a party. At least I was until three minutes ago, when you so unceremoniously summoned me."

I'd never been defiant with Karla before; I didn't think many people were. Maybe it was because of the alcohol sloshing around in my head, maybe I'd finally had enough of all this clandestine nonsense. Most likely it was a messy combination of the two.

She shook an unruly strand of hair from her eyes. "Don't be a dick, Cameron. That isn't you."

Her words cut through my indignation. "I'm sorry."

"Are you? Are you stalking me now? Is this you trying to prove something to me?"

And just like that I was pissed off again. "God, get over yourself. I didn't even know you would be here, and even if I did, do you really think I'd come here just because I…"

I couldn't finish my argument, because she was right. I may not have known she'd be here, but I had come because of her, to show her I could roll with her crowd, that we could be seen together without the world collapsing in on itself like a dying star.

Karla sighed and uncrossed her arms and smoothed the frown from her face. "Look. I like you, Cameron. Really, I do. Just…"

"Not enough to date me."

"I'm not— That's not what I'm saying. We just… If this were a perfect world, and you and I weren't…you and I, then…"

"I get it."

"Do you?" She looked at me with an almost pained expression. I waited, but she didn't elaborate. Instead, she crossed the space between us and kissed me, softly at first, then urgently, like it was for the last time. I felt her tongue against my lips, but when my hands found her waist she pulled away.

"Maybe we shouldn't do this anymore," she whispered heavily.

"Maybe you're right."

She smiled, then slipped past me, stopping with her hand on the doorknob when I called her name.

"Why are *you* here?" I asked. "Lucas is your ex. That's kind of weird, isn't it?"

She chewed her lip. "Everyone's weird, Cameron. Me, you, everyone." She smiled again, and then she opened the door and slipped out into the darkness.

Right. Guess I was just the wrong kind of weird.

D'Anthony might call this the friend zone, but that would be bullshit because (a) the friend zone itself was just something "nice guys" made up to vilify girls who didn't want to date them; and (b) even if the friend zone were an actual thing, Karla and I weren't officially friends to begin with; and (c) Karla did like me, or at least she said she did. The only reason we couldn't date was because of the hierarchy. It wasn't just her friends in the way. G.A.N.U. hated the Caravan, and the feeling was mutual. They'd never let me hear the end of it if they knew about Karla and me.

I sank onto the toilet lid and buried my face in my hands. Weird. Everything about this situation was fucking weird, and I didn't want to even try to make sense of it right now. My head was already swimming.

Someone knocked at the door.

Uh-oh. I stumbled to the door and cracked it open to find

Mackenzie standing there in pajama pants and an oversize sweater with a faded graphic of Shenron, the eponymous dragon of *Dragon Ball*, on the front.

"Why are *you* here?" she said, turning her nose up.

"Why are you here?" I shot back. I was really getting sick of that question. "There's a party going on downstairs, in case you didn't know."

"Yeah, and I get along with precisely zero percent of the people down there."

She had a point. Her and her brother didn't seem to get along that well. In fact, until she'd enrolled at Hilltop I'd forgotten Lucas had a sister, much less a twin. He rarely mentioned her before she enrolled, and when he did, it was to talk about how much of a loser she was. To hear him tell it, Mackenzie was a cross between the Wicked Witch of the West and a bridge troll who was incapable of coherent speech.

I could agree with the witch part, but she was far from a bridge troll. I could begrudgingly admit that good looks seemed to run in the Briggs family, and as much as I teased Mackenzie, there wasn't much in the way of flaws to work with. She was, objectively, pretty.

Unfortunately.

"Later, then." I brushed past her. She was not the person I needed to be dealing with right now.

"For the record," she called after me, "if you need to jack off that badly there's a bathroom downstairs."

I flipped her off without looking back, and I heard her laugh.

D'Anthony was standing next to the fireplace when I came downstairs, cupping a can of Sprite in his hands and staring so intently at something across the room that he didn't seem to notice when I came over and posted up next to him.

"I'm over this," I groaned. "Wanna bail?"

"Hell, yeah," he said without skipping a beat.

"You sure you're good to drive?" I asked as we escaped into the night. "I think I have enough for an Uber."

"And leave my brother's car here so he can literally murder me—"

"You used *literally* wrong…"

He shook his head. "All I had was pop. Beer tastes like piss."

I couldn't disagree, not when it felt like my brain had been frappéed and the inside of my mouth did indeed taste like piss, or at least what I imagined piss would taste like.

I sloshed into my bedroom just before midnight and crashed facedown into my bed with my clothes and shoes still on. Somewhere between drifting in and out of fitful sleep I dreamed that Karla had texted me. Eleven hours later, when I checked my phone notifications, squinting against the brightness of my screen and the throbbing in my skull, I realized I must have looked at my phone at some point the night before, because it hadn't been a dream at all.

Hope you're not too drunk. GN ☺

I rolled out of bed, smiling to myself as I trudged to the bathroom and plucked the aspirin out of the medicine cabinet. Maybe going to that stupid party had been worth it, after all.

Mom was still at work when I got up, but I knew Cassie was home by the sound of Whitney Houston belting out, "I wanna dance with somebodaayy!" blaring from the speakers downstairs.

I thought about taking a shower, then decided not to. I wasn't going anywhere. Instead, I went downstairs and poured myself a bowl of Lucky Charms. One of the great things about having a job was that, in a household where my mother refused to buy "sugary" cereal, I could just buy it myself.

Whitney Houston turned into Billy Idol. Cassie listened to '80s music while she studied, and I had to hand it to her, studying on a Saturday morning was admirable. I ate in silence, listening to "Mony, Mony," until Cassie came in from the living room with her glasses on and her hair pulled into a lazy ponytail. "Well…?" she asked.

I shook my head with my spoon in my mouth, but she persisted, cutting the music off and sliding into the chair opposite mine. "Have you left the ranks of the single?" she asked, grinning from ear to ear.

I sighed heavily. "No."

She leaned back. "No?"

"Forget it, alright? It wasn't even like that to begin with."

She looked up from the phone she'd been texting on and fixed me with a sympathetic look. She looked like Mom when she did that. "You know what girls don't like?"

"When you make blanket statements about an entire gender?"

She rolled her eyes. "When you objectify them. Sure, this girl, whoever she is, is special to you, but don't make her out to be something she isn't. Don't treat her like she's somehow more than human."

I put my spoon down and crossed my arms. "So, you're

saying not to treat her any better than I treat anyone else?" I asked skeptically.

"No, stupid. Just remember that she's a person, and if you're going to go after her, do it because you like who she actually is, not who you think she is. Don't deify her. That's a sure-fire way to scare her off."

I finished my cereal and pushed my chair in with my hip. "There's no girl, Cass."

She nodded, grinning. "I can't wait to meet her."

She cranked her music again. This time it was Pat Benatar. I walked upstairs to her screaming, "Love is a battlefield!"

Pat was right.

I hadn't forgotten about Karla's proposition. I had my work cut out for me. I booted up my laptop. It was time to begin the gross and more than likely fruitless task of preparing for real, actual sex with a real, actual girl, for the first time.

I wasn't looking forward to what the internet had to say on the subject. I felt like Dr. Sattler in the first Jurassic Park movie, when she had to dig up to her elbows in that massive pile of triceratops poop to find out what it was eating that was making it sick. If I sifted through enough virtual garbage and was extremely lucky, I might find some useful nugget of information. It wasn't ideal, but it was a place to start, and I didn't have any other options anyway. I couldn't ask my friends; they were both virgins themselves. My parents were obviously out of the question. My health teacher would only throw condoms at me and probably try to talk me out of it. Even if I knew someone who'd had sex before, what kind of questions would I even ask?

I opened a private window. The last thing I needed was

for Mom, or—god forbid—Cassie, to see my browser history. I braced myself, and typed, "what to expect when you lose your virginity" into the search bar.

Surprisingly, the first two results were from reputable sources—some health care website and Planned Parenthood. The third and fourth were from Seventeen.com and BuzzFeed. I opened tabs for all four and started reading.

After half an hour, a few trends stuck out to me. The first was that most of the articles were geared toward the girl, and what she could expect physically and emotionally. It was useful stuff to know, for sure, and it made sense. It seemed like what the guy had to look forward to was pretty straightforward.

The second was that the awkwardness of the whole thing seemed to be unavoidable, and although it didn't necessarily mean that the first time had to suck, it did seem like the success and enjoyment of the event hinged on how well the people involved weathered those awkward bits, whether or not they could laugh them off and take them in stride instead of letting it rattle them.

Lastly, it was an overarching theme that communication was absolutely key. Without it, you were in for a bad time.

That might present a problem for Karla and me. Talking wasn't quite the hallmark of our relationship; in fact, it seemed like she preferred it when we didn't talk at all.

Then again, when we were doing our thing, we didn't seem to have trouble finding each other physically. We may not say much to one another when we met up, but our bodies didn't seem to have any difficulty communicating. Maybe it would be the same with sex. I could only hope so, but that still led me right into my next line of inquiry.

What if I couldn't last long enough?

I knew enough to know that it was pretty much the unforgivable sin when a guy couldn't keep it up long enough to get the girl off, just like I knew that it seemed to be a very common frustration. I didn't want that to be me. I didn't even care if I finished or not, I just wanted to make sure she did.

After another half an hour I gave up. I was only psyching myself out. When it was time, if we ended up going through with it, we would figure it out.

I checked my phone to see if there were any more messages. There weren't. I sighed. There was one other thing I needed to do today.

Here's the thing.

I didn't hate my dad. Not yet. Everyone who knew about our situation seemed to think it was only a matter of time before I did, but I didn't.

That didn't mean I was cool with him, or that I wanted to talk to him. But Mom insisted that I at least try to keep in touch with him, at least until I was a little bit older, because I "never knew what might happen" and because "a boy needed his father."

He answered just before it went to voice mail.

"How you doing, son? What are you listening to these days?"

His voice seemed almost unfamiliar; he sounded like a stranger. And I hated hearing him say that, but he made a point to always start our conversations like that, and to always use the word. *Son.* I was his son in name only. His offspring, yes. But his *son*? That I was not.

"Same old, same old," I told him.

"Right on," he said, and I could picture him nodding approvingly. Both my parents loved music, and they had passed that on to Cassie and me, but it was Dad who introduced me to hip-hop, or *real* hip-hop, as he called it. Wu-Tang, Talib Kweli, Tupac, and the Fugees. When I was little he'd take us to run errands or just drive around, and he'd play an album—full albums, he insisted, from track one all the way through to the end, the way music was meant to be listened to—and he'd bob his head and rap along to the songs, and he'd always point out an especially meaningful or poignant line or lyric. Those are the ones I memorized.

Mom never really approved of Dad's taste in music, and they'd get into it sometimes over his introducing us kids to that kind of lyrical content. But he'd insist she just didn't understand the culture or the context. These days I could see where they were both coming from. I listened to a lot of local music these days, from longtime Minneapolis acts like Atmosphere, Dessa, and Brother Ali, to The Replacements, and of course, Prince. Music was one of the only things I felt I could halfway relate with my dad about, and talking about it was easy and uncomplicated.

The subject let us dance around the bigger issues, like, *Why the fuck did you abandon us*, or *How does it feel to know you're not taking care of your own goddamn children*, or *How the hell do you manage to sleep at night knowing you're letting your ex-wife do all the things* you *were supposed to help her do?*

"Good. Good. How's Cassie?"

"She's fine, I guess."

That was the other thing. Cassie refused to talk to our

dad. She was the one who hated him, and she made no secret of it. I suppose she had more reason to than I did. She was twelve when our parents divorced, so she got to witness the messiness of it more clearly than I did. She got to see the parts I was shielded from as a seven-year-old. The day after she turned eighteen she'd called our dad, chewed him out for a straight fifteen minutes, and told him she never wanted to see or hear from him again. I'd found her in her room an hour later, still crying.

Aside from music, there wasn't much else to talk to my dad about. I told him I had a 3.5 GPA, that I still worked at Pair-O'-Moose, that I was thinking about majoring in journalism, mostly the same things we always talked about. And then, as usual, I lied and said I had homework to get to, and that it was good talking.

"As always, I'm proud of you."

He always said that, too. Like he could be proud of someone he didn't even know anymore. For all he knew everything I told him was bullshit. I could be a dropout, or a serial killer, and he'd say the same thing.

"Thanks, Dad."

I always felt a little weird saying it. *Dad*. The word felt foreign on my tongue, wrong. It didn't feel right to call him that. He hadn't earned the title. He didn't deserve it. But I didn't know what else to call him, so I just hung up and did my best to forget our conversation, like I always did.

CHAPTER SEVEN

I loved Mondays. I was probably the only person, student or faculty who did. I loved Mondays because those were the days when we met for homeroom for thirty minutes instead of going straight to first period, and Karla and I had had the same homeroom since ninth grade. Aside from our meetups I only ever saw her in passing, but during homeroom I had a solid half hour to be in her presence, breathing the same air and occupying the same space, in a manner of speaking, and it didn't matter that we were ignoring each other from opposite sides of the room with the weight of our shared secret hanging precariously between us like an elephant on a tightrope. During homeroom, we were together.

Sort of. Not really.

I tiptoed to room 305 and hovered at the open door like it was the edge of a pool and I'd never learned to swim. I wasn't sure whether Saturday night had changed anything between us, or if it was business as usual.

Newton's third law of motion stated that for every action, there was an equal and opposite reaction. I'd taken action. I'd gone to that party, and Karla knew it. What happened next? What was the equal and opposite reaction?

D'Anthony and I had the same homeroom, too, and he was already there, leaning back in a chair in the back of the room next to the window. It was 7:25 in the morning, and at this hour he communicated exclusively in caveman, so when I said, "Morning," he responded with a grunt that I assumed meant *You, too*. I dumped my stuff and sat at the desk next to him and waited while Mr. Bender started handing out our new schedules. Karla was always late, and I wondered if it was because she was just that busy or because she preferred to wait to show up until she knew I was already here so there was no chance of our having to interact.

My money was on the first one.

It wasn't like this was a real class. The only things we did here were listen to Principal Standish's weekly announcements (a good 20 percent of which were, just, the worst dad jokes), get our class schedules on the first day of the new quarter, or maybe finish homework assignments we hadn't done over the weekend. Most people just goofed off and gossiped.

The warning bell rang, a muted gong that, on my list of the most annoying sounds on the planet, was just under the frantic shriek of my alarm going off. My eyes were glued to the door, my fingers drumming the tabletop, when Jocelyn swept in, swinging a bulging duffel bag in front of her like a battering ram, which she used to bludgeon the legs of those foolish enough not to yield to her advance as she made a mad dash to our table. "Morning, gentlemen," she said as she hoisted the bag onto the table. It trembled under the weight. Her homeroom class was across the hall, but her teacher never seemed to care that she was over here half the time. "How was the party? Any sordid tales or juicy anecdotes? Did anyone find true love or lose their virginity?"

That last part was meant specifically for me. Whereas D'Anthony wasn't a fully functioning human this early in the morning, Jocelyn was firing on all cylinders; her wit was sharpest before noon. But her comment was enough to rouse him from his fogginess.

"Actually," he muttered, "I decided to obey the Prime Directive, which forbids interfering with less advanced civilizations."

Jocelyn sat down and unzipped her bag. It was crammed to bursting with PVC pipe. "Wow. I surely am sorry I missed that. And while I hate to say I told you so… I told you so."

"How was your weekend?" I asked because I was already sick of thinking about that party.

"I went to a spa," Jocelyn said as she rummaged through the bag. "Then I got my nails done."

D'Anthony frowned. "Really?"

"Of course not! I spent the entire weekend sealing things with Plasti Dip and binge-watching old episodes of *Project Runway* because Tim Gunn is my lord and savior."

"Sounds productive."

"It was. But really, I'm glad you both made it out of there in one piece. *And* with your dignity intact."

I nodded in agreement, although the dignity part was debatable, at least for me, and glanced at the door.

That's when the Caravan rolled up.

I kept my eyes locked on the clock above the door, watching through my peripheral as the girls moved to the table at the head of the room, laughing at something, or someone. Even though they were the last ones to get here, the table was empty. Everyone knew it was the property of the Caravan; no one else would dare dream of sitting at it.

Jocelyn glanced over her shoulder in their direction. "Ugh." Her nose turned up like she smelled something rotten, and she sprang out of her chair. "I gotta go," she muttered with a scowl as she started shoving the pipes back into the bag.

"You good?" D'Anthony asked her. We exchanged confused looks, and I shrugged.

"I gotta get to the tech lab before someone beats me to the 3D printer."

She zipped up the bag and hoisted it over her shoulder, but it was too heavy, and it fell to the ground, which would've been bad enough, had not the bag burst open, sending pipes clattering all over the place and making so much noise that every head in the room snapped in our direction.

There was a moment, *that* moment, a heartbeat, between when people saw that something shitty and embarrassing had happened and when they started laughing about it. If you experienced it enough, you got better at using that sliver of time to brace for the laughter. But it was never enough to insulate yourself completely once it started. D'Anthony and I both jumped out of our seats, but Jocelyn crouched and quickly gathered up the rolling pipes. She shoved them angrily into her bag before swinging it over her shoulder. With her jaw set and her brows pulled into a dark scowl, she shuffled out of the room, kicking the doorstop as she passed so that the door slammed shut after her. The laughter was loudest at Karla's table, with the exception of Lydia, who huffed in annoyance and tossed such an icy glare at Naomi that she froze mid-giggle, and Karla herself, whose eyes followed Jocelyn as she left with a look of pity. Then her eyes flickered to our table, and met mine. She looked away just as quickly, but I could see her blush all the way from where I sat, and I couldn't pull my eyes from her.

For every action, there was an equal and opposite reaction. I should have expected as much.

What happened with Jocelyn was shitty, but it was par for the course, just the latest in the long line of incidents that only fueled the animosity between *us* and *them*.

In biology we'd learned about something called "swarm intelligence," where a large group of organisms, like ants, function as a single unit without any centralized intelligence. It's like everyone in the group instinctively knows the rules and follows them without being told to.

That was the Caravan. One would assume it was Karla who called the shots, but the more I observed, the more I started to understand that she was just as much beholden to the laws of the collective as they all were. She may have been president of the student body at large, but within her own smaller microcosm she was subject to the same checks and balances of power that everyone else was, and it seemed more and more that they kept her from doing what she really wanted to do.

And kept us apart.

There had to be a work-around. There had to be a way to show her friends that I wasn't a threat to their group, that I wasn't a Trojan horse who would somehow ruin whatever they had going for them once I was in good with them.

And there had to be a way to convince my friends that Karla wasn't all bad.

My first class of the day was Spanish II with Señora Chavez. I was nowhere near fluent, and even though my maternal grandparents spoke the language I had no real interest in it, but most of the schools I was applying to required at least two years of a foreign language. I hadn't anticipated the class being stressful in any way, that is, until Mackenzie sauntered in.

I groaned as she walked straight toward me.

"Shouldn't you have a firm grasp on your first language before you try learning another one?" she asked. "I feel like you're setting yourself up for failure."

"Can I help you, Mackenzie?"

"Unless you are a chair, no." She slung her bag down and straddled the chair at the desk next to mine. "It's okay. If you ask nicely maybe I'll tutor you."

"I'll keep that in mind," I said, rolling my eyes. As far as comebacks went, that was pretty weak. But I had other, much more pressing matters weighing on my mind. Like sex. Not the actual physical act. Not that a perfectly naked Karla didn't pop up in my head at regular intervals, but the impact of it, how it could change our relationship, and what would happen after we did it, kept rattling around in my head. Once we had sex, we couldn't just go back to making out in the musty library every few days, could we? That wasn't how relationships worked. That would be going backward.

I was overthinking it. Sex didn't change anything. She'd still be her, and I'd still be me, and we'd still be us. Except that now we'd have just one more secret to keep from our friends. Could I handle that? Could she?

Sex was still on my mind when lunchtime rolled around. *Get in where you fit in.* Too $hort said that, and it was the way of the lunchroom. Nothing said more about where you were on the geopolitical spectrum at Hilltop High than where you ate at lunch. There were some groups, like the cheerleaders, the band geeks, or the theater snobs, who took the same places every day. It made sense; groups like those ran at least five deep at all times, so there was always someone there to reserve their places. Then there were groups like Robotics Club, the debate crew, or my friends and I, who sat wherever it was most convenient because it really wasn't that serious, which left the underclassmen scuttling to stake claim to whatever was left over. Most seniors only ate lunch on campus on days like today, when it was too cold out to leave.

"God, I hate it here," Mackenzie groaned as she sat down at our table for lunch.

"And yet, you're still here," I noted. She was always saying that, since the first time we'd met, all the way back during open house, which was held at the end of August, a week before school had even started. Open house was a chance for incoming freshmen and new students to come and get a feel for Hilltop High, get their schedules, meet their teachers, and visit their classrooms, and for everyone, upperclassmen in-

cluded, to have their ID pictures taken. It was also an opportunity for clubs and teams to meet and recruit potential new
members. Tables and booths lined the walls along the entire
shaft, from the main entrance all the way to the gym, with
the quality of the displays directly correlating to the amount
of enthusiasm the members had for their respective club or
organization. Our display consisted of a laminated sheet with
our name displayed in Comic Sans, and a big anime scroll
Jocelyn had scored at a convention draped over our table.

"Why are we here, again?" I asked. The G.A.N.U. table
was set up in the corner, near the base of the shaft, between
Robotics Club and the mathletes. Jocelyn wasn't exactly keen
on newcomers. She was definitely a quality over quantity
type of person.

"We have to be," she said as she glared at the massive display
Theater Club had set up directly across from us. "Or else we
lose our faculty sponsorship, which means no more tech lab."

Tandy, Miranda, and the rest of the cheerleaders roamed
around in their uniforms, waving their pom-poms, welcom-
ing people and directing traffic. Principal Standish was at the
front doors, shaking hands with people as they entered, while
Vice Principal Reynolds quietly lurked, vigilantly patrolling
and keeping an eye out for troublemakers.

And then, there was Lucas, standing with Lamont and the
others next to the football team setup. He was the only one
not wearing a jersey, except for the tall girl with big curly hair
who was standing beside him with an expression like she'd
rather be anywhere else.

No one had stopped at our table yet.

Which was fine. Jocelyn and I both had our phones in our

laps, while in D'Anthony's case it was his Game Boy. Either way, none of us was really paying much attention to what was happening around us.

"Shouldn't you be with *The Quill*?" D'Anthony asked. "Bringing culture to the unwashed masses and whatnot?"

I looked over at *The Quill's* booth. Amanda was there, recording an impromptu interview with a nervous-looking freshman while his parents looked on proudly. Meanwhile, I kept catching glimpses of Ken, popping his head in and out of the crowds with his camera like a meerkat. "Yeah, hard pass. Besides, you know G.A.N.U. is my first love."

Jocelyn clicked her tongue. "We better be."

"I like the banner," said a throaty voice I hadn't heard before.

All three of us looked up at the same time to see the curly haired girl who'd been with Lucas standing on the other side of the table.

I immediately tensed.

"Come again?" said Jocelyn.

The girl tapped the table. "This banner. It's dope."

"Did Lucas send you over here to mess with me?" I demanded. Of course he had. I knew what this was. Trolling. For whatever reason Lucas tended to make me his special target. I was not about to let him drag my friends into it.

The girl leveled an indecipherable gaze at me, and there was a twinkle in her eyes that I had seen Lucas have a million times before, right before he did or said something he found hilarious. "Yes," she said flatly, "he did. I do everything my stupid brother sends me to do, up to and including messing with complete and total strangers, because what better use of my time could I possibly have?"

So they were related. Of course. The universe hated me enough to send the other Briggs sibling to screw with me.

I could feel D'Anthony and Jocelyn glancing between me and the girl, but I ignored them. They didn't get it. Not yet. But I knew this girl was trouble. She had to be.

"Back to the banner," Jocelyn said with an impatient hand wave. "Are you into *Ghost in the Shell*?"

Of course she's not, I thought.

"Hell, yes," she said. "Major Kusanagi could step on me and I'd thank her for it."

"What did you think of the live-action adaptation?" Jocelyn asked skeptically.

Mackenzie leaned back and frowned. "There was no live-action adaptation of *Ghost in the Shell*."

"Yes, there was," I insisted. It was terrible and problematic, and I'd only watched it on a dare, but it was definitely a thing that happened. "How could you not know—"

"Listen to me," she said firmly, leaning forward and staring intently at me. "There was *no* live adaptation of *Ghost in the Shell*. Not one worth talking about or acknowledging."

Ah. I realized what she was doing now. Oops.

She glanced at our sign. "Geeks and Nerds United? Huh. Is there, like, an application process?"

Jocelyn and D'Anthony said, "Nah," at the same time I said, "Yes!" and then everyone looked at me.

"Can we, um, confab please?" I pleaded nervously.

Jocelyn looked at me like I had lost my mind, and I stared at her with a desperate expression I hoped conveyed the urgency of my request, until she relented, rolling her eyes. "Would you excuse us a moment?"

The three of us ducked beneath the table. "What is your deal?" Jocelyn demanded in a harsh whisper.

I was sure Lucas's sister could still hear us, but whatever. "I'm not sure she's G.A.N.U. material." By which I meant, she was definitely *not* G.A.N.U. material.

"Elaborate?" said D'Anthony.

I was all too happy to oblige. "Okay, well, for starters, how about the fact that she shares genes with Lucas?"

Jocelyn nodded impatiently. "And…"

"*And?* What more do you need?" I glanced at D'Anthony in the hopes that maybe he'd back me up, but he looked just as nonplussed as Jocelyn. "Right, look, you guys don't know Lucas the way I do. The guy is a grade A asshole, and I'm getting the exact same vibes from his sister."

"Whom we know nothing about," D'Anthony pointed out.

"We do know she likes Ghost in the Shell—the manga, not the movie—which means she can't be all that bad," said Jocelyn.

"I completely disagree with you there."

Jocelyn threw up her hands. "Fine, let's vote. All in favor of letting her join?"

She and D'Anthony both raised their hands.

"Of all the times for you two to agree on something…"

This was a mistake. A huge, terrible mistake. But the vote had been cast. I was powerless to do anything. The three of us popped back from underneath the table. Jocelyn sat up straight and clasped her hands in front of her like this was an interview. "So. What's your name?"

"Mackenzie."

Jocelyn nodded. "Okay, Mackenzie. What grade are you in?"

"I'm a senior."

"What brings you to Hilltop High?"

She sighed. "My old school had a total student body population of four hundred. Everyone knew everyone else. My dad thinks I live in a bubble. He wants me to 'broaden my horizons' and learn to interact with different kinds of people and not just my weirdo friends. So, here I am. Needless to say, I'm gonna hate it here."

"I get that," said D'Anthony. "My dad made me try out for the football team last year because he thought it would be good for my anxiety."

I remembered that well. I'd gone to tryouts with him, partly so he wouldn't be alone out there in a sea of angry muscle, and partly because the thought of Lucas's face when he found out made it too hilarious an opportunity to resist.

"Did it work?" Mackenzie asked.

"Yes, being chased and tackled by guys twice my size totally cured me."

Mackenzie smirked. "I like you guys. Except for you." She narrowed her eyes at me. "Kidding. Mostly."

I was legitimately concerned that she was not at all kidding. It would definitely be on brand for a Briggs to dislike me.

"Hate to break it to you," said Jocelyn, "but we're the weirdos around these parts, and we hate it here, too."

Today I hadn't seen Mackenzie since first period, which was still too soon. "By the way," I told her, "you're basically living the plot of *Mean Girls*."

"Yeah, except I wasn't homeschooled or in Africa, dumb ass."

I shrugged. "Broad strokes."

"Wait, doesn't that make us the Plastics?" Jocelyn asked.

"Dibs on being Gretchen!" D'Anthony blurted.

"You do have big hair," I noted, eyeing his afro.

"I say we start wearing pink on Wednesdays," Jocelyn said conspiratorially.

Mackenzie frowned, but not in a way that made me think she was opposed to the idea. Surprisingly. "I don't own a thread of pink," she mused.

"Me, either," I admitted.

"Same," D'Anthony said after a beat. He sounded disappointed.

I still wasn't sure why Mackenzie bothered sitting with us, not when she could pretty much sit anywhere she wanted. As much as she claimed to hate it here, I'd seen her in the hallways and around with other people. She seemed to be one of the few people who could float between cliques and groups without catching any flack for it. I was almost jealous.

Get in where you fit in. That was the way. So when Lucas came around to our table on the far side of the cafeteria, it was something of a surprise, and a mostly unwelcome one. This was definitely *not* where he fit in.

"Guys." He nodded. "Kenzie. This seat taken?"

He didn't wait for any of us to answer, just hunkered down and started in on his burger, like this was a perfectly normal thing for him to do.

All four of us stared blankly at him. I looked around to see if Gerald, Todd, or Lamont would be joining us, as well.

Mackenzie visibly bristled. "What. The *hell*. Are you doing?" she seethed.

Even though both of the Briggs siblings seemed to carry the same sort of diplomatic immunity when it came to who they hung out with or were seen with, I almost never saw the two of them together. Seeing it now felt wrong.

"Eating," Lucas said around a mouthful of food, and then, as if to further illustrate, he crammed another quarter of his burger into his mouth.

"Are you? Really?" Mackenzie fumed. "Because half your food is falling on your shirt, you *freaking* infant."

He ignored her, and looked at me. "So. What'd you guys think of the party?"

D'Anthony and I exchanged wary glances. "It was—" chaotic, abrasive, an assault on the senses "—cool. I had a good time."

Lucas nodded, accepting my half-assed answer wholesale. "Right on."

From across the cafeteria, I spotted Gerald and Lamont. They'd just come out with their trays and were looking around, undoubtedly for their Lord and Savior, Lucas. I prayed they didn't see him over here.

Gerald was, as far as I could tell, an anomaly, a glitch in the system, who had somehow slipped through the cracks and scraped his way to the big leagues. On paper he was more of a loser than I was. He didn't have Lamont's fashion sense— I'd never seen him in anything other than sweatpants, honestly. He wasn't as good-looking as Lucas—his mouth was perpetually hanging open for literally no reason, and his head resembled an upturned kneecap. I at least understood why

Lamont rolled with the Caravan. He was the starting point guard for our basketball team, and I'd never seen him wear the same pair of shoes more than once, and he had an honest-to-goodness six-pack, which I knew because he was always looking for a reason to lift his shirt up to show it off, or just take his shirt completely off. Practice after school? No shirt. Spilled water at lunch? No shirt. The sun is up when school lets out? The shirt was coming off.

I didn't like either of them. They did whatever Lucas did, and Lucas was usually an asshole. After a tense five seconds, they gave up their search and sat down.

I breathed a sigh of relief. Lucas may have been trying to be nice to me now, but I doubted they would follow his lead.

I diverted my attention to the Caravan table. Karla wasn't there, but I wondered what she'd think if she saw Lucas over here with me.

"What are you doing this weekend, bro?" Lucas asked.

It took me a second to realize that he was talking to me. "Come again?"

"We should hang out."

Wait, what? "Hang out?"

"Yeah, bro, come over my place tonight. We can hang."

I tried to think of a reason to say no. I looked at Mackenzie, but she was still fuming.

"You two can come, too," he added, looking at Jocelyn and D'Anthony. "Not you, though, Kenzie."

She flipped him off.

"I'm busy," Jocelyn said flatly.

"Yeah…me, too," D'Anthony fumbled. I knew for a fact that he wasn't, and that he just didn't want to come. I couldn't blame him. Lucas's party had been rough, probably more so for him than me. But more and more I was beginning to accept that maybe Lucas really was trying to turn a new leaf. It was weird as hell, and I just couldn't figure out why he was doing it.

A sudden commotion erupted from the entrance, and the entire student body council rushed in and gathered at the head of the cafeteria like it was the Super Bowl and they were lining up at the scrimmage line. Karla stood at the center, flanked by the others, who surrounded her like her own secret service detail as she took the wireless microphone from the stage. She tapped the microphone she had in her hand, and we all collectively winced at the feedback. "Sorry about that, guys," she said in one of those what-are-you-gonna-do voices. It echoed pleasantly through the PA system. "At least I know you're all paying attention now."

Everyone laughed. Mackenzie rolled her eyes.

"Just a couple quick things, and I'll be out of your hair, I promise."

Everyone laughed again. For some reason.

"First of all, just to let everyone know that tickets for the fall play go on sale tomorrow, and if you buy now you save two dollars off the regular price."

Everyone from the theater snobs' table clapped.

"I hate them," Jocelyn groaned as she served their entire table some of her grade A side-eye. "Like, we've all read Jane Austen—it's required. Don't think you're the shit because you *pretend* to enjoy it."

"Preach," said Mackenzie. They fist-bumped.

"Also," Karla went on, "voting for yearbook superlatives

has officially begun, so don't forget to fill out your vote and turn them in by Friday!"

"As if anybody cares about student body council," Jocelyn grumbled.

"They did lobby to have the lockers painted last year," D'Anthony pointed out. "And they got soda put back in the vending machines."

"As if anybody cares about lockers or vending machines," Jocelyn amended. "Or the fall play, for that matter. It's the same cast every year, anyway. It's like a shittier *American Horror Story*—different stories, all the same faces."

From the stage, Karla smiled, surveying the sea of students whose attention she held captive in the palm of her hand. Her eyes fell on our table, and her perfect smile faltered as our eyes met.

Given time, I'm sure I could have come up with a situation that was more butt-clenchingly awkward as sitting across from a guy you were sure was your worst enemy up until about four days ago and watching his now-ex-girlfriend, who he clearly still had feelings for, and whom you'd been hooking up with pretty much since the day they broke up, walk past and completely ignore both of you while trying not to give away the fact that she was absolutely mortified that the two of you were together, but at that moment none came to mind.

But like the consummate professional she was, Karla recovered it so quickly I was certain no one else had noticed except for me.

And maybe Lucas.

He stared throughout her entire presentation, and he wasn't discreet about staring at her as she handed off the microphone and quickly crossed to the exit with her entourage in tow. If we were in a manga, he'd have heart-eyes.

Gross.

I realized then that somehow, I had to keep him from getting back together with her, and even though this was Lucas, the guy who'd spent the better part of six years making me miserable, I still felt a pinch of sympathy for him, but it was only a pinch.

"I'm good for this weekend," I said. If hanging out meant more face time with Lucas, and a better likelihood of my being able to thwart whatever plans he might have to get back together with Karla, then I was game.

"Cool," he said distractedly as he stood up. He frowned. "What's your shirt say?"

"What?" I looked down, and realized I was wearing the orange shirt stylized with the turtle symbol of Master Roshi, the first master to train Goku in martial arts. "It means *turtle*," I said simply.

I could tell he was resisting his natural urge to say something derogatory. "Oh. Later, bro."

"Yeah. Later."

He was already tossing his tray. He rushed off in the opposite direction she'd gone, exiting through the back door that led to the south staircase, which was supposed to be off-limits to students. Pete the security guard didn't even turn his head.

"That was weird," Jocelyn said.

"I don't know what that was all about," Mackenzie said to me, "but FYI, by 'hang out' he means get high and play *Call of Duty*."

"I don't do either of those things."

"Well, it sounds like you two are going to have a great time," she said sarcastically.

The buzzing of my phone in my pocket derailed my equally sarcastic response. It was a text from Karla.

Meet me at our spot, 5 min?

Based purely on context instead of the fact that her message had no winky faces, xoxo's, or emoticons, I knew exactly what this meeting was about.

I sent back a sure even though it wasn't necessary. Karla had to know by now that her requests might as well have been marching orders. I'd follow them blindly, just like I always did.

"See you guys."

Mackenzie looked up from her sketchbook. "Maybe you should lay off the fiber."

"Maybe."

CHAPTER EIGHT

Summer

By mid-June, I had worked about eleven shifts with Karla, and if that time had taught me anything, it was that she was either high-key fake as hell or low-key kind of a nice person. I'd yet to figure out which was the truth.

Everyone loved her: Oscar, Rebecca—even Stella, our resident grouch, wasn't as chilly toward her as she normally was with people. Half the regulars knew her by name now, and they tipped a little bit more when she was working. She was already garnering me-levels of adoration all across the board. Which was why it was so out of character when she stormed in that Saturday and swept through the lobby and past the bar before slamming through the traffic doors that led through the back room.

Oscar, who was manning the register, shot me a questioning glance. "The fuck?" Stella said from behind the bar. "Not it," she said.

"What?"

"She's pissed, obviously. But in case either of you were about to send me in there to have a 'girl's talk' with her, forget it. Not my circus, not my monkeys."

"Not it," said Oscar.

I balked. "Dude, you're the manager on duty!"

"You know her better than I do. Besides, I need to run inventory. Or take the trash out. Or check the restrooms. Yeah, that one. Let me know when it's over." I watched him in disbelief as he threw on a pair of rubber gloves and strolled into the men's restroom.

"Godspeed," said Stella. She stuck her tongue out at me as I made my way into the back room.

"I'm fine," Karla said the second I opened my mouth, in a tone that most definitely did not sound like she was fine. She threw on an apron and tied a messy knot around her waist.

I held up my hands in surrender. If she said she was fine, she was fine. "I'll see you on the floor, then."

I was relieved. Whatever was enough to piss her off this much probably wouldn't be resolved by talking to me of all people.

"Wait. I'm sorry." She huffed and ran her hands through her hair. I'd never seen Karla angry before, or anything approaching it. She was always smiling, always cool and collected. At peace. That's what it was. She seemed to be in tune with the universe. Right now, the stars were definitely out of alignment.

"Lucas and I aren't on the best terms right now," she admitted with an exasperated groan.

I cringed. Lucas and Karla had started dating in the second semester of junior year, and two weeks later they'd broken up. Four days after that, they were back together. Thus began the most dysfunctional, on-again, off-again relationship I'd ever heard of.

"I'm sorry to hear that." If I didn't sound convincing, it was because I wasn't, really. I'd never understood how the two of them had ended up together in the first place. "Break-ups suck."

"I never said we broke up," she said in a scathing voice.

"Oh. Right. Sorry." Fuck it. I turned back around and started back out. They didn't pay me to be a mediator or a therapist. I had coffee beans to prep and espresso machines to clean. *That* was my job, not this.

"I'm sorry," she said again. I stopped with my toe on the door and turned back around. "I don't mean to snap at you. It isn't your fault. Sometimes I just wanna grab him by the neck and…" She motioned like she was strangling him.

I laughed. "Same."

She cocked her head to one side. "Same?"

I nodded. "Not to bag on your boyfriend, but he's an idiot."

A slow grin spread across her face. "Agreed."

Then why are you dating him? I wondered. I didn't understand the bonds that brought certain people together or compelled them to stay together, even, maybe, when they shouldn't. Regardless of whether or not she was fake as fuck or a halfway decent person, Karla was smart. How she could put up with someone who wasn't on her intellectual level was beyond me, but at least they were trying to make it work.

Not that it was any of my business.

"Well… I'll see you on the floor, then," I said. I started to leave. No sense standing around making it awkward. Besides, I had tables to clear. "We're busing today. FYI."

She nodded. "Hey. Thanks."

I stopped with my foot out the door again. "Not a problem. See you out there."

"Hey, Cameron?"

"Yeah?"

"He's not my boyfriend anymore."

I stood there, thinking of something to say to that. I had no idea what to do with that information, so I just nodded and left.

CHAPTER NINE

I used to be a five.

I knew this because during freshmen year Tandy Lewis and the rest of her cheer friends went through a list of all the boys in our class and rated them on a scale of one to ten. Tandy and her best friends, Miranda and Louise, sat across from me in my second hour social studies class that semester, and since none of them knew how to whisper—either that, or they didn't give a damn who heard them—I got to hear them as they went down The List. When it came to my name, a hush fell over them, and I pretended to be focused on my work.

"Four," said Tandy. "His nose is big as fuck."

"No, it's not," Miranda said. "Still, I give him a five. He's too short."

"Fine," Louise agreed. "He'd be cuter if he got new clothes and cut his hair, though."

Ouch.

There was a special sort of icky feeling that came from knowing that a group of girls were scrutinizing your looks and had come to the conclusion that you were average at best. I looked at some of the guys in my grade, like Lucas, and they already looked like adults. Some of them even had mustaches. I hardly had hair on my legs, and there was no way anyone could mistake me for an adult. But fuck them, I thought then. I may have been able to pass as a twelve-year-old, but I was damn proud of the fro I'd spent the summer growing, and there was no way I was going to cut it because a couple of cheerleaders thought I should.

Still. Ouch.

The cheerleaders did the same thing sophomore year. So I heard. I never found out what I'd ranked that year, and it was probably for the best. The little self-esteem I'd had had already taken a massive hit, and I hadn't quite recovered. By junior year nearly everyone knew about The List. It was like Starbucks's secret menu; officially it didn't exist, unless you knew the right people. Guys like Lucas, they bragged about their ratings. He was a solid nine, and he had a way of bringing it up at exactly the wrong moments, like when I'd had a particularly bad acne outbreak, or was having an off hair day.

The List was like Fight Club—no one was supposed to talk about it. If you had to ask what your rating was, you had no business knowing. But that year D'Anthony was dead set on getting his hands on it somehow. "For science, obviously," he insisted. "This list is allegedly rating attractiveness, but what type? Are we talking about aesthetic attraction, or sensual attraction, or sexual attraction, or a combination of all three? What are the criteria? The metrics?"

"Aren't sensuality and sexuality the same thing?" I'd asked.

"Nah, but pretty much all of society thinks so. It's pretty frustrating, actually."

"Oh. Well, I really don't think it's that deep. The list is just about how hot you are."

"Yes, but what is 'hot'? When I say someone is hot, it means they're aesthetically pleasing and sensually attractive. Like, does it mean I want to sleep with them? No, gross. But would I make out with them, or possibly cuddle? Probably. If I got to be little spoon."

Somehow, he'd managed to get ahold of the list, at least a part of it. An original, if the fact that it was written in Tandy's elegant scrawl was any indication.

He'd nearly knocked me over when he bulldozed his way through the hot-lunch line, waving a scrap of paper over his head. "Dude, this is unreal! You've got to see this!"

"What the hell, man?" He couldn't have got that high of a rank. I mean, objectively, D'Anthony wasn't a gargoyle. But he was heavyset and kind of a mouth breather, two things that didn't exactly bump your numbers with the cheer crowd.

"Look!" he insisted.

He waved the paper in front of my face, and I snatched it from him, frowning as I searched for his name.

"Reed, D'Anthony…six. They spelled your name wrong."

"Not that. *This!*"

He snatched the paper from me and jabbed it. His finger was on my name.

Carson, Cameron…

"Seven-point-five?"

"Fucking *yes!* You sexy mofo!"

"That can't be right."

"It is right! It's right here. Congratu-fucking-lations, my friend! You're certified hot! Whatever that means."

"What difference does it make?"

So what if a couple of girls thought I was cuter now than I used to be? That didn't change anything about my day-to-day, and it wasn't like you automatically got set up with a girlfriend just because you were a certain level of cute. The cheer crowd wasn't exactly my cup of tea anyway.

Eventually, D'Anthony stopped reminding me about The List, and I stopped thinking about it. Until recently.

I knew Karla had access to The List. I doubted she had anything to do with anyone's rank, but she had to have seen it. I was sure Karla and I weren't hooking up strictly because of my looks. It couldn't be that. According to the numbers, Lucas was still better-looking than I was. There had to be another reason why we kept doing this. I'd never asked; some part of me knew that asking her about it would make her realize it was the stupidest thing in the world to be doing and end it. But the longer it went on, the more and more I had to know, and I knew it was only a matter of time before I had to ask her, even if it ran the risk of blowing it all.

"Fancy meeting you here," I said as I joined Karla between the dusty stacks. I said it more often than not when we met here, more a nervous habit than the hopes that it might make her laugh.

She never laughed.

"What's up?" she asked innocuously, swaying from side to side.

That made me extra nervous. This wasn't how it usually began back here. "Um, nothing, I guess? What's— I mean, how are you?"

She shrugged her shoulders and beckoned with a manicured finger. French tips, as always. I'd never seen her with any other type of nail. I moved closer, reeled in like the world's stupidest fish, and she draped her arms over my shoulders. "Question," she said quietly.

"Answer," I said back.

She didn't laugh, but she did smile. Well, almost. "What's up with you and Lucas?"

Oh. That's what this was about. "What do you mean?"

"You two seem to have a bit of a bromance going on. I thought you hated each other."

Was that how she'd always read our situation? A mutual hatred? "Honestly, I don't know what's going on. I mean, last week he was all, 'sorry I've been such a jackass to you,' now he wants to hang out and be chummy. I really don't get it."

"God, I don't understand him," she muttered, shaking her head.

"Hey, Karla?"

"Hmm?"

"This thing. With us. This isn't just to get back at him, is it?"

She met my eyes and did that thing she did sometimes, where it was like she was doing a virus scan, analyzing all of my components, only I never had any idea what she was scanning for. She leaned forward and slipped her hands into my back pockets. "Would it make a difference?"

"Um, *yes*. It really would. I don't want to be your toy."

"Hey, relax. That's definitely not what's going on here. Lucas doesn't even know about this. *This* is no one's damn business, least of all his. That's why I think it's a little weird that you two are suddenly—what'd you call it—'chummy.' I know how boys talk."

"Some boys. Not me. Hell, my friends don't even know about this." A pang of guilt twisted in my guts when I said it, but then she slid her hands out of my pockets and ran her fingers up my back, and I forgot all about that.

"I know," she whispered. "That's not you."

"That's Lucas, though, right?"

She nodded, biting her lip and blushing. "I've dated a lot of guys like Lucas. Different model, same make. After a while I guess you forget that there are..." She grinned.

"Other cars out there?" I asked, laughing. She laughed with me, and somehow it morphed into a kiss, long and slow and breathless.

"Not my best analogy," she chuckled. She leaned in for another kiss, but I straightened up, putting a few inches between us.

"What's wrong?" she asked.

"He wants you back." I couldn't keep that from her, even though I probably should have. "In case that wasn't obvious. I bet he thinks his being nice to me will prove he's changed."

She groaned. "That's so fucking gross. This is what he always does. He makes these empty promises, makes a show of pretending he's so different, and I always fucking fall for it."

"Are you going to fall for it again?"

The air seemed to freeze. Karla raised a single brow, and I couldn't tell whether she felt affronted by my sudden boldness or impressed by it. "I don't know," she said finally, burying her face in her hands. "I don't think so. But I'm never sure."

"I don't get it," I blurted. I was somewhere between irritated and exhausted. "Like, why me? Why *this*?"

The question rang in the air. I felt a weight lift from my shoulders for asking it, but it was chased by a nervous dread.

Karla looked down at her shoes, and when she looked back up at me there was fresh determination on her face. "Okay. So, I have a dog. Mindy. Every morning I walk Mindy before I feed him, and by the time I make his food he's, just, *so* ready to eat. He acts like he's starving, like we didn't do the same shit yesterday. That's what it's like being with Lucas. He's... greedy? He just wanted to feel me up without really paying attention to what he was doing or whether he was making me feel anything. You know? God, I can't believe I'm telling you this, but whatever. Fuck it." She huffed. "The way you touch me, and kiss me...it's like it's all about me. It's like I'm something valuable, venerable. No one's ever done that before. I like it. A lot." She ran her hands through her hair. She was blushing. "Well, there you have it. That's what *this* is. That's why I think that..." Her voice started to trail off, but she shook her head resolutely. "That's why I never slept with him. Not that he didn't want to. Not that I didn't want to sometimes. But I know exactly how that would've gone, and I want my first time to be with someone who would listen and take their time, not someone who's just gonna rush through the whole thing just to say he did it."

I nodded. My throat had gone completely dry by the time she'd finished. So many different emotions were warring inside me—I felt flattered, sad, lucky, anxious, nervous, scared—the cocktail threatened to spill out of me all at once, until one took hold and bubbled to the surface: certainty. I realized in that moment that somehow, I had to keep him from getting back together with her, but even though this was Lucas, the guy who'd spent the better part of six years making me miserable, I still felt a pinch of sympathy for him. But it was only a pinch.

"Give me a couple days?" I asked, embarrassed by the crackle in my voice. "I just, I want to make sure I'm ready. Is that cool?"

The smile she gave me was reassuring. "Of course. I wouldn't want you doing anything you're not one hundred percent comfortable doing." She fixed her shirt. "I like this, Cameron," she said, looking back at me with a smile on her face. "Whatever this is."

I watched her smooth away the evidence of our tryst.

"Do you guys need any help with the play?" I asked as she finished putting on her lip gloss.

She stopped, looked at me, frowned. "Why?"

I sucked in a deep breath. It was time to clear the air again. "Karla, I like *this* as much as you do, but I really like being with you. Not just here. I like being around you. We obviously can't do that out there." I gestured widely. "But helping with the play would give me a reason to talk to you without your friends flaying me alive."

Karla cocked her head to one side, regarding me with a thoughtful expression. "You've never been part of a play, have you?"

"First time for everything. Auditions are until this Friday, right? Maybe I'm undiscovered talent."

"You've never acted."

"I kill at charades."

She sighed. "Auditioning isn't easy. It means performing a monologue. If you get a part you've got two months of nothing but rehearsals. You'll have to memorize your lines, cues, blocking…"

"Are you trying to talk me out of it?"

She smiled and shook her head. "Not at all. Just…you're really willing to do all of that just so we can be together, out there?"

I grinned. "Well, when you say it like that I sound like an absurd person."

"Yeah, you do." She laughed. "Absurd, but sweet."

CHAPTER TEN

Summer

"How's the SAT practice exam treating you?" I asked.

It was the beginning of July. Karla and I had been working together for nearly an entire month. It was strange how working in close quarters could lead to such familiarity between the two of us. It was weird being privy to her life, and having her privy to mine. Strange, but not unpleasant.

Karla groaned. "Kicking my *ass*. I've written twelve different essays on twelve different topics in the span of four days."

"That seems excessive."

"Yeah, well, it's something to do. Lydia's still at her Dramatic Acting workshop—as if she needs to be more dramatic. Naomi is up to her eyes in summer courses at Minneapolis Community and Technical College. Jackie is too busy screwing her boyfriend senseless—"

"I thought she dumped him."

"Yeah, so did I. Maybe they're doing the whole friends-with-benefits thing. I dunno. Live and let live, I guess."

"Sure."

"What about you? How's life outside the world of coffee?"

"Boring." And it was. Jocelyn was out of town visiting family in Washington. D'Anthony's job at GameStop had swallowed up every minute of his free time. That left me with nothing to do but binge all the anime I had missed or fallen behind on during the school year. As of two weeks ago, I was all caught up. "I've been reading a lot." Of manga, which I was not going to tell her. It didn't seem appropriate.

Even with working in these close quarters, and talking about our personal lives, there were things I knew instinctively not to tell her. Things that might remind her that I was not someone who would ordinarily be a part of her world. Like anime. Like manga. Like the fact that I'd found this incredible PVC statue of Goku in his Super Saiyan God form for, like, thirty bucks at Hot Comics.

"That's it?" Karla asked. She actually sounded surprised. "No friends? No *girl*friends?"

"What, like more than one?"

She held up her hands. "Hey, I don't know how you live. Open relationships are a thing."

"Not a thing for me."

She gave a noncommittal shrug. Dating and relationships didn't come up often between us. Karla was evasive anytime we came close to talking about Lucas or the status of their relationship. Not that I ever asked, but I'd be lying if I said I wasn't curious, because the more I got to know Karla, the less I understood how they could ever have dated in the first place. Karla was…cool, and Lucas was not. He was the opposite of cool, its antithesis. Those two were a study in contrasts, and I was grateful to whatever had broken them up this time.

Stella came back in from her smoke break, looking exasperated. "I guess I'm gonna start restocking," she said with a groan. "Since Oscar flaked on it. Little shit."

"Need some help?" I offered. Restocking sucked, but it helped to have more people working it.

"Nah. It gives me something to focus on. Thanks, though." She winked at me, and pushed through the back doors.

"What's up with you and Stella?" Karla whispered, even though we were the only two people behind the bar and no one in the lobby could hear us. "I think she likes you."

That made me laugh. "She definitely does not."

Karla gave me a knowing grin. "You should ask her out. I bet she'd say yes. You two would make a cute couple. I think you should date."

She said the last part like it was a proclamation, like it was a bygone conclusion now that she had decreed it.

I laughed again. "How do you know we haven't already?"

Her eyes widened in surprise. "Oooh, *gossip*. Do tell."

"There's literally nothing to tell."

"There's always something."

"Nope."

She grinned at me. "You know I'm going to bother you about this forever, right?"

"That's perfectly fine by me."

She glared at me, and I stared at her, refusing to break our eye contact. Finally, her frown melted away, and she laughed, shaking her head. "You're so fucking stubborn."

CHAPTER ELEVEN

After Karla left, things went back to normal around The Moose. She'd made a clean break. It was like she had never even been here. Everything was exactly the way it had been before she'd shown up.

Except for me.

Absurd, but sweet. That's what she'd called my plan to audition for the play. Now that I'd had a couple hours to think about what all that actually meant, I was sure she should have gone with "stupid, but sweet," or, "pathetic, but sweet," because it was both utterly stupid and sadly pathetic of me to commit to auditioning for a role I knew nothing about, in a play I knew even less about somehow, all because there was a chance it would mean being in the same room as the girl I was probably, most definitely obsessed with. I'd felt like I was making this grand romantic gesture then, but now I just felt like an idiot.

I switched out the old coffee and started brewing fresh pots, then grabbed a rag and went out to wipe down the lobby. Keeping busy made the shift go by faster, and besides, I was full of nervous energy. The prettiest, most popular girl in the entire school wanted us to lose our virginity together. In theory I should've been over the goddamn moon. I should have jumped at the chance. I couldn't think of a single person who wouldn't, so why wasn't I? Was something wrong with me?

It was Stella and me today, and the new guy who came on as Karla's replacement. Sameer. Nice guy. Quiet. And almost certainly high. But he did what he was supposed to, and what he was told to, so no one cared. Besides, if there was anything that could overpower the smell of weed, it was coffee.

I quickly wiped down the creamer counters and swept the straw wrappers and used sugar packets into the trash, then moved on to the empty tables. I was nervous, that was for damn sure. The prospect of losing my V-card wasn't something I'd expected to confront so soon.

I piled used mugs and plates, ran them to the back sink, and returned to the lobby without really paying attention to what I was doing. Maybe I was being a prude. It was only sex, and it probably wouldn't even be good sex. Maybe I was overthinking it, trying to find a reason to back out of it, to take the cowardly way.

What would Goku do?

The thought made me stop in the middle of wiping down the table in front of me. Goku had thought marriage was some kind of food. He hadn't even known the difference between men and women until he was, like, thirteen. For once, this might be a decision I couldn't rely on Goku's example to make.

Dammit.

I went to work.

To be a good barista you had to be part server, part thera-pist. My regulars were almost like friends, always updating me on what was happening in their lives, whether it was a new pregnancy, the kids graduating, or their getting laid off or a promotion, and in turn I kept them abreast of how school was going for me. Broad strokes, at least. None of them needed to know that, hey, for the past few months I've been hooking up with the most popular girl in school, in secret, and now her ex-boyfriend, who had absolutely no idea, and who I also hated, wanted to be my best friend for some reason. Oh, and she also wanted us to have sex.

I came back to the bar, where Stella was mixing her drink. We got one free drink every shift; Stella's drink of choice was the same as mine—the Bushy Tail Breve, made of espresso and steamed half-and-half, topped by a giant dollop of whipped cream and sprinkled with caramel crumble. The perfect drink for this time of year.

Stella and I worked well together. We had both been here long enough to know what needed to be done and when, and we knew who was going to do what. As a result we could go almost an entire shift with hardly a word said between us. There were some people who made it awkward when they didn't talk. Like they wanted to say something, they just didn't know what to say, and it was making them and everyone else uncomfortable. Stella wasn't one of those people. She wasn't quiet because she couldn't think of anything to say; she was quiet because she didn't feel like saying anything. I was the same. People who insisted on talking just for the sake of it not being quiet usually ended up saying something stupid.

But now, I had something to say, or rather, to ask. The evening rush was over, and most of the people in the lobby were students working on their laptops with their headphones on and not paying attention to anything else that was going on.

"Hey, can I ask you something?"

Stella looked up from the beans she was measuring. "Yeah…"

"It has to do with us, back when we were dating. FYI."

She laughed. "Okay, weird, but okay."

"Was I a good kisser?"

She cracked up and almost choked on her drink. "Is that— Are you serious? Why the heck do you wanna know that now?"

"Just curious."

She shook her head. "God, you're weird." She thought for a moment, sipping gingerly at her drink "But, I dunno. I don't remember you being especially *bad* at it, but I don't remember you being especially *good* at it, either. But we only kissed, what, twice, so who knows?"

"Huh." As far as answers went, it didn't tell me much at all, but at least I could assume that my skills weren't super advanced. "Thanks, Stell."

"Don't mention it," she said as she leaned back against the counter and checked her phone. "Don't feel bad," she added a few seconds later. "What doesn't work for one person may work for another. Mouths aren't one size fits all."

"I see. Thank you."

"I guess."

That was a small comfort. I wasn't some sexual dynamo, or even an above-average kisser, but whatever I did worked for Karla, so I could comfort myself with the idea that if I just kept doing what I was doing, it would all turn out fine.

In theory.

I couldn't decide which character I wanted to audition for. According to my good friend The Internet, you had Elizabeth and her four sisters, her indifferent father and her neurotic mother, and her best friend, Charlotte. Then you had Mr. Darcy, his best friend, Mr. Bingley, Bingley's snob of a sister, Caroline, and Darcy's younger sister, Georgiana. Complicating things was the charming and ultimately dickish Mr. Wickham, whom Mr. Darcy hates and Elizabeth initially has a crush on. There was also Mr. Collins, Elizabeth's cousin who was a priest and weirdly obsessed with the opinion of Lady Catherine De Bourgh, a relative of Mr. Darcy who was somehow more of a snob than he was. Over the course of the story Elizabeth and Darcy came to realize that their pride and their prejudice (Ha! Good one, Jane Austen) were keeping them from seeing who they actually were. They fall in love, get married, and live happily ever after.

Yay.

I was torn between trying for someone with only a minor role, which would make the odds of my being cast that much greater, or going balls to the wall and trying for one of the principal characters, which would be much more impressive.

You know, if I actually landed the part.

Either way, I had my work cut out for me.

Lucky for me I had an in. Maybe. And we just so happened to live together.

I knew for a fact that Cassie adored historical dramas and period pieces. She cried whenever she saw *Wuthering Heights*, and she and Mom used to watch *Downton Abbey* together religiously. I distinctly recalled her raving about *Bridgerton* for weeks on end after she first saw it (although, a lot of her raving was also about how gorgeous Regé-Jean Page was, which, to be fair, was true). Hopefully *Pride and Prejudice* was in her wheelhouse.

Lucky for me she was at home, stretched across the couch in the living room with a textbook in her lap and her phone in her hands.

"Hello, dearest sister," I said in my sweetest little brother voice. "I like your hair. Box braids look good on you."

"What do you want?" she said impatiently and without looking up from her phone.

"You wouldn't happen to like *Pride and Prejudice*, would you?"

The speed with which she whipped her head up gave me my answer. "Why do you ask?" she said, eyeing me with suspicion.

"Will you watch it with me? And explain it? It's for a school project. I need someone who has a deeper insight into the whole thing."

She still seemed suspicious. "You want me to provide context and commentary while we watch one of my top five favorite films of all time?"

"Yeah, basically."

She sat up and closed her book. "Okay. We're gonna need popcorn. And *I* am going to need wine."

★ ★ ★

I had already downloaded both the 2005 version of *Pride and Prejudice*, starring Keira Knightley and Matthew Macfadyen, and the 1995 miniseries with Colin Firth and Jennifer Ehle. I'd also bought *Pride and Prejudice and Zombies*, figuring the gist of the plot would be the same, plus it had the added benefit of zombies. The undead aside, I really didn't understand the appeal. I wasn't really one for period pieces, mostly because any book, movie, or series set before 1863 most definitely featured characters who owned slaves, whether it was explicitly acknowledged or not, and lots of movies set before that had, just, so much casual racism in them. And if there wasn't that, there was the rampant sexism. I mean, according to the Wikipedia entry on the book, the whole reason Mrs. Bennet was so dead set on marrying her daughters off to rich men was because their property was entailed, which meant it could only be passed to a male relative when their father died, which was why Mr. Collins, who was their cousin, would get the land and property when Mr. Bennet died instead of his five daughters. It was a stupid, archaic law, but that was only scratching the surface. Life back then just didn't seem fun. Everyone dressed in eight layers of heavy, itchy-looking clothes, and when they weren't dancing like they'd only recently discovered how to move their limbs they sat around writing letters. Thanks, but I'll pass.

Only I couldn't, because I had to understand this stuff if I expected to be involved in the play.

"What is it you like about these movies?" I asked. "In general, I mean."

"I have a love-hate relationship with period dramas. On

the one hand there's the costumes, the etiquette, set pieces—
yes to all of that. On the other hand, the patriarchy, and the
fact that most of the people of color you see are, y'know, the
help. If they're onscreen at all, that is. But, seeing Colin Firth
in that clinging wet shirt, though… I like that."

"Gross."

"Don't be such a child."

Cassie insisted we start with the 2005 version of the movie,
even though it didn't have Colin Firth and his aforementioned
"clinging wet shirt" scene. It was the "most palatable," she
explained, and with a running time of just over two hours,
it was much more watchable than the miniseries, which was
just under six hours long.

As we watched, I took notes, which I hoped would help
narrow down who I'd have the best chance of being cast as.
A quarter of the way through the movie she suddenly slapped
my knee. "This! Pay attention, this is important!"

"Pay attention to what? Nothing is happening."

She was practically squealing. "The Hand Flex Scene!"

"The *what*?"

We were at the part where Elizabeth and her sister Jane had
been staying at Netherfield, the home Mr. Bingley had recently purchased not far from where the Bennet family lived.
At this point it was already painfully obvious that Bingley
and Jane were into each other, while it was equally apparent
that up until now Darcy and Elizabeth were pretty indifferent
to one another. At the same time, Bingley's sister, Caroline,
seemed to already suspect that there was some sort of connection between the two of them, and she was doing a really

good job of low-key dissing the hell out of Elizabeth and her entire family the whole time they were together.

Now everyone was leaving. Jane and Elizabeth were climbing aboard their horse and buggy. Jane and Bingley were being awkward and lovey-dovey, while Darcy and Elizabeth still seemed like they wanted to physically fight each other.

But then.

As Elizabeth was climbing into the buggy, Darcy suddenly reached out and took her hand to help her in. The two made the barest eye contact before he turned and stalked away, but as he did, he did this weird flex thing with his hand. I assumed that's what Cassie was talking about.

"Did you feel that?" she shrieked, bouncing up and down and spilling popcorn all over. "The electricity? The will they—won't they. It's a slow burn. When you watch the movie, it's clear there's some level of attraction between the two. But they both absolutely refuse to acknowledge it, and the tension is just…delicious."

"I got none of that."

"That's because you're young and uncultured. Here, try again."

She rewound the scene and replayed it, then paused it again.

"Did you catch it this time? That one, tiny gesture expresses all of Darcy's anguish and turmoil and longing for Elizabeth. There's so much raw, aching desire. Ugh, it's such a beautiful, poignant moment."

I could kind of see what she meant. And even I had to admit, it was a gorgeous movie. Beautiful lighting, big, sweeping sets, and subtle, intimate camerawork. It felt surprisingly… relatable? I mean, considering that these were characters I had next to nothing in common with, inhabiting a world I literally couldn't exist in. I had to admit, I was emotionally invested, even if part of me kind of wished we'd watched the version with the zombies in it. A little too poignant for my taste, and I really just wanted to turn on some anime, but still… I felt some sort of connection to the story here.

"I think I get it," I said. "At least, I'm starting to."

Cassie shrugged as she poured herself more wine. "Eh, that's better than nothing."

I could only hope she was right.

CHAPTER TWELVE

My friends and I didn't see each other much during the day. I still took the bus to school, while D'Anthony and Jocelyn both got dropped off by their families. Taking the bus meant I was part of the first wave of students to arrive, so the vibe on campus was way more chill than it was during the rest of the day, mostly because most of us weren't fully awake yet. When I arrived on Tuesday I headed to the cafeteria, which was the least crowded place on campus this early. There were small pockets of kids here and there, but there was plenty of open real estate, and even whole empty tables.

I bought a carton of milk and scanned the room for the most optimal seat, where I wouldn't be bothered, but instead I spotted Mackenzie, sitting alone at a table in the middle of the cafeteria with her sketch pad and a plastic bag of apple slices. By the time it occurred to me that she might also want to be left alone I was already headed in her direction, and before I could stop and pretend not to have seen her she had glanced up and spotted me.

Smooth, Cam. Super freaking smooth.

When I got to her table I didn't sit down. I just stood there, hovering across from her. "Good morning," I said awkwardly.

She nodded. "What's up?"

Was she waiting for someone? "Do you always eat breakfast by yourself?"

She bit into one of her apple slices. "Only when I don't feel like being bothered or annoyed."

"My bad. I'll, uh, leave you alone."

She laughed. "Sit down, Cam. You don't bother or annoy me. Mostly."

"Oh. Cool." I settled in and opened my script. For my audition monologue, I'd chosen the scene about halfway through the story when an anguished Mr. Darcy confesses to Elizabeth that despite that her family was poor and her sisters were an embarrassment and basically none of the people in his social circle would ever approve, he was in love with her and wanted to marry her.

She says no, because *obviously.*

The scene was one of the more poignant and popular ones in the story, and the confession itself was only a short paragraph long, so I figured it would give me the chance to pack as big of an emotional punch into my audition as possible without my having to bake my brains trying to memorize pages of complicated dialog.

There was just one problem—now that Mackenzie was here, I had precisely zero interest in any of the words on the paper, and I couldn't for the life of me force my brain to focus on them.

Ken's sudden and unwelcome appearance didn't help anything. I tried to avoid eye contact as he passed by with his tray, but when he glanced in my direction he paused. "Reading more about dragons' balls?" he asked with a chuckle, like he'd just dropped some highbrow humor on us. "Wait, is that— Whoa, don't tell me *you* are auditioning for the play."

"Nah, I'm reading this for absolutely no reason. I'd offer to let you borrow it when I'm done, but there are some big words you probably won't understand."

"That's cute," he said with a scowl as he flounced away.

Mackenzie leaned back. "Okay. That was actually awesome of you."

"Thanks. I think?" Was this compliment of the backhand variety?

"Dragons' balls? For real?"

I sighed. "If I had a nickel for every time he's said that I could pay for college with that money."

Mackenzie shook her head, and seemed to notice my script for the first time since I'd sat down. "You're auditioning for the play, though? For real?"

"I know, it's off-brand for me."

"I wouldn't be so sure about that."

"What do you mean?"

She shrugged, chewing thoughtfully on her last apple slice. "I dunno, for someone who clearly considers himself an outcast, you have a lot of connections around here. G.A.N.U., the paper, now the play. I think maybe you're more well-liked than you realize."

"I'm pretty sure the same could be said about you."

"Probably. I guess I still feel like the new kid on the block here. I'm not sure I'll ever not feel like that."

"Hey, if it makes you feel better, I still feel like that, too. We can both be the new kids on the block, like that old boy band."

She stood and stretched her long arms. "Wow, Cam. Just… wow."

"You know what I've noticed about Lydia?" I asked as I watched her table during lunch. "She never dates. Have any of you ever seen her with a boyfriend?"

"Girlfriend," Jocelyn said with a scowl. "She's made it very clear she's very gay, just like she's made it very clear that no one here is good enough for her."

Her words rang in the ensuing silence.

I wasn't sure how people became part of the Caravan. It seemed like the core members had always been there. I knew of people who clung to it, like Ken, but Ken wasn't truly a member; he was a hanger-on. If he stopped rolling with the Caravan today it wouldn't make a difference to anyone. Karla, Lydia, Naomi, and maybe Jackie—they made up the core, the nucleus, of the Caravan.

Jackie was a cello prodigy and a mathlete, and when she wasn't talking calculus or music she was running Yearbook Committee. She and her boyfriend Phillip broke up and got back together almost as much as Karla and Lucas did. Phillip was student council treasurer and was almost never on campus since he was taking college courses at Minneapolis Community and Technical College as part of the postsecondary education program. They were a dead end. Naomi was a promising lead. I suspected that the only reason she was part of the Caravan was that she blindly did whatever Lydia wanted her to. Getting in good with her might be easier, but ultimately Lydia was the key. If I could impress her, then the others would accept me, and Karla and I were as good as dating. The problem was that Lydia was scary. She was one of those people who just looked cunning. It was probably the way her eyebrows were perfectly arched. She always had this aloof, calculating look on her face that was downright intimidating. When she looked at you it was like she could see right down to your molecules. Jocelyn was the same way. Maybe that was why they hated each other so much.

"Makes sense," said D'Anthony.

"Why do you care?" Mackenzie asked dryly. "You trying to date her? Sounds like an impossibility now."

"No. I just don't get her, that's all."

Mackenzie raised an eyebrow. "And you thought she's the way she is because she isn't getting any?"

"*No.* God. I thought maybe she was having relationship problems or something. And for the record, she's not my type."

Mackenzie leaned forward, smiling wickedly. "Oh really? And just what is Cameron Carson's type, exactly?"

"I don't have to answer that." I could feel my cheeks beginning to burn under her mischievous gaze.

"It's a valid question," D'Anthony was gracious enough to point out. "I don't think I've ever heard you mention being interested in anyone here."

This was not where I wanted this conversation to go. But

all three of them were looking at me, waiting, and it was clear I couldn't wriggle myself out of this one. "I don't have a type," I said. "If I like someone, I just do. There's no set of traits I actively look for."

It was kind of true. Before Karla happened. Like Stella. There was no one thing that had made me want to ask her out. I'd just thought she was cool. I still did, even though it hadn't taken either of us long to realize we were better off keeping things platonic. It was different with Karla. Everything about her was everything I wanted, and I couldn't imagine being happy with anything or anyone else.

"Everyone has a type," Jocelyn said. "Whether they think they do or not."

"Not everyone," D'Anthony interjected. "That's some amatonormativity bullshit, right there."

"Okay, my bad. *Most* people have a type," Jocelyn amended.

"If I have a type, I'm not sure I've figured out what that is yet," I said. But that was a lie. I very much knew what my type was: Karla.

"What about you, Mackenzie?" I asked.

"What *about* me?" she asked without looking up from her sketch pad.

"You started this conversation. Don't think you get out of it. What's your type?"

"Someone who's not an idiot."

"That can't be all. That's way too wide."

She popped a french fry into her mouth. "Is it, though? I'd say at least 95 percent of the people here are idiots."

"Okay, but," I pressed, "how do you sort the remaining 5 percent? There's, what, two thousand people that go here?

That means you'd date a hundred people. There has to be a more narrow qualifier."

"Well, I'm not into girls, for one thing."

"Okay, so that's fifty people. How do you sort them? Let's say you had to date one out of those fifty—how do you choose?"

I wasn't about to let her off the hook, not after the grief she'd given me. And then there was the fact that I was actually curious to know what kind of guy could possibly impress her enough for her to want to date him.

"I wouldn't choose any of them," she replied, "because no one here is my type."

"That's a cop-out!"

"Says Mr. I-Haven't-Figured-It-Out-Yet."

Whatever.

"Jocelyn. Your turn. Let's hear it."

"She has to be true to herself, for one thing."

"That's vague," said Mackenzie. "Fair. But vague."

"That's my only stipulation," Jocelyn said. "There are too many fake people out there. To find someone who isn't is a rare thing."

We all nodded in agreement. She was right. But some people were worth faking it for.

"In vain have I struggled. It won't—it *will not* do. My feelings will not be repressed. You must—wait, yeah—you *must* allow me to tell you how ardently I admire and love you."

I had spent the entire week preparing for my audition. It had been a toss-up between Mr. Bennet, Elizabeth's father, and Mr. Darcy. In the end I'd decided to audition for Darcy because (a) he was one of the only male characters in the play who wasn't skeevy, and (b) I couldn't think of a better way to assimilate myself into Karla's crowd than winning the role of one of the play's leads. I wasn't about to impress anyone as Mr. Bennet, who hardly had any lines, even in most of the scenes he was in.

Was I tall, dark, and handsome? Not really. An eligible bachelor? No. Rich? Ha ha. Also, no. But could I pretend to be all of those things? There was only one way to find out.

No matter how hard it get, stick your chest out, keep your head up...and handle it.

A little inspiration from the late, great Tupac. That's what I needed to do right now. Handle it.

I paused to find my place on the page again. "I have waged a great war with these feelings almost from the first moment—sorry, *moments*—of our acquaintance. I—"

"That's great, Cameron. Thank you."

I stopped midsentence, and bowed awkwardly, alone on the stage, and looked down at Mrs. Vernon the theater arts teacher and director. She was looking at me with a drawn, measured face.

"That was...well done," she said. "Yes, bravo." She clapped furiously. "Tell me, Cameron, what made you decide to audition?"

I cleared my throat, fishing for a plausible lie. "Well. It's something I haven't done. It looks fun. Interesting, I mean."

Mrs. Vernon nodded, and jotted something down in her notepad. "You're auditioning for the role of Mr. Darcy, who plays a critical role here as the main love interest. Why do you think you'd be a good fit for the role?"

I thought about it for a few halting seconds. The stage lights were blinding; I could hardly make out their faces in the glare. In a way it helped.

"I'm willing to put in the time and effort needed to do justice to the character. I want to put my own spin on him, make him my own. I want to completely immerse myself in this production, and I believe this role will let me do that. I don't want to just be a minor character, floating in the background, anymore."

Even to my own ears, that sounded super fucking awful.

"Uh-huh." Mrs. Vernon took more notes. Even in the glare I could tell she didn't look impressed. "Well, it takes bravery to step onto this stage, and I thank you so very much for having the courage to do so, Cameron."

She smiled tightly, and I knew that was my cue to leave. "Thank you." I bowed again, like an idiot, and climbed off the stage. Honestly, it had gone about as well as I had expected it to.

Which was, of course, astronomically, *astoundingly* horribly.

Maybe Karla was right. Maybe I was absurd for doing this. Either way, I'd done it. I could only pray Jane Austen's ghost was on my side.

CHAPTER THIRTEEN

It was one of those cold, wet afternoons where you could feel something was going to come down from the sky, but you couldn't be sure whether it would be rain or snow. Or hail. Or all three. That had happened before.

I gave Cassie a twenty-dollar Pair-O'-Moose gift card to get her to let me use her car. The roads were slick but not icy, but I still drove the old Saturn with extra care. I was a decent driver, but I was on edge, and not because of the weather.

It was weird enough having been to Lucas's house once already, but to be here a second time? My past self would not believe me if I went back in time and told him this would happen, and I wouldn't even have to travel back that far. Three weeks, tops. But then, past me wouldn't believe a lot of the things happening now.

I got up to the porch, and it took longer than it should have to decide whether to knock or ring the doorbell, and in the end I landed on ringing. It was a big house, and there was no telling if they'd hear me knocking. I wasn't sure who I hoped would answer the door more. Being around Lucas still made me nervous, but there was something about Mackenzie that threw me off-balance. I still wasn't quite sure what to make of her.

I was somewhat relieved and more than a little disappointed when it was Lucas that answered. "Sup, bro," he said as I stepped inside. He didn't look like he'd been awake that long; he wore gray sweatpants and a Hilltop Hawks hoodie, his hair was a mess, and stubble lined his jaw. He did, however, smell like weed, so it could have been that he was just high, not tired.

"Smoke?" he offered.

"Nah." *Called it.*

"Right on."

I kicked my shoes off and hovered in place. It looked different in here. Clean. Without a million people crowding around, the place bordered on opulent. It made me wonder what their parents did for a living, but it at least explained why they never seemed to be around; you couldn't afford to not work if you lived in a place like this.

I wondered where Mackenzie was. The hallway and kitchen lights were on, but it was eerily quiet, the way big houses tended to be sometimes, even when people were home, which I assumed his parents weren't.

"You play *Call of Duty*, right?" Lucas asked.

"Which one?"

Mackenzie appeared from somewhere within, in jean shorts

and a white T-shirt. She frowned when she saw me. "You actually showed up. Color me surprised."

I had no good answer, so I just nodded. I couldn't be mean to her, not in her own home. It felt weird.

She nodded. "I heard someone say *Call of Duty*? I'm in. But, here's a concept—we play *Mario Kart* on my GameCube, and I kick both of your asses."

"That actually sounds great," I said, relieved at the suggestion. I hated first-person shooters.

Lucas snorted. "That's how it is?"

She nodded on her way to the other room. "That's how it is. Let me get it all set up."

She disappeared again, and I assumed we were supposed to follow her.

"Hey." He stopped me and waited a few seconds. "You're not trying to get with my sister, right?"

There was a protective edge to his voice, but none of the usual threat that I'd grown accustomed to.

"What? Hell, no!"

Where the fuck had *that* come from?

"I'm just asking, bro."

"Why?"

"I dunno."

Was it not abundantly obvious that Mackenzie and I could hardly stand one another? I mean, every conversation we had was at least 30 percent us just dissing each other. People who liked each other didn't talk to one another like that.

I followed him down to the split-level basement, which ran the entire length of the house. The lowest section, which took up a little less than half the floor space, had been outfitted to be the game room to end all game rooms. There was a pool table and an air hockey setup to my left, and farther in was a leather couch and sectional arranged in front of the TV. Except they didn't have a TV. They had a ridiculous ceiling-to-floor projection screen. On either side were matching state-of-the-art speakers, and to the left was a display shelf that housed every console from the last ten years. Next to that was a solid black desk, and underneath was a gleaming gaming computer.

Mackenzie had already set up a GameCube. She picked up one of the four controllers she'd laid out and handed one to me before plopping on the ground in front of the couch.

"You want in?" Mackenzie asked, waving a third controller at Lucas.

He hopped onto the couch with his phone. "I'm good."

"Cool." She sounded happy he'd declined. "Last chance to back out," she told me giddily as she booted up the game.

"I'll pass, thank you very much." I sat cross-legged in front of the sectional. It would take some getting used to, playing on a screen this big, but I'd make it work. If anything, it might improve my game.

She smirked when I chose Yoshi, my old standby, for his speed and dexterity. "You would," she said as she selected Bowser.

"Interesting choice," I noted.

"It's all about raw power."

"What good is raw power at the expense of agility? Can't hit what you can't catch."

"I don't want to catch you. I want to beat you. Just do me a favor—don't let me win."

"I don't let *anyone* win."

"Good."

Our first match was on Luigi Raceway, a simple enough track, and a perfect place to feel out each other's styles.

It was a close match, and a part of me felt bad when I beat her. Not bad enough to keep me from gloating, but almost.

"You might want to rethink your strategy," I said, then shrugged. "Or, you know, come up with one."

She stared straight ahead and didn't respond, and I worried that I'd gone too far and pissed her off. "Okay," she finally said, in a voice completely devoid of emotion.

The next track was DK's Jungle Parkway, definitely not as simple a track as the first. Neither of us changed racers, and I settled in, prepared to beat her again, but hoping she would at least make it challenging for me.

She then proceeded to soundly kick my ass.

"What...was that?" I said in astonishment once the race ended.

It was her turn to shrug. "I dunno, maybe you shouldn't give me a chance to study your technique next time."

A cold chill ran down my spine.

What followed was what could only be described as all-out, brutal mayhem. Back in the day, Cassie and I used to race each other for hours at a time, and it got intense, so intense that our games almost always ended with either one of us switching the console off, unplugging the other's controller, or throwing ours at them. Mom had had to step in and break things up on more than a few occasions, and I rediscovered the joys of single-player RPGs shortly thereafter.

That was nothing compared to this.

I quickly learned that Mackenzie was methodical, merci-
less, and cruel. Over-under passing, screen watching, precision shell shooting—she knew all the tricks, and she crushed
me on Sherbet Land and Banshee Boardwalk. I managed a
win on Waluigi Stadium, but only just barely. She destroyed
me in Bowser's Castle—"Home court advantage, baby," she'd
said with a gleeful chuckle—and I had to pull out all the stops
to catch a break on Rainbow Road. She took a special interest in toying with me on Yoshi Circuit, and the irony of the
defeat in my symbolic home was not lost on me.

"She beat you again, bro?" Lucas said from where he was
still lounging on the couch.

I'd forgotten he was still here. "Mostly."

He laughed, and then his phone went off.

"Dammit." He sprang off the couch.

"What's up?" Mackenzie asked in a tone that sounded like
she couldn't have cared less. He didn't answer as he moved
quickly to the stairs.

"Karla? Hey, listen…" He bounded up the steps, and I
couldn't hear what else he said.

"Good talk," Mackenzie muttered blandly.

A few seconds later I could hear Lucas shouting from upstairs. Mackenzie groaned. "I don't get that," she remarked
without taking her eyes off the screen.

"Get what?"

"Those two, Lucas and What's-Her-Face."

"Karla?"

"Yeah, Karla. That relationship has died more times than
every *Dragon Ball* character combined. I honestly don't un-

derstand what he sees in her. Like, I get it, she's hot, but beyond that?" She shrugged.

"She's nice," I said after a moment. "Or, she can be, when she wants to be."

What the hell was wrong with me? Why was I defending her?

"Let me guess," Mackenzie said dryly, "you're under her spell, too?"

Yes. "No. I mean, I don't get those two, either. Like, get over it, y'know?" I sounded stupid, even to myself, but I also felt like a gigantic hypocrite, because I had been under Karla's spell for months now.

"What, she's not your type?" Mackenzie grinned sidelong at me.

Yes. "Not really."

She raised a doubtful eyebrow. "You don't like perky tits, a perfect ass, and a pretty face? That doesn't do it for you, huh."

"No. I mean, yeah, I guess, but…you know."

"I don't, actually."

I was getting flustered. Between her precision green shell shooting and the barbed questions she was casually throwing at me, I was losing the battle on all fronts. Before I knew it, she'd crossed the finish line.

She mic dropped the controller. "Maybe next time you should pick a not-so-garbage character," she said smugly. "Oh, and I was just bullshitting you with the Karla stuff. Had to get under your skin, make you sweat a little bit."

"That's…dirty," I said, even as I breathed a sigh of relief.

Mackenzie laughed and poked my shoulder. "This is warfare, my friend, psychological warfare. Or did you think this was a game?"

"Yeah, well, maybe you shouldn't have given up your tactics, because they won't work again."

She picked up her controller. "Oh, don't you worry. I've got a few more tricks up my sleeve."

"That's a short-sleeved shirt."

She looked at me, and grinned. "Touché."

Something crashed over our heads, and I heard Lucas mutter a string of profanities. Mackenzie gave an exasperated sigh, one I recognized all too well. It made me think about my sister and me. We weren't always the best of friends, but we never shunned each other, or acted like the other didn't even exist. My friends knew her, and I had met most of her friends, too, at least the ones she brought to the house. I couldn't begin to understand why Lucas would be ashamed of Mackenzie, especially given that, as far as I could tell so far, they weren't all that different from each other. She was nicer, that was for sure, but if there was some gene or a combination of genes that made a person cool, she definitely had them.

"Why don't you two get along?" I asked. I couldn't help it.

"We get along more than he'd have people believe," she said. "But he's got his image to maintain. My parents used to always say, 'Mackenzie was born first, but Lucas came out making more noise.' He's always been the bigger, louder one, and you know what they say about the squeaky wheel. Everyone assumes he's the gifted one because he's an extrovert, you know? Like, he knows how to work a crowd, make people laugh, and play sports."

"For what it's worth, I don't think he's funny at all."

"That's either because he makes fun of you specifically, or the reason he does it. He doesn't 'get' me, he claims. Or people like me, for that matter. All the 'nerd shit' I'm into, as he so delicately puts it."

"Nerd shit?"

"Right? No points for creativity there. He's never been mean about it, though. Not that I'd let him. I don't know how you put up with him."

"Honestly, he's made life suck for me pretty much since the day we met. Literally. He's only started being nice to me about a week ago or so."

"For real?"

I nodded. "Honest to goodness."

"Makes sense. He calls it him 'turning over a new leaf,' but I doubt it'll stick. He's been a dick for way too long to just turn it off and quit cold turkey."

"Has he always been like that?"

"Pretty much," she said. "Same old story, really. Jock masks his insecurities behind false bravado. Honestly, it's kinda sad."

"What insecurities does Lucas have?" Of all the people I knew, Lucas had the least reason to be insecure about anything.

Mackenzie shrugged. "He knows it's all downhill from here. Even if he hadn't got kicked off the football team, he knows he's not good enough to earn an athletic scholarship, or even make starting line at any college. He's not an idiot, but he's no genius, either, so he'll never be, like, a lawyer or anything. The most he can look forward to is working for Dad and being under his thumb forever or becoming some doughy middle manager stuck reminiscing about the 'glory days' after he graduates. High school is his peak, and he knows it, so he figures he might as well live it up while he can."

"Wow, that *is* sad."

"Tell me about it. Up for another round?"

"You know it. I have a sister," I said as Mackenzie set up the game. "She's older, and she doesn't let me forget it. But she's alright. Don't tell her I said that, though."

Mackenzie smirked. "Well, if I ever meet her, I'll be sure not to."

The thought of the two of them meeting each other made me squirm because I was certain it would immediately become The Roast of Cameron Carson, and I would not survive with my feelings or dignity intact.

That was when Lucas came bounding down the stairs, freshly shaved and in a different outfit, a cleaner, more typical outfit. "I gotta go," he announced.

For a second time a chill ran down my back. "You good?" I asked. "I mean, is she…" I couldn't come up with a way to ask about Karla without sounding like I was vitally concerned, which I was.

"I'm good, bro. I'm out."

"You're leaving *now*?" Mackenzie demanded.

"I should probably get going, too," I said.

"Oh. Okay." She shrugged and stood up. Maybe it was just me, but she sounded disappointed.

Lucas didn't wait for either of us. He bounded up the stairs and vanished again, leaving me in a state of near panic. I stopped myself as I instinctively reached for my phone. I needed to know what was happening, and I had no way of finding out at the moment, due to me being at her ex-boyfriend's house, hanging out with said ex-boyfriend, and it'd be hella suspicious if I suddenly texted her to ask her about a situation I shouldn't technically know about.

"Well, this was fun," Mackenzie said, stretching her long arms. "At least, it was for me. I don't know how much fun you could've had getting beat so many times."

"I know how to bow gracefully," I said with a laugh. This was nothing like when I used to play with Cassie. Those games were competitive, but malicious. This was different. It had been intense, but it *was* fun. *Mackenzie* was fun.

She pretended to dust off her knuckles. "Yeah, well, I *suppose* it's only polite to say you aren't half-bad, either."

Lucas was long gone when we got upstairs. I slipped my shoes on, trying not to think about where he was going, or what he might do when he got there. Getting myself worked up about it was pointless right now.

The rain had receded into a thin mist at some point during the evening, and it was cool out, but not cold, that serene chilliness that sometimes followed the storm, like the earth was taking a deep breath before exhaling. I had only parked at the end of the driveway, but Mackenzie walked with me to my car anyway.

"Hey, thanks for the save, by the way," I said. "I really hate *Call of Duty*."

She shrugged. "Don't mention it. You don't seem like a *COD* guy."

There she was being right in her assumptions about me again. It made me wonder what else she knew about me.

"Hey," she said abruptly as we reached my car. I pivoted to face her. She shoved her hands in her pockets and rocked back and forth on the balls of her feet. "I'm doing this art thing. An exhibit. At my old school. Tomorrow. You should swing by."

That caught me off guard. "Yeah?"

She laughed. "No, I'm bullshitting you. *Yes*. It'd be nice to… I dunno…unless you don't want to, in which case—"

"I'll be there."

She blinked. I'd never realized how thick her eyelashes were. "Yeah?"

"No, I'm bullshitting you. Yes, I'll totally be there."

She smiled, a slow smile that started on one side and worked its way across her lips like they were fighting its progress. "Cool. So…you should probably take my number."

"What for?"

"God, you're stupid." She scoffed, but there was a little less venom in the insult than usual. "So I can text you the time and location? Unless you can read minds."

I grinned as I got my phone. "Not sure I want to know what's in your head, Mackenzie."

I handed her my phone, and she put her number in. "You'd be surprised what you'd find up here."

She gave me my phone back, and I took it from her hand and stood there, not knowing what to do.

She cleared her throat. "Well, I guess, see you around?" She was looking at the ground, nudging a rock with her toe.

"I'm always around," I said, and then felt immediately stupid about it. I swept around to the driver side and threw myself inside. She'd returned to the house by the time I'd backed out of the driveway.

I was aching to text Karla and find out what was happening between her and Lucas, but I couldn't do that without giving away that Lucas and I were hanging out, and that wasn't something I felt like telling her. Even though I'd ended up spending the whole time with Mackenzie, which hadn't been nearly as horrible as I would have imagined. As a matter of fact, it had actually been kind of nice.

CHAPTER FOURTEEN

Mackenzie texted me later that night with the time and the place. She'd ended the text with a smiley face, which was a very un-Mackenzie thing to do. I pondered that smiley face until I passed out at close to one in the morning.

As a general rule I didn't get up on Sunday mornings until the morning was over. And yet here I was, up and showered and dressed at 11:45, on a smelly, creaky old city bus on my way downtown.

Interdisciplinary Downtown School was an art magnet off of Tenth Street, right in the heart of the city, in a four-story building that was in reality a converted parking garage. It was connected by the skyway to the Art Institute of Minnesota, and within walking distance of the performing arts district, home of the Orpheum, the Guthrie, the State, and the Pantages theaters. I could totally picture Mackenzie here, right in the thick of it all. It was an artist's paradise, nearly as eccentric and bold as she was.

I understood now why she hated Hilltop so much.

I got off on Hennepin Avenue and Nicollet Mall, and shuffled into the giant, two-story Target store to get the skyway. From there it was only a ten-minute walk to the school.

The ground floor of the school still had a slight incline from when it had been the entry level of a parking garage. It had been converted into a wide-open gallery. Cream-colored partition walls had been arranged in a loose maze, and each was lined with colorful framed works, rich, textured landscapes, soft, languid pastels, and vibrant, abstract shapes. Display stands staggered throughout the floor held sculptures, small statues, and busts. The lighting was soft, warm, and perfectly accentuated the works it was illuminating.

The crowd was decidedly casual. Mackenzie had been absolutely correct when she'd suggested I dress like I was "going on a first date with a girl you really like but who you're pretty sure is slightly out of your league," which was a very un-Mackenzie thing to say. But I was glad I had thrown on the only blazer I owned. There was a palpable energy pulsing through this place that gripped me like a Van de Graaff generator as soon as my foot hit the polished wax floor. It was crowded but not claustrophobic, kinetic instead of chaotic, noisy without being loud. For a moment I was lost in the ebb and flow, swept up in the spectacle, and I forgot I was here to see Mackenzie. But as I wandered from display to display, absorbing the sights and the sounds, the hum of conversation and the gentle vaporwave music lilting from the sparse speakers high in the ceiling, I began to feel the buildup of some unseen force, a pull that was drawing me toward some inexplicable end. I made my way inward, surrendering to the pull without being consciously aware of it, and then I saw her, in an orange slouchy beanie that matched her sneakers and the square patches in her denim overalls. She was standing in front of a massive, seven-by-four-foot portrait. It was a collage of faces, some animated, some nearly photorealistic. Wonder Woman, Eartha Kitt, Motoko Kusanagi, Maya Angelou, Rosie the Riveter, Marilyn Monroe, Gloria Steinem, Michelle Obama, Supergirl, Virginia Woolf—and woven between and around the faces were elegantly written words. I couldn't make them out from where I stood, but I couldn't take another step closer. It was beautiful. I felt like a pilgrim who had journeyed to pay respects to a shrine that I was unworthy of nearing. There was also a small crowd of admirers gathered around Mackenzie, and I didn't want to intrude or interrupt.

I was content to observe.

Mackenzie seemed to have two settings. The first was this almost aloof, it's-whatever-I'm-doing-me version of herself, the version that reminded me the most of Lucas, and then there was the fangirling, manga-referencing übernerd who gushed about her hobbies without shame or self-consciousness. That's who I was seeing now, as she engaged the slew of people who swarmed around her like paparazzi. That's who she'd been last night. I wondered which one was the real one.

I worked up the nerve to step closer, and I realized that the words on the portrait were quotes. Before I could read any of them, someone called my name.

"Hey! You're here." Mackenzie had spotted me, and now that her fans were leaving she was coming over to where I was admiring her work. "You actually came. I gotta admit, I wasn't sure you had it in you."

"I'm a man of my word," I said with a laugh. "Apparently you are, too. Not the man part. I mean, um—your art is amazing, is what I'm failing to say."

She shook her head and laughed. "Thanks. Nerd."

I laughed, and shuffled in place. I had no idea how I was supposed to act with this version of Mackenzie.

"So, um, tell me about your work." It was the only thing I could think of.

I couldn't be sure, but I thought she might have blushed. "It started with this quote I read, from Gloria Steinem— *Girls actually need superheroes much more than boys do.* That got me thinking about how even from a young age boys have all these powerful figures to look up to, and girls don't. Girls aren't taught to be powerful or strong or self-reliant. Society doesn't really enforce that concept. This was me wanting to celebrate the women of power that we do have to look up to, whether they're real people or not."

I moved closer, studying the pictures and the words. Many of them were from the late Maya Angelou. One quote stood out to me.

When you know you are of worth...you just are. And you are like the sky is, as the air is, the same way water is wet. It doesn't have to protest.

"Mackenzie, this is incredible," I said as I studied the words up close.

"Thank you," she said, beaming proudly. "I mean, it's a little on the nose, but I felt like it needed to be."

"No, this is great. I love it."

A girl with purple hair in a blazer skipped over and tapped her shoulder. "Kenzie! Some people from the Art Institute want to ask you a couple of questions."

She lit up. "For real? Let's do it. Oh, Laya, this is Cameron."

Hearing her say my full name sounded strange, and I realized that she usually called me Cam, just like my other friends did. How hadn't I noticed that before?

Laya waved and smiled tightly, and I could tell she was anxious to take Mackenzie with her.

"I'll, uh, I'm gonna look around," I said. I didn't want to hold her up.

"Okay. Hey, come back around if you decide to stay."

"I will."

She smiled quickly, and then hurried after Laya.

For the next forty-five minutes I meandered the floor, taking in the different pieces, drinking the grape juice, and wondering if I should stick around longer or hit the road. I was still trying to decide what to do when someone behind me tapped my shoulder. I spun around, and it was Mackenzie. She'd changed into jeans and a T-shirt, and her hair was pulled into a curly ponytail. "We're going to lunch. You're coming with me."

She linked her arm in mine and started leading me toward wherever lunch was. I didn't protest. I was too swept up in this new Mackenzie. "Who's we?"

"You, me, and some friends of mine."

"Oh nice," I said weakly. I had the sinking feeling that this wasn't going to go over well. I wasn't good at meeting—or making—new friends, especially the kind of friends Mackenzie probably had.

Before I realized what had happened we were surrounded by seven smiling, laughing faces. Names were thrown at me faster than I could catch them, hands were shaken, hugs were exchanged, and then I was caught up in their momentum and we were moving, out the doors and up the escalator and into the skyway. Energetic conversation bounced back and forth from every angle.

We ended up at a small family-run pizza parlor not far from the school, where one of the girls (her name may have been Esther) and one of the guys (Yusef, maybe?) dragged a trio of tables and their chairs together so we could all sit together. I was the newcomer, and had no idea what the pecking order or the usual seating arrangements were, but Mackenzie grabbed me by the arm and pulled me into the seat next to hers. It was such a nonchalant motion that I was sure no one else even noticed it, but I was grateful.

Grateful. To Mackenzie. Fucking weird.

Once everyone knew where they were sitting, they split up to get food. Mackenzie and I, along with two other girls (Mariah? Christina?) stayed behind to watch the purses and phones. Maybe-Mariah, who was sitting across from Mackenzie, leaned in past Maybe-Christina, who was texting furiously on her phone. "Kenzie tells me you're into anime?"

I nodded. "To put it mildly."

"Uh-huh." She waited expectantly, and I realized she wanted me to go on. I wasn't used to that, to people other than Jocelyn and D'Anthony giving a shit about my hobbies.

"He's obsessed," Mackenzie said. "Like, me-levels of obsessed."

"God. I didn't think that was possible."

They both laughed.

"You go to the same school, right?" asked Maybe-Christina, who I was beginning to think was actually named Catalina.

"Hilltop High," I said. "It's in Robbinsdale. Not too far from here."

"I think I have a cousin who goes there. Do you know a Tandy Lewis?"

I bit back the involuntary grimace that started to form on my face. "I know of her," I said. "We're not close or anything."

"That's good. She's a bitch."

I laughed, relieved that I wasn't the only one who thought so.

Once everyone was seated and eating the conversations became impossible to keep up with. It was like starting a TV series in the middle of the second season; most of the references and in-jokes went over my head, but it was still fun, and it didn't take long for me to at least pick up on the main threads.

The girl I thought was named Mariah was actually Mercedes, and she and Catalina were dating. Ashanti had graduated last year and was now attending Saint Thomas, pursuing a degree in engineering. She loved college, but the workload was ridiculous. Laya was a junior and Yusef's younger sister. Samuel had placed nationally on their school's bowling team and was hoping to go pro, which I didn't know was a thing.

Just when I thought I was beginning to get a handle on who everyone was, two more guys and another girl joined us. They were soon followed by three more people. It was too much to stay on top of, but somehow Mackenzie did it. I shouldn't have been surprised; this was her world and these were her friends; I just hadn't expected her to have so many of them.

It was the weirdest thing, watching someone straddle these two worlds, worlds I thought were mutually exclusive. How was this even possible? She was wearing a Capsule Corp jacket. She freely and frequently referenced all sorts of manga and anime—and not even the obvious stuff; obscure shit, shit I didn't even catch at first. And yet here she was, surrounded by the same kind of people Karla might be seen with. This, what I was witnessing, what I was experiencing—this was something new entirely. Two worlds, blended seamlessly into one cohesive whole.

My mind kept coming back to Maya Angelou's words. *When you know you are of worth…you just are.* Mackenzie didn't try to prove anything to anyone. She just *was.* It was incredible. I started to realize that there weren't two separate parts to her. It was all her. That overlap of self-assuredness was all her, too.

We spent an hour at that table, until one by one people began to break away, and I was surprised and slightly unsettled that as they said their goodbyes everyone seemed to remember my name.

Mackenzie and I parted ways with Mercedes and Catalina at the top of the escalators, and then it was just us two, and I was finally able to come up for air.

"Hey," she said. She chewed her lip before speaking again, as if she wasn't quite okay with what she was trying to say. "I really appreciate that you came. It…kinda means a lot."

I wanted to shrug it off, say it was no big deal, like it was something I would have done for any of my friends. Only I wasn't so sure it was.

"Anytime. It was a lot of fun."

"Don't get it twisted, though," she said, grinning. "You're still the worst."

I laughed. "Likewise."

She smiled and nodded, and I smiled and nodded, and even though I knew this was the part where I was supposed to leave, I couldn't. I stood there, frozen at the top of the escalator, still smiling like a doofus, and then she stepped forward and pulled me into what was part bro hug, part real hug, and it caught me so off guard that I couldn't even hug her back before she'd pulled away.

"See you around," she said.

I stumbled backward onto the escalator, dazed and confused. "Yeah. See you around."

Instantly, my mind went back to when I'd watched *Pride and Prejudice* with Cassie, and how she'd gushed about the Hand Flex Scene. I remembered the look on Elizabeth Bennet's face when Darcy had taken her hand to help her into the carriage, and suddenly I understood exactly what she must have felt in that moment, because I was feeling it now.

CHAPTER FIFTEEN

I was disappointed but honestly not at all surprised when I stopped by the auditorium on Monday to see that my name wasn't on the cast list. Not after my train wreck of an audition. I only wished I hadn't wasted so much time with it. The list was a who's who of the Theater Snobs circle, because *of course*. Again, no real surprise. And anyway it didn't matter, because if Lucas and Karla were back together it would have been pointless regardless.

I'd spent half of the last thirty-six hours composing a text message asking what was up, and whether she and Lucas were a thing again and if we were through, and the other half of it talking myself down from hitting Send. She'd tell me, one way or another, and when I did find out I wanted it to happen in person.

But I broke when I spotted Lucas outside the gym at school that morning before classes started. I'd never been so relieved to see that asshole, even if he was flanked by his three idiot flunkies, because if he was with them it meant that he wasn't with Karla, and today that was good fucking news. I called his name and walked right up to them.

"Sup, bro?" he muttered. He looked hella stressed, and not at all like he and Karla were back together. The others fell back as he stepped forward, and we did that stupid bro-hug thing again. "I'll catch up with y'all later."

The three of them looked at each other, then reluctantly wandered off.

"You good?" I asked Lucas. He definitely didn't seem like it.

He cupped his hands over his head and groaned. "I think we're over," he said numbly.

"You mean you and Karla?"

"Who else?"

"Huh." An uncomfortable blend of satisfaction and guilt frothed in my stomach. If Lucas had finally given up hope, then... "Why do you say that?" I asked. I had a fairly good idea of why, but I wanted, *needed*, to be sure.

"It's never gone this long," he said. "We should be back together now. We were only supposed to be taking a break. That's what she told me. Only a break."

Jeez. He sounded like he was on the verge of a nervous breakdown. He reminded me of Vegeta, the once mighty prince of all Saiyans, after Frieza had beat the shit out of him and left him to an ignoble death, and how he'd begged Goku, pleaded with tears in his eyes, to avenge him and his people. It had been tragically touching then, and the beginning of his transition into a more sympathetic character in the series.

Right now, it was only tragic. And awkward, all things considered.

"Sorry to hear that," I said, even though I really, truly was not.

He shook himself, and tried to muster some of his signature bravado. It didn't quite work. "It's whatever, bro."

"Hey, man, don't force it," I said. "If you two are meant to be together, you'll work it out."

I couldn't believe I was saying this.

Lucas leaned his head back, then chuckled. "That's some Hallmark movie–type shit, bro."

I couldn't help laughing myself. "I might actually have gotten that from a Hallmark movie. That, or a Lifetime one."

The warning bell rang, and all at once the mad dash to get to class on time began. "Catch you later," I said. I needed to get moving.

"Thanks, bro," he said, and the note of sincerity in his voice gave me pause.

"No problem," I said, and then I rushed away as if I would be able to outrun the guilt that had suddenly settled in my stomach.

The realization that what I'd just done was a hard-core dick move hit me like a fast ball: hard and with pinpoint precision. Maybe that's why I had this icky feeling in the pit of my stomach. Looking him in his eyes and telling him not to give up on the girl I was trying to be with was pretty fucked-up, I could admit that. I wasn't even sure why I'd said what I'd said to him. This wasn't supposed to be about getting back at

Lucas for all the shit he'd done to me over the years. This was supposed to be about Karla. Maybe I was losing sight of that.

Or maybe it was all of it. So much was happening at once. Between Karla and me, *and* between Lucas and me.

I've got three lives balanced on my head like steak knives. Frank Ocean wrote those lyrics, and I felt them now.

But then there was *Mackenzie* and me.

The icky feeling twisted into apprehension as I entered Spanish class. But what the hell was wrong with me? This was Mackenzie. We argued and traded insults every day. We got on each other's nerves every time we saw each other. This was stupid. *I* was stupid.

She wasn't here yet. I went to my desk and sat down, but my anxiety didn't go away. I couldn't stop thinking about the way she'd hugged me. We'd hugged. I'd gone to her art show, and we'd hugged.

When she finally showed up, she wasn't alone. There was some guy with her, a tall and good-looking guy with dimples, which I only knew because he was smiling. They both were. And laughing. About what was anyone's guess and absolutely none of my business, but for some reason something about them didn't sit well with me. Maybe it was because I'd never seen Mackenzie smile like that before, or maybe it was because I didn't recognize the guy she was with, or maybe it had nothing to do with that situation at all and it was just my nerves and stress throwing me off.

Whatever the heck was happening, I was still watching them lingering inside the doorway when the warning bell rang, and Mr. Dimples reluctantly departed. Mackenzie seemed to watch him for a while before turning and making her way to her desk. My heart stopped, and so did I.

I stared at my hands, and I felt like I was breathing extra loudly. I should say something. It would be weird not to say something. But I didn't know what to say. I didn't know where we stood with each other. Was I supposed to do the usual, throw some snarky shade her way? Was she going to do it to me if I didn't do it first? If I was being truly honest, I liked the Mackenzie I'd met at the art show. She was…nice? Pleasant, even?

"Hey," I croaked, immediately torpedoing any hope I had of having a normal interaction with her.

She shook her hair out of her face and looked over at me. "Hey."

Maybe I had imagined it, but I could swear she'd said it almost like a question, like maybe she didn't know where we stood with each other, either.

I swallowed. She nodded. The bell rang, and I stared straight ahead for the rest of class.

This was weird. I couldn't not notice her sitting next to me, taking notes like the rest of us. The way she held her pencil, how she hunched over her desk and let her hair droop down and almost cover her face. She smelled good. Something clean, like fresh linen. I'd never noticed that before.

"It's raining," I said in a weak attempt to fill the pressure cooker silence between us.

"You know," said Mackenzie with a grin, "turkeys are so unintelligent that they'll stare up at the sky with their mouths open until they drown."

I looked over at her. "I'm pretty sure that's a myth."

She looked up from her sketchbook. "Maybe. But I know some people who are probably foolish enough to do it."

"Jerk."

"Gobble, gobble."

I rolled my eyes, but I laughed. This was closer to normal for us. Close, but not quite there.

Five minutes before class ended my phone vibrated. I glanced at the screen under my desk. It was Karla.

Meet after class?

A flush of relief surged through my nervous system.

I typed a quick reply. Cool.

I put my phone away and sat up straight, and when the bell finally rang I gathered my stuff and stood up, just as Mackenzie was doing the same. We filed up the aisle and left the room, almost shoulder to shoulder. I moved to go left, and she moved to go right, and we bumped into each other.

"My bad," I said frantically.

"You're good."

We looked at each other.

"Well," I said.

She nodded, rocking on the balls of her feet. "Well…"

"I'd better…"

"Yeah, same."

We stood there, shuffling our feet awkwardly.

I couldn't take it.

"Have you heard of the Christmas Truce of 1914?" I asked "During World War One the British and German troops who'd been fighting each other for months stopped fighting to celebrate Christmas Eve together?"

"I've heard of it, yes."

"Well…"

The frown melted away from her face, replaced by a triumphant smile. "Are you thinking of conceding victory?"

"A temporary cease-fire," I amended.

"Why?" she asked. I supposed she had every right to be suspicious.

"I don't know." I didn't, not at the moment. "I just figured…"

"Because we're friends now, right?" she asked dryly.

I nodded reluctantly. "It just feels weird now, I guess."

"It's not like we weren't friends before."

I raised a brow. "We've been friends this whole time? That's news to me."

"That's because you don't pay attention," she said with a cheeky smile. "I'm mean to all my friends. Sarcasm is how I relate to my surroundings."

"Oh. Wow."

"I accept your surrender, though." She smiled proudly as she brushed past me. "It takes a big person to admit they've been beat."

I turned after her, grinning. "*Temporary* cease-fire. This isn't over."

I bolted to the library, still feeling weird about what had just happened. But any lingering thoughts about that weirdness evaporated when I saw Karla waiting for me in the stacks. "You're late," she said, and before I had the chance to even come up with a reason she had shoved me against the wall. We slid to the ground, and she climbed onto me.

I tried not to be like guys like Lucas, the way they talked

about girls, or the way they didn't even try to be discreet about drooling over them. They acted like the Jawas from Star Wars lusting after a shiny droid. There was a time and a place for that sort of thing, and I tried hard not to have a case of what my mom called "wandering eyes."

But right here, right now, this was that time and that place, and my eyes were most definitely wandering. My eyes, and my hands. She was soft and firm, salty and sweet, and I loved the way her body responded to mine, the way her perfume filled my head, the way her tongue tasted on mine.

Something was different about the way she kissed me this time. There was a frantic, greedy feeling to the way she touched me. She was moving faster than I could keep up with, and then without warning she stopped, pushed me down, and pulled her shirt up over her head and off. Before I could process what was happening, she was reaching behind her back, and then her bra came undone. Slowly, she let it fall. I heard a sharp inhale, and realized it was me.

There was a world of difference between seeing boobs in a bra versus seeing them out of one. I'd seen Karla's boobs in a bra before. It was a lot like seeing them in a swimsuit; it was great, but if you walked around sprouting a boner every time you saw cleavage you had a problem, or several. But seeing her boobs free and unclasped, and only inches from my face, was something different entirely, something I couldn't begin to describe. My higher brain function completely shut down, probably because my dick was so hard against my jeans that I could actually feel the strain of the zipper.

"Sorry," I stammered.

"For what?"

I sat up. "I was thinking," I said between gasps of air.

"About what?" she asked, her breath warm on my neck.

"About us."

She stopped kissing me and straightened up. "Us?"

I nodded. "I think we should…you know…"

"Say it," she demanded. "I want you to say the words."

My cheeks flushed, and butterflies took flight in my stomach, but my mind was made up. I wanted this. God, I wanted this.

"Sex," I said, and the word felt new and strange, "I want us to have sex."

Karla smiled, and rewarded me with a slow, deep kiss. "Tonight? My place. My folks will be out. We'll have the whole place to ourselves."

"Hell, yeah." I hadn't expected it to be so soon, but I was ready.

"Hell, yeah." She kissed me one last time, and slipped back into her bra and pulled her shirt back on. "Six o'clock? Don't disappoint me."

"I won't," I said, stifling a nervous laugh.

I hoped I wasn't lying.

CHAPTER SIXTEEN

I got home and took the longest shower I'd ever taken, and then I spent nearly just as long shaving. My face, my nuts—I'd never shaved my balls before, and I hoped when I finished that it wasn't something I'd ever have to do again. I briefly considered jacking off before I left—I'd read somewhere that that could help keep from finishing early—but I decided not to. With my luck, and the way my nerves were now, I'd somehow manage to break my penis and ruin the whole night.

Two more gift cards got me Cassie's car for the evening. My teeth rattled so hard as I drove to Karla's house that I could barely hear where my GPS was telling me to go. Never in a thousand years would I have guessed I'd end up outside Karla's door, but that's exactly where I soon was, just over an hour after I'd come home from school. At least I knew she was home; her Malibu was parked in the carport when I pulled in. I took a moment to cram half a pack of Tic Tacs in my mouth before getting out.

I felt the weight of each step I took up the driveway. I rang the doorbell, completely expecting to have somehow come to the wrong house, but then the door opened, and Karla was there, smiling.

"Hi," she said.

"Hi."

I took a deep breath, and hadn't realized I hadn't moved until she said, "Did you wanna come inside?"

Right. Shit. I stepped in, and when she closed the door behind me I caught the light scent of shampoo and soap.

"So," she began, "how…are you?"

"I'm…okay. You?"

"I'm fine."

We stood there, both of us staring at the ground, and I noticed how she was playing with her fingers, and I realized that she was just as nervous about this as I was. It was almost comforting.

"I, um, brought condoms." From health class. They gave them out like candy.

She seemed surprised. "Oh. Cool. I did, too. Just in case."

"Oh. Cool."

We were still standing in the living room.

Was this what it was like the first time? So far, we were off to a slow, painfully awkward start. Hopefully this wasn't what we could look forward to the entire time.

"So," Karla said, breaking our awkward stare-off, "should we…go somewhere, or…"

"Yeah. That'd be cool."

She rubbed the back of her neck. "Okay. Follow me."

I did, and she led the way in and up a flight of steps.

I hadn't been in too many girls' bedrooms, so I had no frame of reference now. Hers was big, with a queen-size mattress, a walk-in closet, and a thirty-inch TV on one of the dressers on the far wall, which was next to a set of massive white bookshelves. There was a display case with all of her awards and trophies, and above the headboard of the bed was a big world map cluttered with photos and sticky notes. Everything smelled like Karla's perfume, a pink bottle of which was on the night stand next to her bed.

"Your perfume is called *Bombshell*?"

"Appropriate, isn't it?" Karla replied with a wink.

I'd run through this exact scenario at least a hundred times in my head since this afternoon, but now that I was here, and this was really happening, all my mental preparations went up in smoke.

And then I spotted something I never in a thousand years would have expected to see anywhere near Karla's room: *Star Trek: The Next Generation*, the complete DVD collection, sitting on one of the shelves like it was supposed to be there, not even hidden.

"Seriously?"

"What?"

I pointed at the DVD. "This whole time you've been a secret Trekkie? What the hell, why didn't you ever tell me?"

This was bullshit. All this time my friends and I had been ostracized because of the things we enjoyed, because we were too "nerdy," when all the while she was hiding the fact that she was just as nerdy as we were. All of this secrecy, this pretending, was pointless, because she was just like me.

"I didn't tell you," she said slowly, "because I'm not a *Trekkie*."

"Oh really, because the special edition of the original se-ries says otherwise."

She sighed. "Cameron, let me ask you something. Have you ever wondered why most of the kids at school treat you the way they do?"

"Because 99 percent of the kids at our school are assholes."

"No. Well, maybe. It's not the fact that you like the stuff you like that makes it weird. It's the fact that you're *so* ob-sessively into that stuff that weirds people out. Like, it's your *whole* life. It's possible to enjoy something without being *completely* obsessed with it, without it being the *only* thing you ever talk about. So yes, I like *Star Trek*, and I watch it, *casually*, but I'm not so wrapped up in it that it's the only thing I care about. Do you understand the difference?"

I scowled. I was trying very hard to discredit what she'd said. It was no excuse for the way they treated me and my friends, for the way they ignored us. But at the same time, and even though I hated to admit it, a tiny part of me acknowl-edged that on some level, at least the rationale behind it made some sort of sense.

"Hey." She cupped my face in her hands and guided me toward the bed. "Hey. None of that matters right now. All that matters right now is you and me."

She took my hands in hers and pressed them against her chest. I could feel her heart beating rapidly as she wrapped her arms around my neck.

My hands found their way to her waist, where my fingers curled around the hem of her shirt. Her stomach was soft and warm as I inched her shirt up, pausing just slightly at the slow reveal of her bra, and she let go of me and tugged the shirt up and over her head herself, before pulling mine off. It was strange being shirtless in front of her, but I was only fleetingly self-conscious when I saw the way she looked at me. We crashed into one another, and she wrapped her legs around me as I laid her down on the bed. This felt just like it did when we were in the library. I was lost in the moment, and I wasn't worried about what was happening, or what could happen, or what might happen. This felt right, and nothing else mattered.

I felt her hands at my hips, and then her fingers working as she unhooked my belt buckle. I straightened up and undid my fly as she watched with eager eyes. I kicked out of my jeans and stood there in nothing but my boxers, unsure of what to do next. Karla grinned as she reached back and unhooked the clasp of her bra. My breath caught in my throat at seeing her completely naked from the waist up for the second time. I was relatively certain it was something I would never get used to.

She slid to the edge of the bed and stood up. Slowly, she started inching her panties down.

That was when her phone went off.

"Shit." She straightened up, pulled her panties back up, and snatched her phone off the dresser, pausing to clear her throat before answering. "Yeah? Hey!"

I used the interruption to try and catch my breath and gather my wits. My head was swimming, and every muscle in my body felt electric. So far, this seemed to be going alright. I hadn't done anything stupid or embarrassing, yet. Maybe this was going to go alright, after all. While I caught my breath, I took the opportunity to get a better look at her room. Karla had *a lot* of books, and the spines were meticulously arranged according to size and color. A lot of the titles were science-fiction works, many of which I'd never read or never even heard of. I had no idea Karla was such a fan of the genre, and I never in a million years would have guessed as much.

What else didn't I know about Karla?

She was pacing in a tight circle on the other side of the room. I glanced up at the map hanging over the bed, and upon closer inspection saw that some of the locations were circled in green marker. Some of the photos were of famous land-marks, like the George Washington Bridge in New York, or Cloud Gate in Chicago, or the Griffith Observatory in Los Angeles. Dublin and Paris, Quebec and Belize, London and Egypt—places I hardly thought about, much less imagined visiting. It had never occurred to me that Karla had put so much thought into leaving.

On the other side of the room Karla suddenly stopped pacing and sighed. "I thought…yeah…I have a friend over…No, that would be great!…'Kay, see you in a bit. Love you, too."

The second she hung up her shoulders dropped, and she groaned loudly. *"Dammit,"* she muttered.

"Is everything okay?" I asked, even though I had the sinking feeling that I knew exactly what was going on. I recognized the talking-to-your-parents voice.

"My folks are on their way home," she said, confirming my suspicious. "Both of them. They were supposed to be going out for dinner tonight, but they changed their minds and want to eat in. They're stopping to pick up a couple of pizzas first. *Dammit.*"

"Should I go?"

"No," she said as she went into the closet. "They'll think something's up if they come home and you're gone already.

I was hoping telling them I had company would keep them away, but I guess not. Fuck my life."

"So…you want me to stay…and meet your parents?" That couldn't be right.

She came out of the closet in a pair of sweatpants, and pulled a hoodie on over her head. "It'll be fine. They're used to me having people over. Lucas practically lived here."

"That's something I definitely needed to know," I said dryly.

Karla sighed. "I said 'lived' as in past tense. And we never did anything, remember? I mean, not like what you and I were doing. Or, about to do. God, I'm so irritated. Like, the one night I actually want my parents to be away is the night they decide not to be."

"Are you sure you don't want me to leave?" I asked. If she was already annoyed, I really didn't want to be around to accidentally add fuel to the fire. I always felt a little awkward around families when there were two parents. I usually ended up ignoring the dad altogether. Not intentionally, of course. I just…didn't know how I was supposed to interact with fathers.

"Did you…want to leave?" Karla asked.

Kind of. "Nah."

"Great. You should probably get dressed, though," she added with a grin as she threw her hair up in a quick ponytail.

"Right." I gathered my clothes, fresh panic churning in my guts. Meeting Karla's parents had absolutely *not* been what I'd planned on doing tonight. In fact, it was the complete opposite of what I'd planned. I was *so* not ready for this.

We were sitting across from each other—with a completely platonic we-totally-weren't-about-to-fuck-each-other distance between us—at the dining room table, pretending to be working on homework, when her parents came home with two extra-large pizzas.

"Hey, guys. This is Cameron," Karla said in a completely casual, almost offhand tone.

I stood up. Karla looked like both of her parents somehow. She had her mother's dark hair and her father's bright, friendly eyes. They were dressed like they were supposed to have been going somewhere fancy, and they looked like models from a Macy's commercial.

"Hi, Cameron," said her mother.

"Good to meet you," her father said jovially. "Hope you two are hungry."

I responded with a nervous nod, even though eating was the last thing I wanted to do right now.

The first several minutes of our dinner were spent in complete silence, with everyone looking down at their plates. I couldn't taste the pizza. I was too busy wondering how long it would take for one of her parents to realize that all of the notebooks and textbooks we'd cleared aside were hers, and not mine. I wondered if it was my presence that was making it so weird, and how much longer it would be until it was safe for me to excuse myself and escape.

Finally, someone broke the silence.

"So, how long have you two known each other?" her mother asked. The question seemed to be more directed at me than Karla.

"Ninth grade. I think," I added, so it didn't sound so horribly pathetic.

"Oh, that's a while," her mother said, and I completely understood where the surprise was coming from. If I was supposedly one of Karla's friends, why hadn't I ever been around before now?

"Has it been that long?" Karla asked, with almost as much surprise as her mother. "It hasn't been that long, has it?"

"Yeah, it has," I said quietly. At least I could confirm for an absolute certainty that she'd forgotten all about that day when we'd first met, the day that was etched so remarkably clearly in *my* memory.

"What are you into, Cameron?" asked her father.

I swallowed the automatic response: anime.

"Writing," I offered instead.

"He's on the school paper," Karla added. "He's good." It was almost exactly what Mackenzie had said, except there was something different in the way Karla said it; it was kind of like she'd thrown it out there to end the conversation, like, *He's good, okay? Let's drop it.* I figured she was doing it for me, trying to take some of the heat off me and not leave me to field her parents' questions on my own. I should've been grateful, but instead I was, slightly, resentful.

Her father nodded. "Big plans after you graduate?"

"I don't know if they're big, but I've definitely got plans." I took another bite of the pizza I still couldn't taste, looked up, and saw that all three of them were waiting for me to elaborate. "I'm going for journalism," I croaked. "I'm hoping to get into the University of Minnesota." I doled out each bit of information carefully, unsure of how it would be received.

Her mother smiled. "What an interesting choice," she said, and I realized where Karla got her politician's voice.

"Why journalism?" asked her father, and I wasn't sure

whether I imagined it or not, but I thought I saw Karla's mother toss him a dirty look.

"I guess, I like the power of the written word," I said, trying to choose my words judiciously. This was the first time I'd really said any of this out loud to anyone other than my adviser at school. "I think it's cool how what we read, like how it's worded, can impact how we process information. Two articles can be about the exact same thing, but if one is well-written and the other isn't, it can change everything. I think that's cool."

Her father nodded approvingly. "You've got a good head on your shoulders. I like that."

He directed that last part at Karla, who rolled her eyes, and it dawned on me that her parents might have thought I was her boyfriend. The idea filled me with a strange sort of pride, as if, maybe, if her parents approved of me, the idea of us actually dating wouldn't seem so far-fetched.

Of course, their approval would be short-lived if they found out or suspected what I'd actually come here for, but it was far too late to worry about that now, so I focused all my attention on eating pizza in a totally normal, not-at-all-nervous way. Whatever the hell that looked like.

After dinner Karla walked with me to the carport. By now my nerves had settled, and now that my anxiety was fading I was left with only the exhaustion.

"That didn't seem so bad," I said.

Karla shrugged absently. She'd been uncharacteristically quiet throughout the entire evening.

"I mean, other than the whole 'plans being ruined' part. But we can try again, right? If you still want to?"

"Um-hmm."

I huffed. She was angry. It wasn't fair of her to be all pissy toward me. I wasn't the one who screwed up tonight. If anything it was her fault. Maybe she should've been sure her parents weren't coming home so early tonight.

When we got to my car I wordlessly unlocked the door. Fine. If she didn't want to talk, I wouldn't, either.

"They liked you," she said just as I was about to climb in. I stopped. She was hugging herself, her expression cloudy. "More than they liked Lucas."

"Oh." I felt like there was something else I should say, like there was something I wasn't picking up on. "That's a good thing, isn't it?" Shouldn't you want your parents to approve of the guy you were sort of hooking up with? Or was that the problem, that their approval was reserved for the guys she was actually dating?

"It's just…that was the first time my parents actually sat down together like that without it ending in a screaming match in I don't know how long. It reminded me of how things used to be."

"Oh." It all clicked, the tension I hadn't quite realized I was sensing, that feeling of mild discomfort. I felt like the world's most perfect asshole. "I'm sorry."

She shook her hair against the evening breeze, and it was like she was shaking off her sadness, shedding it like a skin. "This was fun," she said, suddenly and unnervingly cheerful. "I mean, it wasn't a complete disaster. Things could've gone a lot worse."

I nodded in agreement. "Crisis averted, I guess."

"Maybe," she said.

It didn't seem like she wanted to go back inside.

"Wanna get in?" I offered.

She tilted her head to one side. "What, like now?"

"Why not? It's—" I glanced at the passenger side, where there were only a few straw wrappers and receipts scattered on the floor "—pretty clean in here. Decently clean."

She shook her head, smiling, but then she came around and climbed in. "I don't think I want to lose my virginity in the back seat of your car," she said slowly. "If that's what you had in mind here."

"No, that totally isn't what I had in mind," I said, laughing at how ridiculous of an idea it was. "We both have pizza breath, for one thing, both your parents are waiting just inside, and this is my sister's car, which I definitely could not expose my genitals in, even if you wanted me to. I just... wanted to talk."

She arched a skeptical brow. "Talk? About what?"

I shrugged. "About you."

She squinted. "Me?"

"Yes, *you*. Not us, not sex, just...you."

She bit her lip as she thought it over. "Okay," she said, shifting in the passenger seat so we were angled toward each other. "What do you want to know? Ask me anything."

I grinned. This was like what we used to do when we worked together, taking turns asking silly questions to make each other laugh. Only I wanted to know things that mattered now.

"Tell me about the map in your room."

"Oh that? It's just a reminder. Something to look forward to. I have all these things I want to do, and sometimes it's like the rest of the world isn't moving fast enough. I'm restless, you know? Okay, but think about it. This time next year we could be doing things we've never done before with people we haven't met yet. I can't wait for that. Like, this is only senior year of high school, and I know a lot of people are like this is the 'end of an era' or whatever, but it's really only the starting line. We haven't even *started* living. Sometimes this all feels like...practice."

"So, you're just biding your time and counting the days until you can get away from here?"

"Well, yeah. Cameron, we're on the verge of a brand-new chapter in our lives. I don't want to get there and still be dragging all the baggage from before with me."

I frowned. "You think everything you've done up until now is baggage?"

"Of course not. You *know* that's not what I mean. I'm just...over it."

"Over what?"

She waved a hand vaguely. "Everything. I've done all there is to do. It's time for a fresh start."

I thought about all the trophies and awards in her room. All the accolades she'd earned over the years. "You're bored."

She leaned back and sighed deeply. "Yeah. Maybe."

I used to think I was just made to be a loner. That who I was and who I wasn't would always drive people away. That I was never going to be enough to be accepted. But that was before I met Jocelyn and D'Anthony. Before I had G.A.N.U. I couldn't imagine saying goodbye and completely cutting ties with them without ever looking back.

"I'm excited to see what's next for you," I said.

"Thanks." She smiled as her text tone rang, and she reached for her phone.

"You still keep it in your back pocket, huh?"

"It feels wrong keeping it anywhere else," she said as she read the screen.

"Your parents?"

"Student council stuff. We're putting together another fundraiser and they need me to weigh in on whether to do a bake sale or some sort of auction or a raffle. I'd better go."

She slipped out of the car, and I rolled the window down when she came back around to the driver side instead of going back inside.

"You aren't baggage," she said. "I hope you know that. And even though tonight didn't go the way it was supposed to *at all*, I'm glad you were here. But that does leave us with some unfinished business…"

"It does indeed."

"Unless you're having second thoughts?"

"Definitely not. Are you?"

She reached down and kissed me. "Definitely not. See you around, Cam."

It wasn't until I was halfway home that I realized this was the first time she'd called me Cam, not Cameron.

Only my friends called me that.

Was that what we were now? A slow burn, like Darcy and Elizabeth?

CHAPTER SEVENTEEN

"I finally saw *Pacific Rim*," D'Anthony said during breakfast. "Oh, I'm sorry, I meant, I finally saw Guillermo del Toro's Shameless Rip-off of *Neon Genesis Evangelion*. Can I just say that I think it's unforgivable that in this day and age we don't have mech-technology yet?"

I couldn't help laughing at D'Anthony's rant. It was just the sort of normalcy I needed right now in these weird times. "Would you trust anyone you know, any of these people—" I waved my arm to indicate the swath of people pressing in on us in the hallway "—with a giant weaponized robot?"

"I wouldn't," D'Anthony said, "but that's why we would have mech battles. I have a laundry list of people I'd love to demolish with an arm cannon or shoulder-mounted torpedoes."

"Okay, Char Aznable, press the breaks on those homicidal tendencies."

"You know you'd do the same—your laundry list is probably longer than mine."

"Maybe." A couple of weeks ago, that might have been true. But these days I wasn't so sure who my enemies were and who my friends were. The lines were blurring.

My mind was still stuck on last night. In a way, I was glad we hadn't been able to go through with it. Suppose Karla and I did have sex. Where did that leave us? We weren't a couple, that much was certain, and I wasn't delusional enough to pretend that we were, but we were definitely more than friends, even though I didn't know whether we even considered ourselves friends or not. That left us in some sort of nebulous, nameless relationship that defied definition or classification. Were I a romantic, I would've thought of us as a modern-day Romeo and Juliet, only hopefully without the whole suicide pact at the end. As it was I was only a regular idiot, and I knew that this thing between Karla and me had little to do with romance.

And besides, at least Romeo had Mercutio to back him up. I couldn't even tell my best friends about us, even though I sure as hell could use their advice right now.

Or maybe I was thinking about the wrong piece of classic literature.

Something Cassie had said came to my mind. She'd called the relationship between Mr. Darcy and Elizabeth Bennet a "slow burn." Was that what Karla and I were? A real-life slow burn?

A loud commotion erupted behind us, and we pressed ourselves against the wall as the Caravan passed by. Generally it was best to avoid the Caravan if you weren't a part of it; the last thing you wanted was to make yourself a target. Most of them were content just ignoring the common folk, but there were a few among their number who actively sought someone to make the victim of their games. Today's toxic mix didn't include Lucas or his cronies, but a shark missing some of its teeth was just as dangerous.

My stomach twisted. That was the group of people I needed to ingratiate myself with.

"God, I hate them," D'Anthony muttered.

"Do you ever wonder if maybe they aren't as bad as they seem?" I asked. "Like, maybe we just don't understand them, and they don't understand us?"

D'Anthony laughed sourly. "Oh, I understand them perfectly. That entire clique is full of nothing but stuck-up douchebags, girls included. They've been like that since forever—they aren't ever going to change."

It was easy to forget that D'Anthony, like Jocelyn, had grown up in Robbinsdale, and this was mostly the same group of people they'd grown up with. The smart thing to do would be to believe them, but I couldn't, and I used to justify that because I knew Karla better than either of them did, but last night made me realize that wasn't necessarily true. I knew the Karla that everyone knew: the president. The cheerleader. The assistant director. She of the perfect hair and flawless face. But that wasn't all there was. I couldn't claim to truly know her as a person just because we made out sometimes. I kept telling myself that I wanted to be with Karla, but could I really claim to want to be with someone I hardly knew anything about?

The staff of *The Quill*, Hilltop High's student newspaper, met regularly in room 308, on the third floor of the left testicle, in what we called the bullpen, but what was really just an open room with all the desks pushed against the walls. There were ten of us in total; six reporters, two photographers, our cartoonist, and our student editor-in-chief, Amanda, who ran the paper like she was the love child of Captain Ahab and J. Jonah Jameson.

"Alright, team, let's get to it," she barked. "I want to leave this paper in better shape than I found it. From here on out, no more puff, no more fluff. We're doing this for real now."

I groaned. The first issue of the paper was always the most boring. It was geared almost entirely toward incoming freshmen, which meant articles like "Steps to Success: Navigating the Staircases," or "Hot or Cold: A Guide to Lunchtime." My contribution had been a nice little piece called, "Don't Hold It: How to Find the Nearest Bathroom." It included such sage advice as "check paper before you sit down," or "play something loud on your phone so no one hears the splash-back."

Truly the height of journalistic excellence.

I joined *The Quill* my junior year for the elective credit, and because, as Cassie liked to say, I had strong opinions about things most people didn't care about. Sometimes I reviewed new albums or movies, and every so often I'd get to write about a new or upcoming anime or manga. Usually, though, I was assigned boring stuff like interviewing the kid with the highest GPA that quarter, or covering the renovations to the tennis court. Still, it was an easy enough gig, even when Amanda wasn't being an absolute tyrant, or giving the best assignments to Cleft-Chin Ken, as he was known among G.A.N.U. members, on account of the extreme crevice of a dimple that nearly split his chin in two. Also because he was

an asshole. He insisted that he was both a reporter and a pho-
tographer, even though he wasn't all that great at being either.
He'd interviewed us once before, and he'd made it very clear
that (a) he couldn't have cared less what we had to say about
our group, and (b) he was only talking to us in the first place
because Amanda had forced him to.

"I was thinking about covering the fall production," he said
now. "I know most of the cast and crew, after all."

I almost snorted. Cleft-Chin Ken was Caravan-adjacent—
not officially a member, but sycophantic enough to have
latched himself on to them like a barnacle. Ken was all about
appearances, which was why he dressed like he owned a yacht
and insisted on only being seen with the right people. It was
also why he'd insisted on being assigned the sports beat. Sports
articles wrote themselves, and he'd lobbied hard for it since
that meant not having to struggle to come up with anything
original to write while still guaranteeing his name was in
every issue of the paper for at least the whole semester, which
would look better on college applications.

Now he wanted the play, too.

"No can do, Ken," Amanda said. "I'm putting Cameron
on it."

I did a double take. "Huh?"

She scowled at me. Having to repeat herself was a special
pet peeve of Amanda's. "You. Cameron. Will cover. The fall
production. Did you catch all that?"

I nodded.

"I don't want you skimming the surface on this one, either. Enterprise copy. I want you following the entire show,
from rehearsal to performance. Got that?"

I nodded again, confusion and excitement warring inside me.

"Good." Amanda clapped her hands and pointed at T.J., who was sitting in the corner across from me. "I'm giving you the exchange student feature. *Feature*. Got that, T.J.? Give me feeling, not just facts and figures."

"I'm on it," T.J. said excitedly, jumping out of his seat so fast he nearly knocked over his laptop.

What the hell?

Everyone knew T.J. was into Klaus, our exchange student from Germany. Giving him the feature was a huge favor. Just like giving me the play. Amanda had never been big on favors.

What was going on?

I could feel Ken staring daggers at me, but I was honestly too confused to care.

"Movie night, my place," Jocelyn announced that Friday. She was shaping strips of plastic into what looked like armor. "I am in *desperate* need of a distraction. I physically cannot touch another piece of PVC."

"Count me in," said D'Anthony. He was on his Game Boy yet again. *Yuri!!! on Ice* played from the wall-mounted TV, but none of us was really paying attention to it. I assumed we'd all already seen it.

I glanced at Mackenzie. She was hunched over her sketch pad, a latte on the desk beside her. "What are we watching?"

Movie night was sacred to G.A.N.U., and I didn't take missing it lightly. Neither would the others. But I didn't have any other choice. There was a read-through tonight, and I couldn't miss it. I'd decided to take the piece seriously, and, if I was being honest, I was looking forward to seeing Karla. My maybe-friend.

"I was thinking maybe *Gunbuster*," Jocelyn said, "Maybe *Bubblegum Crisis*."

"Subbed or dubbed?" D'Anthony asked.

Not this again.

"Are you a sub or a dub person?" I blurted at Mackenzie, my sort-of-friend.

I'd much rather hear her thoughts than listen to Jocelyn and D'Anthony retread their same tired arguments. Jocelyn sat up straight, and they both waited. They reminded me of the scientists at NASA command center, waiting for confirmation that the Apollo 13 mission had landed safely in the ocean.

Mackenzie chewed her lip thoughtfully, and I realized I was just as eager to hear her response as they were.

"Well, in my opinion it depends on which one you get introduced to first," she said. "Like, I think the *Sailor Moon* sub is superior, but I first started watching the old *Toonami* dub, and to this day that's the version I prefer because it's what's most familiar to me. I think as long as you're enjoying what you watch, it doesn't matter whether it's subbed or dubbed."

"But wouldn't you agree that subs are more accurate and closer to the source material?" Jocelyn countered.

"Maybe, but not always, especially with the newer stuff that's a lot of times written specifically with an international audience in mind."

"That's true, but even so, lots gets lost in translation."

"Yeah, but not enough to take away from the experience. Someone watching dubs doesn't come away with a completely different understanding of the story than someone watching the sub."

"In most cases."

"True, but I feel like in those cases it's because of the way it was dubbed, like if the voice acting sucked, not the fact that it *was* dubbed."

Jocelyn frowned, and I held my breath, ready to break up the argument if it started to get heated. "I guess that makes sense," she said, to my absolute shock.

And, apparently, to D'Anthony's, too. "What?" he said, setting his Game Boy aside. "Hold up, so you agree with her, but not me?"

"*She* makes valid points, *you* never do."

"Wow." He picked his Game Boy back up, pretending to be indignant. Jocelyn went back to whatever it was she was working on.

Another beat of silence. I supposed this was as good a time as any to break my news.

"Guys, I can't make it to movie night."

I waited, bracing myself for the shock and outrage, but all I got was Jocelyn's half-hearted "Oh, okay."

"I got assigned to cover the play. Rehearsals start tonight."

Still nothing.

"Hey, Jocelyn, why don't you ever work on the play?" I asked her. "You could do set design, or set construction. Or both."

"Hmm, let me think, there's the fact that I hate everyone involved, for starters. It would mean taking time away from my cosplay work, for another. Oh, and also because I would rather do *literally* anything else."

She had a point.

"No one's gonna miss you," said Mackenzie. "If that's what you're wondering."

It was weird how much that stung. But she grinned. "I'm messing with you. Sort of."

CHAPTER EIGHTEEN

After school I hurried down to the auditorium, where the theater kids were setting up. The entire cast and crew was already crowding around the front of the stage and the first several rows. I made my way down the aisle, the clipboard rattling in my hand. This was enemy ground. Hostile territory. Every theater snob in this entire building was here, mulling over thick scripts or huddled in groups having quiet conversations among themselves. This was concentrated snobbery, thick and rich. Heads turned and noses turned up as I approached. I was a foreign pathogen here, and this body was about to reject me. Aggressively.

"What's *he* doing here?" I heard someone ask.

"He's not on the cast list," someone else said.

I squared my shoulders, scanning the crowd for a friendly face. There were none.

They formed ranks as I descended the aisle, and I felt like I was facing down an army. Alone.

"Hey, guys. I'm the, uh, correspondent. For the paper. *The Quill?*" I waved my trusty notepad.

Four people crossed their arms.

"I thought *Ken* was supposedly the correspondent," Lydia said with a voice dripping in scorn.

"I'll handle this." The crowd parted, and Karla emerged, holding a book and her own clipboard to her chest. "Walk with me," she said as she brushed past me.

I did as I was told, and followed her back up the aisle. She turned to face me when we were well out of earshot of the others. Her expression was unreadable. I couldn't tell whether or not she was annoyed.

"Look, before you accuse me of stalking you again, I didn't ask for this assignment," I blurted. "Amanda gave it to me. I can let Ken have it if you want. If it's going to be weird."

Karla crossed her arms, the clipboard dangling from one hand. "Do you *want* this assignment?"

I sighed, glancing behind me. The swarm had gone back to what they'd been doing before, but some of them were still tossing suspicious eyes my way. "It could be interesting. If they don't end up sacrificing me to the ghost of Jane Austen."

Karla laughed under her breath. "Good. In that case, congratulations, and you're welcome." I frowned. "I *might* have had a word with Amanda," she explained with a sly smile. "I'm the production manager. That means I'm your point of contact. Feel free to ask me anything. Anytime. You and I are going to be spending a *lot* of time together. That's not going to be an issue, is it?"

"What if it is?"

She bit her bottom lip. "Then we should probably talk about it later. In private."

I felt my cheeks flush, and averted my eyes, focusing instead on my notepad. "Okay. So, why this play?" I asked, eager to divert attention away from my nervousness.

"We felt it was relevant, thematically," Karla began in her Student Council President voice. "At its core, it's about these two people who completely misunderstand each other, and over the course of the story they learn to overcome their pride and their prejudices in order to see each other for who they really are. It's a nice reminder that our first impressions of people aren't always right, and in fact sometimes they're completely wrong."

"So, a slow burn?"

She raised an eyebrow. "Yeah, I guess you could call it that. Sure."

"There's more to it than that, isn't there? I mean, there's a whole class system between them, too. Everything about how their world is set up says they can't be together. But they make it work, in the end."

"Yes," she said slowly. "In the end, they do."

"Wow," I said as I finished my notes.

"What?"

"Oh nothing. It's just, that sounds like a certain situation I know of."

"What, us?" she asked, dubiously.

"Why not?"

"Because we didn't hate each other. Did we? I never hated you. Did you hate me?"

"No." But I was supposed to. Jocelyn had once said that G.A.N.U. was meant to be the antithesis to everything the Caravan was. We weren't meant to like them or be like them. From what I always understood, the feeling was mutual.

I decided to change the subject. "What are you reading?"

Karla looked down at the book she was holding as if she'd forgotten it was there. "Oh. *Death on the Nile*. It's one of my favorites."

I thought about all the books she had in her room. And the map with all the notes and photos. "What are your other favorites?" I asked. "Like—okay, name your top three favorite books."

"Top three? That's tough." She clicked her tongue as she thought about it. "Okay, so *Frankenstein* is one. Did you know Mary Shelley started writing it when she was only eighteen? Wow, right? Then there's *Dawn* by Octavia E. Butler. And then…this is hard. Does it have to be three? What about top five?"

"Nope. Only three."

She laughed. I liked how serious she was taking this. It meant I might actually learn something real about her.

Suddenly, she stood straight up, shaking herself and squaring her shoulders. In an instant she had formed herself into the Karla she was whenever we weren't alone. The one everyone else knew. I glanced over my shoulder to see why: Lydia was approaching, taking crisp strides until she was standing with us.

"Like I was saying," Karla stammered, "the show debuts on the Friday of Thanksgiving break, meaning we've got a little less than a month to perfect the production. There are five types of rehearsals—the first are the read-throughs, where everyone gathers and just reads through the script, like tonight. No acting, no movement, just everyone reading through the play. Once read-throughs are done, we start what we call blocking rehearsals, where the actors practice their movements and start to figure out who needs to be where in each scene."

"What's taking Mrs. Vernon so long?" Lydia asked Karla without acknowledging I was even standing there. "We've got a lot to do."

"I'm sure she's on her way," Karla said. Her face was beet red and her eyes were bugging. I'd never seen her look so nervous.

I glanced back and forth between them. Lydia stared down her nose at me, a sneer on her lips. Karla wouldn't look up from her clipboard. Lydia looked at her, then at me, then turned on her heel and left.

"God. How are you friends with her?" I asked under my breath.

"She can be cool," Karla said. "Sometimes. Like, she isn't mean, she just doesn't put up with anyone's BS."

"I've noticed. She reminds me of one of my friends, actually."

It was a fairly common trope in manga and anime that the Student Council—and especially its President—were the most respected and feared people on campus, even more so than the teachers. The President was usually upheld as the paradigm of perfection, academically and in their personal life. They called the shots and made the rules, and the rest of the Council enforced them. No one crossed the President, not if you valued your continued well-being.

I'd always assumed the Caravan was like that, but now, more and more it seemed Karla was only the face of the group, the mascot, in a way, and Lydia was the true puppet master, the Emperor Palpatine, or, as D'Anthony might say, the Final Boss.

"Right. So…"

"You can watch, if you want. You can sit next to me."

"That sounds good."

Suddenly, Mrs. Vernon came storming in, clapping her hands over her head, and everyone stopped and waited for her direction.

"Let's get started, folks! We've got a lot of ground to cover. You again? Lovely to see you again, dear, but I didn't think we gave you a part this time around."

I froze, sputtering, and Karla took a step forward. "He's the correspondent for the paper. He's going to be following the production."

Mrs. Vernon looked up at me through her half-moon glasses. "Just make sure not to get in our way, you hear?"

I nodded quickly. "Yes, ma'am."

She nodded curtly, then made her way to the stage. Everyone clustered around her.

It was strange seeing everyone crowding together like this. Mrs. Vernon directed everyone to stand in a wide circle, in the spots she'd designated for them, with the main cast closest to her, and everyone else in descending order depending on how much they appeared in the play. The lighting and technical crew were farthest from her. I stood off to one side, outside the circle, hovering next to Karla. Mrs. Vernon went around the circle, introducing each member of the cast and their role in the play. I took careful notes.

Lydia, naturally, was Elizabeth Bennet, while Naomi had been cast as Jane. I only paid cursory attention to the rest of the cast because they were the ones I needed to focus my attention on.

Pride and Prejudice had three acts, and tonight Mrs. Vernon wanted to focus on getting through half a dozen scenes that made up act one.

"What we're looking for here is accuracy, folks," she said as they all opened their scripts. "Don't worry about anything else. Remember, this is a *read*-through. We're not acting yet, folks. Let's start with the narration. Wyatt, if you would be so kind."

Wyatt nodded, cleared his throat, and began in a voice that was not unlike that of a news anchor. "It is a truth universally acknowledged, that a single man in possession of a good fortune, must be in want of a wife."

"My dear Mr. Bennet," Jackie, who was playing Mrs. Bennet, said, reading her lines carefully, "have you heard that Netherfield Park is let at last?"

Mrs. Vernon tapped the table. "Alright, folks, do we know what Mrs. Bennet means when she says Netherfield Park is 'let'?"

Lydia raised her hand. "It means the property is occupied," she said smugly.

"Very good. Continue."

"I had not," said Kevin Jackson, who was playing Mr. Bennet.

Mrs. Vernon held up a finger. "Remember what we talked about. I need you to project, Kevin. We can't hear you up here. Remember, everyone, there are two dozen rows in that auditorium—that's twenty-four rows of people who need to hear what you're saying."

Everyone nodded, and Kevin continued, slightly louder this time. "I had not," he said.

As I watched, the seeds of a plan began to take root in my head.

Karla's friends were the reason we couldn't be together. They hated me, or at the very least didn't like me. But what if I changed that? What if this was my chance to change their minds about me? It would be a long shot, that was for damn sure. But I had to try.

The read-through lasted just under two hours; in that time the cast had gone over the first act almost three times. "Excellent work, people," Mrs. Vernon said as they all packed up and mulled toward the door. "I want to see the same enthusiasm when we start blocking!"

Karla lingered with me while everyone left, pretending to be preoccupied with her phone. "What'd you think?" she asked.

"It's a lot more than I thought it'd be," I admitted. "You all have your work cut out for you."

She nodded. "That we do."

I looked down. Lydia and a couple of the others were quietly talking halfway up the aisle. Lydia tossed a not-so-covert glance our way. Karla sighed. "I'd better go," she said.

"Are you afraid of her?" I asked quietly.

Karla jerked her head in my direction. "Lydia? Of course not," she hissed. But then she huffed. "I mean… I don't know. Why would you ask me that?"

I shrugged. "I dunno. I mean…you're student body president. Don't *you* make the rules?"

"Please tell me you don't actually think that's how government works. The president isn't a monarch or an emperor. I was elected, and when you're elected you have to do certain things, behave a certain way, and uphold a specific set of ideals."

"Or else you get impeached, yeah, I took AP Government Studies, too. It's required."

"But we're not really talking about government, are we?"

I shrugged. "I just figured people would do whatever you tell them to, you know? March to whatever drum you beat."

Karla inspected one of her nails, and I assumed this conversation was over. "It's not that simple," she said after a moment of silence. "What about *your* friends? Would they be cool with *us*?"

She had a point, and we both knew it. There was the social order, and all of its nonsensical, inescapable rules. The more I learned about Jane Austen's work, the more I was starting to think little had really changed between her time and ours. "Hey," Karla said. "Text me tonight?"

"Sure." She'd been right when she'd said the play was relevant. It definitely was. Depressingly relevant. I just had to remember that Darcy and Elizabeth did eventually get their happily-ever-after. Hopefully Karla and I would get ours, too.

She hopped off the stage and met the others. I watched them leave, and wheeled around when I heard someone walking behind me. Naomi was emerging from backstage, frowning and staring down at her phone.

Here was my chance to put my plan into motion. "Hey! Naomi!"

She didn't stop at first, so I tapped her on the shoulder. She turned, annoyed, and groaned. *"What?"*

"I wanted to get your thoughts on a couple of things, if you're cool with that." She didn't look like she was, so I launched into my question before she could respond. "What made you decide to audition for the role of Jane? Was it something that drew you toward her character?"

"I didn't," she said flatly. Her eyes darted down the hall, in Lydia's direction, and I understood. She'd wanted the role of Elizabeth, but Lydia got it instead.

Interesting.

"You know, there are some who would say Jane is the emotional backbone of the story."

She turned her nose up. "Who says that, *SparkNotes*?"

"Well, think about it. The plot begins with Jane. Sure, Mr. Darcy and Elizabeth resolve their differences and get married, but I would argue that the true through-line of the play is Jane's arc. Everything ties back to her. Which, in a way, makes her the most important character in the play, as far as I'm concerned."

Naomi cocked her head to one side and looked at me like I'd only just started speaking. "I would never have assumed you had more than a passing familiarity with Austen."

I shrugged. "Her work is important. Not just to literature, but to history, art, music—everything."

She raised a brow, and I hoped I hadn't laid it on too thick. "I like that," she said. "Important. That's the perfect word."

She nodded approvingly, and I breathed a sigh of relief. That relief was short-lived, because I'd just doomed myself to becoming intimately familiar with everything Austen had ever written if I wanted to keep myself in Naomi's good graces. At least all the research I'd done up until now wouldn't go to waste.

CHAPTER NINETEEN

Summer

"Okay, so tell me this. Why do girls keep their phones in their back pockets? It only takes once to sit on it and, just, *obliterate* your screen."

We were closing down for the night. Stella was up front, kicking our last few customers out, but in a nice way, which for Stella wasn't really nice at all. But she was effective, which was why it was her who always did it.

Karla and I were washing the dishes in the back. I passed her another platter. She rinsed it off and placed it neatly on the drying rack. "Because those are the only real pockets on women's pants," she said. "If we even get those."

"What about putting your phone in your purse?"

"Uh-uh. My turn. What's with hairy legs? Doesn't that bother you, feeling all that under your jeans or against your socks?"

I laughed and passed her a plate. This was an extension of

the game we'd been playing. She'd ask me a question, completely random, about boys, and I'd ask her one about girls. It was interesting, getting an inside look into the workings of a girl's mind aside from my sister's, interesting and intriguing. "I can tell you with absolute certainty that no guy has ever been bothered by his own leg hair."

"Okay, but what if your pants are really tight?"

"Nope. Question for question. Them's the rules. Heels. They look painful. Why do you wear them?"

It was her turn to laugh. "Pain is beauty, my friend. Besides, they make your calves look fucking amazing."

"Fair enough. Last one." I handed her the final clean cup and pulled the plug and watched the water swirl as it drained from the sink. "I still don't believe you about the pocket thing, though."

"Really? Feel my pocket. See how shallow these shits are."

I rinsed the suds off my hands and patted them dry with a towel. "I'll take your word for it."

"Nope. You doubted me. Put your hand in." She jutted her hip at me. I couldn't tell if her pants were actual pants or leggings, but her legs looked fine without her wearing any heels.

"Really, I—"

"Do it!" She gave me a playful scowl, but she wasn't budging.

I gave up. "Okay…" I tossed my towel over my shoulder. "This is hella weird."

"It's only a pocket."

Easy for you to say, I thought.

I braced myself, and slid my finger into the tiny pocket. I barely got past the first bend. "Damn, these are shallow."

"Yeah, now imagine that's how every pair of pants you own were."

"That's tragic."

Our eyes met, and I didn't dare so much as twitch my finger. My cheeks burned, and I just knew I was blushing. People assumed brown folks didn't blush, which was absolutely stupid because (a) blushing was a physiological response to psychological duress, which had nothing to do with melanin, and (b) of course we fucking did.

I snatched my finger out of her pocket like it was a hot stove top. Karla laughed.

I backed away, and moved on to rearranging the tubs of chocolate. Not because they needed to be. I needed something to do with my hands because the room had suddenly become a very small space.

Karla opened the fridge and started rotating the milk cartons, sorting them according to expiration date and bringing the oldest ones to the front.

"So…" she began while she worked. "You and Stella…"

"Nope." I crouched and started on the tubs at the bottom of the storage rack.

"Come on," she whined. "It can't have been that bad."

I started to move past her, but she closed the refrigerator door and blocked my path. I was cornered.

I groaned like I was annoyed, but I was anything but. "Fine. We went on a few dates, hung out a few times, realized we were better off as friends. No big deal."

"Was it a physical thing? Like, were you a bad kisser or something?"

I shrugged. "You'd have to ask her. Actually, please don't do that."

"Oh, but I'm curious now."

"Sucks to be you."

I tried to push past her, only for her to close the space between us. "Let's find out," she said.

"What do you mean?"

She moved even closer. "Kiss me."

"What?" My heart jumped into my throat. "Are you... Do you really..."

"Yeah, you said you didn't know if it was because you sucked at kissing. Kiss me and I'll tell you."

I tried to read her expression, tried to figure out if she was serious or if this was some sort of joke. But she waited, standing right in front of me. I could feel my heartbeat in my ears, pounding like I was running.

"Close your eyes," she said softly.

I did as I was told, feeling like a complete moron. But I felt her move closer, then a finger on my chin, and I tilted my head down, and she pressed her lips softly against mine.

I wasn't sure how long the kiss lasted, but when we pulled away from each other it felt like it had lasted an entire, perfect lifetime. But as soon as we let go of each other the reality of what had just happened went off like a bomb in my head.

"What was that?" I demanded frantically.

"Not bad," she said, her lips curling into a grin. "But once could be a fluke. We need a larger body of work before we can make a conclusive decision."

By the time she'd finished her sentence she had her arms locked around my neck. I pulled her into me, and when we kissed again, it was like the world had split in two.

★ ★ ★

"Hey. Gimme your phone."

We were outside the storefront, Karla and I, waiting for our rides while Stella locked up for the night. I shook my pocket, finding my phone among the wads of crumpled bills and jangling change. It had been a good night for tips.

"What for?" I asked. I knew for a fact that she had hers on her; I could see it poking out of her back pocket.

"Ohmigod, just let me see it." She stomped her foot impatiently, and I handed it over. "You don't keep it locked?"

"What for?"

"Um, so someone can't steal it and have access to all your shit. Duh."

I shrugged. "Maybe I like to live dangerously."

"Or stupidly," she said with a smirk.

A shiny gray SUV pulled slowly into the lot.

"That's me," Karla said. She handed my phone back. She'd put her number in and hit Dial. I frowned in confusion and looked up. She was halfway to the car. She glanced over her shoulder and answered her phone. "Smooth, right? Text me sometime."

"I… Sure?" My brain was still catching up with what was happening.

She smiled and hung up, leaving me dazed. I sat on the curb, staring at her number, saved to my contacts.

"She's just bored," Stella said as she joined me on the curb. Her eyes were glued to her phone, but she sat down cross-legged beside me. "You do know that, right?"

"What are we talking about?"

"The Princess. Don't give me that look. I see you two. Everyone does. Just...don't get too caught up in it, alright?"

Her mom's car rolled up next. Stella stood up and yawned, her eyes still glued to her phone.

"Thanks, Stella," I told her.

"Just looking out for you. You didn't need a ride home, did you?"

"I'm good. Cassie's on her way."

"Cool." She hopped in the back seat of her mom's car, and I watched it peel off. Then I sent Karla a text.

Maybe this wasn't the end, after all.

CHAPTER TWENTY

It was a strange week.

"We missed you at movie night," Mackenzie said as she slumped into her chair next to me in Spanish on Monday.

"No, you didn't."

"You're right," she said, grinning.

"Hey, how's Lucas?" I asked. I hadn't run into him lately, and I wasn't sure if it was coincidence or because I was subconsciously avoiding him.

"Why don't you ask him?" she asked pointedly. "Aren't you two bros now?"

I laughed uncomfortably. "Not exactly. I wouldn't call us bros."

"You're not really anything like the kind of people Lucas typically hangs out with."

"Is that a good thing or a bad thing?"

She shrugged. "Probably a good thing. I'm undecided."

★ ★ ★

"Well, if it isn't Cam the Man," Ken said mockingly when he saw me that Tuesday.

I groaned as he came sauntering to meet me, slicking back his shimmering hair. We never spoke to each other outside of *Quill* meetings, mostly because of his being a giant tool, so I assumed this was about to be a weird conversation.

I was not wrong.

"Listen, I just want to make sure everything is copacetic," he said, propping himself against the lockers. "That means satisfactory."

Here's the thing about Cleft-Chin Ken: he treated mansplaining like it was a competitive sport. If it were, he'd be an Olympic-level athlete.

"I know what it means. What the hell are you talking about?"

"Oh, I think you know," he said, a snakelike smile spreading across his thin lips.

"I promise you I don't," I assured him.

He leveled a smug gaze my way. "I know Karla talked to Amanda about giving you that assignment. Why would she do that? What's up with you two?"

My blood ran cold in my veins. How the hell had he found out about that? I struggled to gather myself. "Ken, if you spent as much time on your writing as you did on your ridiculous conspiracy theories, you'd be the editor."

He recoiled. He'd actually tried for the editor position last year, but he was absolutely not at all qualified. "Watch your back, Cameron," he warned.

I was sure he meant it to be threatening, but it came off as clichéd. Who even said that in real life?

★ ★ ★

It was going to take a lot of faking to get in good with Naomi. She'd never been my favorite person. Unlike Lydia, who was never overtly malicious, but rather let her glare do most of the talking for her, Naomi could be very mean and very loud. But the thing was, I'd always suspected that she didn't intend to be, either; that she just didn't have a filter.

Naomi and I had fifth period web design together, a fact that neither of us had acknowledged yet, mostly because we never, ever talked to one another despite the fact that she literally sat right next to me. Whereas before I couldn't have cared less about our sharing a class, I saw it now as a golden opportunity.

I got to class a full six minutes before anyone else. I set up shop, booting up my desktop and emptying the contents of my backpack onto the desk, which included a worn copy of Jane Austen's *Emma*, which I laid on the corner of the desk. It was only worn because I'd found it at Half Price Books for, like, a nickel over the weekend, and apparently Stacey, the person whose name was scrawled on the inside cover, was a big fan. I'd never actually read it, but I was armed with all the knowledge Wikipedia could provide me on the book, or at least what I could remember, which, honestly, wasn't a lot. I knew that the eponymous Emma got herself into trouble trying to set her friend Harriet up with the wrong guy, and that she herself almost fell for the wrong guy, but ended up realizing that the guy she should have been with all along was the guy she routinely got into arguments with.

Or something like that.

I placed the book carefully, positioning it so it looked like it was left there casually, as an afterthought, like I might just have been reading it, and not so it was obvious I wanted anyone to clearly see what it was. It was a matter of degrees. One millimeter in the wrong direction would fuck the whole thing up. Naomi was no fool.

She came into the room, talking to Jackie, and neither of them so much as looked my way.

I waited, barely paying attention to my work, fidgeting with my hands, playing with my pen, anything that might catch her eye.

Nothing.

Fuck.

I waited all class period for her to look in my direction, trying all kinds of tricks. I crumpled up a piece of paper, loudly. She inclined her head, but didn't look over. I got up to throw the paper away in the waste bin at the front of the room and came back, making as much noise as I could when I sat back down. Jackie looked at me with a what-the-fuck look, but Naomi still didn't glance my way. I peered at the clock. Class was halfway over. There was no point in my having brought this stupid book here if she wasn't even going to notice it, and I didn't want to have to repeat this whole thing tomorrow.

I had to do something drastic.

With five minutes left to go, I started packing up to leave, and I watched from the corner of my eye as Naomi did the same.

I had to time this just right.

I watched the second hand arrow make its slow circle around the clock. With thirty seconds to go, I lifted my backpack while I looked at my phone, as if I wasn't paying attention to what I was doing.

The bell rang. Still looking at my phone, I pushed my backpack across the desk, nudging the book off and onto the floor just as Naomi was sliding out of her seat.

The book landed right at her feet.

I jerked upright, trying my hardest to act surprised.

"Oops. My bad."

She rolled her eyes, and started to step over it. But then she saw the cover. *"Emma?"*

I stooped down and scooped up the book, pretending to be embarrassed. "Yeah. It's my favorite. I reread it in my downtime."

She frowned at me, but it wasn't an angry frown. She frowned the way a person might when they were solving a math problem, or studying a menu. A calculating, decision-making frown. "Why have I never seen you with it before?"

Shit.

"I guess I try to keep it to myself. Don't want people thinking I'm some kind of nerd."

A smile almost materialized on her face, and the frown did soften, which I took as a definite win. "There's nothing nerdy about *Emma*. I love that book. It's actually my second favorite, next to *Sense and Sensibility*."

"Really? I like that one, too." I had it in my backpack, as a matter of fact, and I'd also read the Wikipedia entry on it. I shoved *Emma* into my backpack. "Sorry to hold you up."

"Don't worry about it." She didn't sound annoyed anymore. I bowed to let her and Jackie pass by, waited until they'd passed through the door, then shouldered my backpack and headed out, too. I couldn't help but smile. *Operation Emma* was a success—not a perfectly executed success, but a success nevertheless.

CHAPTER TWENTY-ONE

I headed to join the cast and crew after school on Thursday without any real game plan. Maybe I'd interview some of them, so I could actually start the article I was supposed to be writing.

Everyone was on the stage when I arrived. Mrs. Vernon was darting back and forth, guiding and positioning people like chess pieces on a board.

Karla was nowhere in sight.

I sat down in the second row from the front and tried to figure out how long I had to wait before leaving without it seeming like I didn't give a shit. I did, sort of. This whole process was fascinating in its own way. It was like watching the behind-the-scenes featurette of a movie. I had to admit, it was a lot. The actors not only had to memorize a book's worth of dialogue, but they had to know when to say what they were supposed to say and where to be when they said it. There was more precision involved than I would have ever guessed.

"It's important that we all think big," Mrs. Vernon said as she placed people. "Everyone in the audience needs to be able to see what we're doing up here, so let's see some big, bold choices! Ah, there she is."

Karla was coming in from the side door near the stage with a large Pair-O'-Moose drink in each hand. "Sorry I'm late," she said as she handed Mrs. Vernon one of the drinks. "The line was ridiculous."

"That's quite alright. Thank you, darling."

I watched her carefully as she made her way off the stage and came around to the first row. She was good at hiding it, but I knew something was amiss. I saw it in the way she held herself, in the slight incline of her neck. There was less pep in her step, less sparkle in her eyes. I tried to catch her eye as she descended the stage, but she either didn't see me or was ignoring me, because she sat down in the first row on the opposite side of the aisle.

What the heck had happened between her and Lucas?

All I could do was speculate. They weren't back together, that was for sure. I tried to remember how it went the last time they'd broken up and got back together, but I hadn't ever paid it enough attention to know if this was normal for them or not. They had been apart since this summer, which was a record length of time. Lucas had said they were only supposed to be on a "break," whatever that meant. That was new information to me. Karla had told me they weren't together anymore, full stop. The way she'd said it made it sound like the breakup was of the permanent variety. Or maybe that was just my wishful thinking.

But whatever was going on, I was worried about her. I

didn't like seeing her like this. I wanted to do something, to help somehow, but I didn't know how or where to begin. So I did the only thing I could do right now: settled in and devoted all my attention to the rehearsal unfolding in front of me.

It was like a dance. The actors ran through the first act over and over again, each time trying new movements and gestures, or taking a few steps in a different direction, or positioning themselves at a slightly different angle. When they got a sequence right, Mrs. Vernon made a note of it, and they put markers down to remember what they'd done and where. Then they did the whole thing over again, until I lost track of how many times they did it. When they finally stopped for a break, I caught up with Naomi as she made her way off the stage.

"Hey. Quick question?"

She stopped and looked at me. "Hey. *Emma* fan. What's up?"

I was relieved that her opinion of me seemed to have softened. "Let me ask you this, now that you've gone through the play a few times, at what point do you think Mr. Darcy starts falling for Elizabeth? I mean, to go from thinking she's ugly to proposing to her is a pretty huge leap."

It was a question I'd come up with while I was rereading the Wikipedia entry.

Naomi smiled. "It's weird, because everyone seems to think that that first spark is when he notices how pretty her eyes are, but I think it's deeper than that. To me the moment that really marks the beginning of his feelings for Elizabeth is when he starts eavesdropping on her conversations and realizes how intelligent she is, contrary to his initial assessment. That's what I love so much about their romance—he falls in love with her mind. Yes, he notices that she's prettier than he first thought she was, but he doesn't fall in love with her looks so much as her personality. I think that's profound, or important, like you said before."

"Interesting," I said as I jotted down my notes. I hadn't expected her to give me such a detailed response. I paraphrased what she said as best I could. "So despite her social standing, that they belonged to different worlds essentially, he was willing to ignore all of that because he was in love with her. I think that's a powerful message. What matters is who a person is on the inside, not where they fit in the social hierarchy. Would you agree?"

She didn't seem to know what to think about that. "I guess you could say so," she admitted. "Hey, can I ask you something? What's with this?" She gestured at my shirt, which had the word *Otaku*—which could roughly be translated to mean "hard-core anime fan"—in block lettering on the front. "I mean, why are you so into all this?"

"Do you want the long answer or the short one?"

"The honest one."

I shrugged. "I haven't always had a lot of friends, and to me, friendship is one of the biggest themes of *Dragon Ball*. A lot of Earth's biggest threats end up becoming its greatest defenders, all because they were given a shot at redemption and friendship. I like the idea that it's possible for anyone to find friends. To find a family, I guess. Sometimes with the last people you'd expect."

Someone called her name. Naomi sighed. "Well. This has been…enlightening."

I nodded. "I wrote a primer on the top five best series for people looking to get into anime. You could go back and read it."

"Do people read papers anymore?"

"It's archived online, too. Or you could come by a G.A.N.U. meeting one of these days. They're pretty low-key."

"Maybe."

"Cool."

I was shocked. I hadn't expected this to go that well, and I was even more surprised at myself that I actually hoped she did show up.

"Hey!" Karla tapped me on the shoulder. "Making friends, I see. Naomi doesn't seem to hate you."

I shrugged. "Just doing my job."

She nodded, and bit her lip like she was thinking about something. "Are you alright?" I asked.

"Of course," she said just a little too quickly. "Why?"

"You seem a little…well, not okay."

"I'm fine. Really." To prove it, she flashed me one of her ultra-smiles, but it didn't quite reach her eyes.

I knew this wasn't the time to argue, so I didn't. "Well, I'm gonna go see about talking to some of the crew now," I said because there didn't seem to be anything else to say.

"Cool. I will see you around, then."

She smiled, and skipped off.

It was unnerving how she could just turn it off and on like that. Sometimes it made me think that I didn't know the real Karla at all.

"You did *what*?"

Jocelyn clutched a permanent marker in one hand, and I worried she might attack me with it. Judging from the look on D'Anthony's face, he'd probably approve if she did. Her entire corner of the room was covered in crumpled newspaper and piles of cardboard and sheets of foam. She'd latched a couple of desks together and was stooped over them, glue gun in hand, hovering over what looked like a pair of robotic boots. With her goggles and her glue gun, she looked like some mad scientist, and I supposed that in a way she was.

"Come on, it's just an invite," I said. "Odds are she doesn't even show up."

In hindsight, I probably should have talked it over with them before inviting Naomi to a G.A.N.U. meeting. It was sort of a closed club.

"Then what's the point?" Jocelyn demanded.

"I'm with her on this one," said D'Anthony. "I expressly recall her calling you and me 'a pair of fucking nerds' on more than one occasion."

"Dude, she said that because we were *Naruto*-running down the hallway."

"Fucking nerds," Jocelyn said with a dry chuckle.

"Isn't that what we are? What's wrong with introducing someone else to our culture? Who's to say she won't end up really liking what we're into?"

"You still haven't answered my question," said Jocelyn. "What's the point? Even if she becomes the biggest weeb in the world, who cares? What difference does it make to any of us? It's not our job to try to change assholes or convert them, and it's not our job to defend ourselves to them. If she was supposed to be a member of G.A.N.U., she'd have found us…like Mackenzie."

"Thanks," she said dryly without looking up from her sketch pad.

"Whatever," Jocelyn blurted. "Did you invite her to movie night, too? Not that I care. I'm not going tonight anyway."

"Why not?" D'Anthony asked as he rummaged through his backpack until he found his Game Boy.

She gestured at the boots. "Con crunch. I'm behind. It took longer than I thought for my Worbla to get here."

"What's Worbla?"

"Thermoplastic," she said, as if that explained everything.

"You can bring your cosplay stuff with you," I offered. I was hosting tonight, and I was looking forward to us all hanging out at my place.

Jocelyn scoffed. "You really want all this in your house?"

"I really don't—"

"No. The answer to that question is no. Everyone thinks they wouldn't mind, but they do. They always do. Anyway, it's just one movie night—which is sacred, I know—but seeing as you bailed last Friday, I think I'm entitled to one transgression."

She had a point, as usual. "Fair enough."

"Well, this is awkward," said D'Anthony. "I was gonna say I can't come tonight, either. Now I don't feel so bad about it."

I turned to face him, shocked. D'Anthony never missed movie night. He'd shown up sick on three separate occasions. "What's your excuse?" I demanded.

"Work," he said casually.

"Since when do you have a job?" Jocelyn asked.

"Since tonight. It's my first shift."

We all nodded, and the conversation unraveled into that strange, almost awkward silence between one topic and the other. Jocelyn went back to working on her boots, D'Anthony inserted his *Pokémon* cartridge and started up the game, the 8-bit theme puncturing the silence. Mackenzie was looking at her phone, but I couldn't tell if she was reading or watching something.

"Hey," D'Anthony said suddenly, "what's up with you and Stella?"

Jocelyn paused with her hand hovering over the left boot. Mackenzie didn't move, but she raised a single brow.

"What do you mean?" I asked. Stella came by for movie night every once in a while, but for the most part she was busy. It had been months since she'd come. I forgot D'Anthony even remembered who she was.

"Well, do you think you'll ever patch things up with her?"

Mackenzie cocked her head to one side.

My stomach twisted. "We're still friends—there's nothing to patch up."

"I worry. There's gotta be someone for you."

"I'm good, man. Don't sweat it."

"You're right," he said. "You're a seven-point-five. You've got options."

"Hold on." Mackenzie sat up straight, a disbelieving grin spreading across her face. "Seven-point-five? Really?"

I held my hands up. "Hey, I didn't write the list. Take that up with the cheerleaders."

She cracked up. "That shit is real? I heard about this alleged 'hotties list,' but I didn't think it was an actual thing. That's so sad."

I rolled my eyes. Whatever. And whether I had options or not didn't matter so long as Karla wasn't one of them. Yet.

"Let me guess, you're gonna bail, too."

She shook her hair and shrugged. "I'm still down if you are."

"I knew— Oh. Wait, for real?" I looked at her, scrutinizing her expression for any indication that she was being extremely sarcastic. It was hard to tell, since that was her default setting.

"I mean, it's not like I have anything else to do tonight," she said casually.

"You're sure?" I was still trying to figure out if this was a joke.

She leveled an annoyed look at me. "Yes. Cam. I'm sure."

It isn't a date, I kept telling myself that night. It wasn't a date, so there was nothing to get bent out of shape over. This wasn't any different than when I'd gone over to Mackenzie's house, or if it was Jocelyn or D'Anthony coming over. Which they would have, had they not bailed on me. Assholes. It was only Mackenzie. There was no reason to be as nervous as I was, and yet, I couldn't figure out why I was still so jittery.

I waited in the living room for Mackenzie to arrive. It had rained pretty bad, but it wasn't terrible out, not enough to have the roads blocked or for traffic to be backed up. Still, I couldn't help checking my phone every four minutes, hoping to get a text saying she couldn't make it, or she had something better to do, or something else had come up.

"What's your deal?" Cassie said when she came downstairs and saw me perched on the edge of the couch.

"Just waiting for someone."

"It's a girl, isn't it?" She beamed.

"Whatever." I waved her away, but she hovered behind me.

"Remember in *Scott Pilgrim vs. The World*, when Scott ordered a package from Amazon just because he knew Ramona Flowers would be the one to deliver it, and then he sat directly in front of the door waiting for her?"

"No," I lied.

"Yes, you do, and that's exactly what you're doing now. Question is, who's your Ramona Flowers?"

"There is no Ramona," I snapped. "I'm just having a..." Friend? Acquaintance? Frenemy? "I'm just having a person over, not that it's any of your business."

"Is this 'person' of the female persuasion?"

"I don't have to answer that."

"Which in itself is an answer. Who is she? Do I know her?"

"No, you don't, and hopefully it'll stay that way."

"Oh my god, do you have a secret girlfriend? Does Mom know? How long has this been going on? Wait, is this the girl from the party?"

"There's nothing secret about it, alright? She's *just* a person, who happens to be a girl, and she's *just* coming over to watch TV."

"That sounds *just* like a date."

The doorbell rang, and I bolted off the couch. "Don't you have somewhere else to be?" I hissed at her as I moved to the door.

"I did," she said as she plopped down on the chair and took out her phone, "but this is gonna be much more interesting."

"I hate you."

"No, you don't. Now open the door—don't keep your lady person waiting."

I rolled my eyes, and opened the door. Mackenzie was waiting with one hand in the pocket of her red jacket, which had four gold belt buckles down the right side, and which I immediately recognized as being from *Akira*. I had to admit it was a pretty badass jacket. The other hand was holding a box of cookies.

"Hey," she said as she shook the rain off and stepped inside.

"Hi." I shut the door behind her and glared at Cassie, who was watching us with a Cheshire cat grin, like she just couldn't wait to pounce. I figured I might as well beat her to the punch. "Mackenzie, this is my sister, Cassie—Cassie, this is Mackenzie."

"Mackenzie, so nice to meet you!" Cassie smiled, and I couldn't tell if she was being facetious or genuinely polite.

"Likewise," said Mackenzie, and whether Cassie was being actually nice or not, I wanted to get us away from her as quickly as possible.

"Are you hungry? I ordered pizza. We have pop, too. Pepsi, Sprite, and root beer, I think."

"Oh. Root beer sounds nice."

"Awesome."

For some reason I didn't know what to do next. Maybe I was still adjusting to the fact that Mackenzie Briggs was standing in my living room.

Mackenzie shifted from one foot to the other. "So… I brought these." She thrust the box of cookies at me. "I wasn't sure what kind you liked, so I got a bunch of different ones. There's chocolate chip, snickerdoodle…"

"No oatmeal raisin, right?"

She blinked. "Um, no. Do you…like oatmeal raisin?"

"No," I said, grinning. "Oatmeal raisin cookies are literally the worst thing in the world. Snickerdoodles are my absolute favorite."

"Oh," she said. "Good."

She sounded relieved, and I felt just a little bit bad for teasing her. "So. Um. Right this way."

I ushered her forward, through the dining room and into the kitchen. I was ready to physically fight with Cassie if she followed us, but, mercifully, she didn't. Instead, she sent me a text that said, She's cute! Nice work!

"Ugh," I groaned.

"You alright?" Mackenzie asked.

I grabbed a pair of cups. "Yeah, just, that one—" I jerked my chin back toward the living room "—is driving me up a wall."

"I know how that is," Mackenzie said wearily. I wondered which of us had it worse.

Probably her.

"I like your jacket," I said as I poured our drinks.

"Thanks."

"You know, the first time I saw that movie I was like, 'what the hell did I just watch?' I had to see it, like, three more times to make sense of it."

She laughed. "Same. It should come with CliffsNotes."

This was weird. Normally we were at each other's throats on sight, but for some reason—maybe she was exhausted, maybe because I had home court advantage here—Mackenzie was being halfway decent.

Cassie peeked her head around the corner, that stupid smile plastered across her face.

"Shall we?" I asked Mackenzie. I had to get her upstairs, *now*, before Cassie could corner us in here.

Mackenzie didn't seem to notice. "Sure. Let's do it."

CHAPTER TWENTY-TWO

I'd spent a good half hour getting the den ready, which was about double the amount of time I'd ever spent cleaning up here, even when Jocelyn and D'Anthony were coming over. It was nothing fancy, but our TV, like the den itself, was big enough, and at the very least the space was clean. I'd arranged the furniture so that the couch and the love seat were an optimal distance from the screen, and placed the coffee-turned-serving table between the two. And since I hadn't been sure what we'd end up watching, I'd made sure to arrange my DVD collection in an easily accessible order. I'd even brought up some of the ones from my room that I deemed too valuable to keep in the common area. All this added up to my not being too embarrassed to bring Mackenzie up here. I mean, there was some embarrassment, but it was of a manageable level.

"This is cool," she said as she looked around. I waited for the punch line, but it didn't come. That was…reassuring?

"Oh my god," she blurted.

"What's wrong?" Here it comes.

She bolted to the bookshelf and snatched a DVD off the shelf. "You have *Little Nemo: Adventures in Slumberland*?"

I couldn't tell what kind of reaction she was having, so I decided to tread lightly. "I really like the movie," I said carefully, defensively, "and I know a lot of people don't consider it a true anime film, but it was produced by Tokyo Movie Shinsha, so it counts to me."

"Hell, yeah, it counts! It was released in Japan before the US. I *love* this movie! And I thought *nobody* loved this movie!"

"That's how I feel, too. Like, I can't tell you how many times I've tried to convince D'Anthony and Jocelyn to watch it with me, but they never even make it to the part where the dirigible gets to Slumberland."

"No way, that's when the movie actually starts."

"Right?"

"Well, they're totally missing out." She carefully put the DVD back in its place on the shelf, then studied the rest of them, listing the names off to herself. I'd never been more nervous about someone else scrutinizing my collection.

"*Robotech, G-Force: Guardians of Space, Metal Armor Dragonar, Mobile Suit Gundam, Neon Genesis Evangelion*—somebody has a thing for mecha." She glanced over her shoulder at me, then went on. "*Cowboy Bebop, Gungrave, Fullmetal Alchemist, Hell Girl, Death Note, Bleach, Trigun, Ergo Proxy, Gurren Lagann*, and my personal favorite, *Ghost in the Shell*—wow, Cameron, I'm actually impressed."

"That's a relief," I said, and I absolutely meant it. "Guess we can call a cease-fire, then."

"For now," she said with a grin. "Someone with tastes this good can't be *all* bad. So, what are we watching? *Dragon Ball Z?*"

Huh. My knowledge of Mackenzie could be summed up thusly: she was Lucas's twin sister, she liked anime and manga as much as I did, if not more, and we categorically didn't get along. Until now, all of those things had been true.

"We don't have to. I had it in earlier. I pretty much keep it on all the time, to be honest. Helps me work or think or whatever."

"No, it's fine, I love the Frieza saga."

Huh. Just. Huh.

"You do?"

She hopped onto the couch and stretched her long legs across the ottoman. "Are you kidding me? The Ginyu Force, Vegeta joining forces with Gohan and Krillin, Goku's first transformation into a Super Saiyan? Who *doesn't* like the Frieza saga?"

She had a point.

"Cool." I gingerly edged my way onto the opposite side of the couch, which had never before seemed so small, and pressed Play.

I'd left off on season three, episode ninety-six: "Explosion of Anger."

There was a lot of backstory.

Frieza was an evil alien who razed entire planets in order to sell them on the galactic market. He'd employed the Saiyans to do his dirty work, but thirty years prior, when he realized they could become a threat to his power, he destroyed their entire planet, killing all but a few of them.

At first, Goku had been completely outmatched during their battle. But when Frieza killed Krillin, Goku's best friend, Goku's anger caused him to transform into the legendary Super Saiyan, giving him enough power to defeat Frieza, who claimed to be the most powerful being in the universe. These episodes were the climax to their epic battle on a dying world.

"This is why Goku will always be my hero," Mackenzie said as we watched. "This. Despite how carefree or airheaded or just plain stupid he can be, at the end of the day and when push comes to shove, this is who he is, and this is what he fights for. Hands down one of my favorite moments in the entire series. That's why no other anime character comes close to comparing to Goku. Except *maybe* Trunks."

"What's up with you and Trunks?" I asked. "Not that I want to start a debate or anything, I'm just curious."

Mackenzie crossed her legs and dangled one of her sneakers on her toes. "I like Trunks because he's from the future. He's always a couple steps ahead of everyone else. That's what I aspire to be—ahead of the curve."

I nodded thoughtfully. "Wow. That's profound."

She tilted her head toward me. "What, did you expect me to say it's because he's hot, or I like his fashion sense?"

"No," I said quickly. "I just…"

"Relax," she said with a grin. "I'm joking."

"I knew that," I said in a voice that made it obvious that I hadn't.

"I mean, both of those things are true," she added when we'd both settled back into the couch. "He's got a badass jacket, and he really rocks the yellow boots. And those purple bangs? He could get it."

I laughed.

"What about you?" she said in a more serious tone.

"I've never been overly attracted to him, but I mean—"

"Not that, nerd! I meant, aside from Goku, who's your next favorite anime character?"

I didn't even have to think. "One Punch Man."

One Punch Man was a newer series, and it featured a bald superhero who was so powerful that he could defeat any villain with a single punch.

"Really?" Mackenzie propped her head on her arm. "Do tell."

I thought carefully. "I like the simplicity of it, I guess. One hit, it's over. I wish more problems could be solved like that."

"What, with punching?"

"With a single, swift solution. Things can be so muddy sometimes, so complicated. It's easy to lose sight of who you're fighting and why—it'd be so much easier if the answers were a simple, direct line."

"That makes sense," she said approvingly. "You know the thing I hate about One Punch, though?"

"How people are always debating who would win a fight between him and Goku?"

"*Yes! I hate* that shit! Like, I love *One Punch*, but it's a satire. A send-up. You're not supposed to take it that seriously, and that's why you can't have a serious debate over who would win a fight between them."

I nodded in agreement. "The laws of their respective worlds are incompatible."

"Exactly! Nobody gets that."

"Right? I hate it."

"I'm glad you see the truth," she said.

"Likewise."

I laughed, and then she looked at me, and I looked at her, and I realized that in an alternate reality, the two of us might have been more than sort-of-friends. Maybe there we were good friends, possibly even close friends. Maybe that wasn't entirely out of the question in this reality.

And then my phone went off.

A quick glance told me it was from Karla. My blood ran cold, and I sprang off the couch.

"You good?" Mackenzie asked.

I looked up in surprise and nodded frantically. "Oh yeah, totally. Hey, do you want popcorn? I sure do."

"Um, sure?" she said, giving me a weird look. "You sure you're okay?"

"Yep," I said over my shoulder as I hit the stairs. "Be right back."

It was all I could do to make it to the bottom of the stairs before taking my phone back out.

I almost ran face-first into Cassie's gleefully grinning face. "How's your date going?" she asked, singing the word *date* just a little too loudly.

"Like I said before, it's not a date," I said calmly as I side-stepped her and unlocked my phone. Now was not the time to engage, but to absorb and deflect. Especially since I needed to read this text ASAP, and even more especially since Mom was coming in from the garage.

"Hey, Mom," I said.

"Hey," she said as she slipped off her shoes and her jacket. "What's this about a date?"

"It's nothing," I said with a sigh.

"Oh, it's definitely something," Cassie said. "Cameron's got a girl over."

"Is that right?" Mom eyed me.

"It's not what it sounds like. She's just here for movie night. D'Anthony and Jocelyn couldn't make it, so it's just us two."

"He didn't want them messing up his date," Cassie asserted smugly.

"I don't want to add fuel to this fire," Mom said, smiling, "but technically the definition of a date is a social *or* romantic appointment. It is only the two of you."

She and Cassie looked at me with the same expression that read, *I wasn't born yesterday.*

But I had stopped paying them any attention, because I was too engrossed in Karla's text.

Lucas wants to get back together.

My blood ran cold. He'd asked her out, like I knew he would, like he told me he was planning on doing.

Now what? I typed, and my thumb hovered over the send key for a full four seconds before I hit it. This was bad. If she'd said yes, and they were back together, it was all over.

Her reply came quicker than I expected.

I said no. Obviously.

It was like I could breathe for the very first time. She'd said no… She'd actually said no. To Lucas, the guy she'd been dating on and off for more than two years. As far as I was aware, the way it worked was that they'd break up, get some space from each other, and then they'd patch things up and get back together. But this was different. Something had changed. Did that something have to do with me?

I couldn't be sure, not now. Maybe I would ask her the next time I saw her, maybe I wouldn't. All I knew was that if her mind was truly made up about this, then mine was, too.

"Just so you guys know, you both suck." I put my phone away and retreated back up to the safety of the den.

It was a lucky thing that, right after the Frieza saga ended the Trunks saga began. After Goku's epic battle with Frieza, he's left to travel home alone in a beaten spaceship. Frieza, who somehow survives the battle, beats Goku to Earth. But Trunks is already waiting for him, and he reveals that he, too, can transform into a Super Saiyan before singlehandedly killing Frieza and his minions. When Goku arrives, Trunks explains that he came from the future to warn him that in three years' time two powerful androids would arrive and kill them all and plunge the planet into chaos. His warning enables Goku and his friends to train until they are powerful enough to confront the androids, changing history and their fates.

Naturally, we watched the five episodes it took for Trunks to be fully introduced before Mackenzie and I finally called it quits. I hadn't realized how late it was until it was time for her to head out.

I'd been dreading this because it meant having to introduce her to my mother, who could be just as bad as Cassie when it came to people they thought I was interested in. For the longest time she'd insisted Jocelyn and I were either already an item or were going to end up as one. That had only stopped when I'd told her Jocelyn was gay.

Mom and Cassie were in the kitchen when we came downstairs, and they were waiting. "Hey, Mom. This is Mackenzie. Mackenzie, this is my mom."

"Nice to meet you, Ms. Carson," Mackenzie said. It was still weird, seeing her be polite.

I kept moving in the hopes we wouldn't linger and that this would be a quick hi-and-bye, but I should've known better.

"Call me Hilary," Mom said graciously. "Good to meet you, Mackenzie. Oh, aren't you gorgeous! Isn't your friend gorgeous, Cameron?"

Fuck.

I couldn't believe she was doing this. Cassie sat at the table with a self-satisfied grin. She must have expected this, too.

"Thanks," Mackenzie said politely. If she felt at all as awkward or mortified as I did she sure as hell did a better job of hiding it than I could.

"We go to school together. Same grade. We have a class together, and she's a member of G.A.N.U. Sort of."

I figured if I blurted enough factoids Mom wouldn't have the chance to ask anything.

Mom nodded, still looking at Mackenzie. "Well, dear, you are welcome here anytime. I mean that." She wagged a finger. "*Any*time."

"I appreciate that," Mackenzie said with all the aplomb I could never muster when I met someone else's parents.

"We'd better go," I said, trying not to sound like I was in a hurry even though I wasn't. "The rain's picking up out there."

I steered Mackenzie toward the living room.

"Nice meeting you," Cassie called. I could hear the smug grin in her voice.

I came back to the house to find Mom and Cassie in the living room, idling suspiciously like they'd been watching us through the bay window.

"Tell me you two weren't spying on me."

"I don't know what you're talking about," said Mom. "She's pretty."

"Yeah, we were just watching the rain," Cassie added, even though there was barely any.

Neither of them could contain their giddy little smiles.

"Seriously, guys," I groaned. "I told you, she's just a friend, and we were just hanging out." It felt weird calling Mackenzie a friend, but I couldn't think of a word that fit better.

"That's usually how it starts," Mom said with a chuckle.

"She definitely likes you, that's for sure," said Cassie. "You should have seen how you were looking at each other."

"Gross. She doesn't like me. Not like that. God, you two are so embarrassing."

I stalked off toward the den and away from all this nonsense.

"For what it's worth, I like her," Cassie called after me.

"Ditto," yelled Mom.

"Nobody says 'ditto' anymore," I muttered as I made my way back upstairs.

CHAPTER TWENTY-THREE

"How was work?" I asked D'Anthony when I got to homeroom.

He shrugged. "I don't know. It wasn't horrible. I'm on the fence. It was mostly paperwork and getting to know the store. Could be fun. I'll make it work."

"Nice."

Jocelyn came in fifteen minutes before homeroom let out. Her hair wasn't pink anymore, but a loud, shimmering green struck through with dark streaks of black.

"Looks good," said D'Anthony as she sat down.

"Thanks. I was going for 'evil mermaid,' but it's more like 'slightly irritated mermaid,' which I'm okay with."

"It looks badass," I said. She seemed to be in a better mood than she'd been in lately. "How's your cosplay build coming?"

"Good," she said, beaming. "I was behind schedule, but I caught up. For once, nothing screwed me over."

"Nice."

Over her shoulder I happened to catch sight of the Caravan table. Lydia was staring at our table, her expression unreadable. When she saw me looking she jerked her head away.

"How was movie night?" Jocelyn asked with a grin. "Was it as horrible as I imagine?"

"God, did you guys spend the whole time yelling at each other?" D'Anthony said, shaking his head.

"Actually, it was alright," I said matter-of-factly. "She brought cookies."

Jocelyn squinted suspiciously at me. "She brought *cookies*?"

"Yep."

"That's weird," Jocelyn said with a frown.

For some reason I didn't want to talk about it. It felt like something private, something between the two of us. It just didn't feel right.

I bombed my Spanish quiz. At least it felt like I did. My head was too full of what had happened during movie night with Mackenzie to allow space for verb conjugations in another language. To be honest I'd been suffering from a severe attention deficit ever since she'd left my house. I was still running on autopilot, and when class let out, I packed my stuff and shuffled out of the room by muscle memory alone. I was in a daze, a fugue state, catatonia. Someone tapped my shoulder, and I jumped.

Mackenzie laughed. "¿Qué pasó?"

Just like that, everything snapped into focus. "¿Qué pasa? ¿Cómo estás?"

"Estoy bien. ¿Y tú?"

"Estoy bien, gracias."

She smiled broadly. "Sounds like we're both passing this class."

"Maybe," I said with a shallow grin. And then we did The Thing, where we both just sort of stood there, neither of us saying anything, but not leaving or ending the conversation for whatever reason. It almost felt like she was on the cusp of saying something that she never did.

"So..." she started. "Did you hear about this year's prom theme?"

"Oh, '80s Madness? Yeah, whose idea was that?"

"Right? I think I might still go."

"Really?" I wondered, instinctively, if Karla was going.

Ew, gross. Why did that thought feel so gross?

Mackenzie shrugged. "Yeah. I mean, most of the proceeds go to charity, and if I had to pick, the '80s would be my favorite decade. You know, minus the racism and homophobia and the Gulf War."

"Don't forget the rampant sexism," I added.

"Right, can't forget that now, can we?" The Thing happened again. I was beginning to feel like I was missing something important. Was it her who wasn't saying what she wanted to, or was it me?

"Why the '80s?" I couldn't help asking.

"Well, art was better then, for one thing," she said. "Whether it was actual art, like Jean-Michel Basquiat, or anime, like *Akira, Fist of the North Star, Dragon Ball*... Not to mention, that was the decade that gave us two of the greatest albums of all time."

She was speaking my language now. "What albums do you mean?" I asked with bated breath.

She scoffed. "*Purple Rain*, by Prince, and Michael Jackson's *Thriller*, of course."

Wow. Just, wow. I mean, I couldn't agree more, I just wouldn't have assumed she would think so. If I had to guess, I would have thought her musical tastes would veer more into the obscure and indie.

Mackenzie tilted her head to one side. "What's that look for?"

"What look?"

"You were giving me a funny look just now."

"Oh. I guess I don't know you as well as I thought I did."

"Well," she said, rocking back and forth on her feet, "maybe you should work on that."

"Is that an invitation?" I asked. I'd meant it in a teasing way, but it came out sounding like an embarrassingly earnest question.

It didn't help that the only answer Mackenzie gave was a vague shrug that told me absolutely nothing.

"Right. So…how does this cease-fire work?" I asked. "We never established the terms."

"I dunno. It was your idea."

"Right."

"I'm fine with it being an indefinite cease-fire," she said carefully. "I mean, unless you say something stupid and start the whole thing over again."

"Same."

The warning bell rang, and we both looked up at the clock. Had it already almost been five minutes?

"Well," Mackenzie said, backing away with her binder folded in front of her, "My class is in the left ball, so…"

I pointed my thumb behind me. "I'm in the shaft."

"Cool." She nodded.

"Cool."

She swatted a curl from her face, and then wheeled around and rushed into the stairway.

With work, class, and rehearsals, the next two weeks seemed to blow by. Production was getting down to the wire. There were only ten days until the show debuted, and tensions had never been higher.

Karla was waiting for me next to the auditorium doors when I got there. "Come with me," she said, and she started walking.

"Where are we going?" I asked as I followed.

"Costume shopping. We're way behind schedule."

"Wait, just us?"

"I wish," she said. "Simone and T.J. are heading the costuming department, so they're coming, too."

"Yay," I said sarcastically.

"Same," said Karla.

They were waiting for us in the parking lot next to Karla's car. "About time you showed up," said T.J. through chattering teeth. "I'm freezing my nuts off."

"Same," added Simone.

"No one told you two geniuses to wait outside for me," Karla said coolly as she unlocked the doors.

"Shotgun!" T.J. shouted. He moved to the driver's passenger side.

Karla snapped her fingers at him. "No. He's up front." She pointed at me. "*He's* the correspondent. *You* play the back."

T.J. balked. "That a problem?" Karla asked, eyeing him

and Simone, who hadn't said anything yet but who looked like she had plenty to say about it.

"Nah. We're good."

"Good."

There was a Goodwill a mile up the road, in the same complex the McDonald's and the Pair-O'-Moose everyone who left campus at lunch inevitably ended up eating at.

"Remember, guys, we can be *on* budget," Karla said as we approached the entrance. "We can be *under* budget, but we absolutely cannot go *over* budget—not again. Let's not have a repeat of the *Hamlet* incident."

"What's the *Hamlet* incident?" I asked.

"Basically we ended up spending double our budget on dresses for Ophelia because someone—who shall remain anonymous—insisted that a true lady would never be seen in the same outfit more than once."

I laughed. "Sounds like this anonymous person is a real prima donna."

"It's been suggested. Come on."

T.J. and Simone went their own way, toward the women's formal wear. Karla took my hand and led the way in the opposite direction, toward the back of the store, where we stopped in front of the towel racks.

"Do any of these scream, 'landed gentry' to you?" she asked as we scrutinized secondhand towels and blankets.

"Most of these scream 'I was used to dry mop water.'"

She laughed, and we spent the next hour and a half gathering old blankets, dresses, fabrics—anything that could be used to transport the cast back into the nineteenth century. Personally, I didn't know how that could be done given the items we bought and the time frame, but I supposed that was why I wasn't a part of the costuming department. It was a shame they didn't have Jocelyn. She could dress every single member of the cast on her own with time to spare. I'd seen her make an entire dress in one afternoon.

"I didn't thank you for the other night, with my parents and all that," Karla said quietly as we shopped. "That was a lot to put on you."

It felt like that night had been a lifetime ago. "It's cool. Your mom and dad were nice. Dinner was cool. Who doesn't love pizza?"

"Not that part," she said, dropping her voice even lower. "Afterward, what I told you about my folks. No one else knows, I mean, I've never told anyone about it. Not even Lucas. Thank you for not, I dunno, being freaked out."

My nerves abated by a few degrees, overcome by a wave of sympathy. No, *empathy*. "My parents got divorced when I was seven. It sucked, hard. It was like everything I knew was being sliced right down the middle, like how Future Trunks did to Frieza when— Anyway, I can relate, is what I'm trying to say."

"That's very sweet," she said, and her expression clouded over. But just as quickly as the storm came, it passed, and she smiled brightly. "I like you."

"Your friends don't."

"They'll come around."

I had my doubts about that.

Karla parked in the back of the school, next to the tennis courts, so we could haul our seven plastic bags full of clothes into the auditorium.

"Polishing rehearsals," Karla explained to me, "are when

we run through the play from beginning to end and make whatever final tweaks and changes we need to before tech rehearsals. No scripts, no cues."

"Sounds terrifying," I said.

"We gotta take the leap at some point. Besides, if we've all been doing our jobs, it'll be a breeze."

"Here's hoping, then."

During their break I decided to try my luck again with Lydia, to ask her a few questions, maybe show her that I wasn't some idiot who'd been snooping around this whole time. She looked at me the way someone might look at a piece of gum they'd accidentally stepped on. "Yes?"

The agitation in her voice was obvious. I cleared my throat. "I, uh, just wanted to ask you a couple of questions. For the feature?"

"Okay." She faced me. She was almost my height. For some reason, she'd always seemed taller.

I fumbled with my notepad. "You've been in every school play since your freshman year. Acting is clearly something you enjoy. How did you get into acting? What drew you to it?"

To my surprise she seemed like she was actually thinking about it. "I dunno. I guess I like the idea of being someone else. Onstage I can be whoever I want, or do anything I want to. It's liberating."

"Very cool."

"It is."

I took a second to scribble that down. "Alright. What would you say is the biggest thing you have in common with the character, versus the biggest difference?"

"That's easy. The biggest thing I have in common with Liz is that we both believe we're good judges of character. The biggest difference between us is that she really wasn't, and I definitely am."

"Oh. Wow. Must be nice."

"It is. There are way too many fake people out there to not be."

I quickly jotted down my notes. "One more question."

She crossed her arms. "Fine."

"The play deals a lot with romance. Do you use your own romantic experience to inform your portrayal?"

Her eyebrows knitted together. "Liz was lucky. The person she thought she could never be with turned out to be the one she was meant to be with all along. Sometimes it's the opposite, and the one you're sure you're supposed to be with ends up being the one you can't ever be with."

Without asking or waiting to see if I had any follow-up questions, she walked away. But then she stopped and turned back around. "Let me give you a piece of advice—it isn't worth it. This thing you're trying to do, it's not what you want. Trust me."

I frowned, confused and somewhat afraid. "What…is it you think I'm trying to do?"

She gave me a look that was mostly annoyance with just a pinch of pity. "Let's not play that game. You may be able to play it with them, but you can't with me. Look, if this—" she made a sweeping gesture with one arm "—is what you want, I'm not going to try to stop you. Just know that it isn't worth it. It's never worth it."

I lingered when rehearsal wrapped up, waiting for everyone else to leave. There was something deflating about watching them all go. It felt like closing time.

"Hey." Karla met me at the head of the auditorium, where I was leaning against the stage. She poked my arm. "Do you want to hang out?"

I frowned. "What do you mean?"

She got a panicked, almost horrified look on her face. "Are you serious?"

I couldn't help laughing. "No, Karla, I'm not."

She breathed a sigh of relief. "Cool. We'll do it this weekend."

"This weekend?"

"Unless you're busy, I mean." The way she said it left no doubt that she knew full well I was going to go whether I had plans or not.

"No, I'm free."

"Great. I'll text you later to figure out the details. Maybe afterward we can…" She bit her lip and looked me up and down. She didn't need to finish that sentence.

"Sounds like a plan to me."

"Good." She smiled as she started walking. "I look forward to seeing you then," she said over her shoulder.

She sounded like she sincerely meant it.

CHAPTER TWENTY-FOUR

With the holiday coming up, none of our teachers were giving out homework, and class work consisted mostly of running out the clock until the break. Mackenzie spent most of Spanish class drawing, and I spent it watching her draw. There was this face she made when she was drawing; her eyebrows puckered together, and she bit her bottom lip in concentration. It was like nothing else in the world around her existed; all of her focus was laser-tuned on the paper in front of her. I wasn't meaning to watch her, and I assumed she didn't notice, until without warning she flicked her curly hair and looked me dead in the eye. "That bored, huh?"

I jumped, banging my knees on the underside of my desk. That made her laugh.

When class let out we left the room together.

"Any plans for Thanksgiving?" I asked, shouldering my backpack.

"Aside from pretending to get along with my extended family? Nope. You?"

"Same. At least this year I'm with my mom's side of the family."

She tilted her head to one side. "Your parents aren't together?"

"They're divorced."

There was a time when I wouldn't have been able to say that so casually. A time when I was embarrassed by it, ashamed in a way. Even now it wasn't something I broadcast; it didn't exactly come up in normal conversation. Usually.

"My parents aren't together, either," she said plainly.

I nodded. This was nice. Some people were weird about this kind of thing, like it was something they needed to walk on eggshells about. And I guess for some people it was. But my dad wasn't dead, he just wasn't around, and I felt like that was a big difference. But there was no weirdness between Mackenzie and I. Just an unspoken, mutual understanding.

I swallowed, feeling suddenly restless. "Hey, do you want to go get coffee or something? I could *really* use a coffee."

Her eyebrows drew together. "Are you asking me on a date?" she asked with that familiar grin.

"Yes," I blurted, even though I knew she was joking, same as always. "Yes, this would technically be considered a date."

She stepped back and looked at me in surprise. "Wow. Okay. Wasn't expecting that. Are you okay?"

"Never better," I said, nodding frantically. My mind was racing because I had no idea why I'd decided to ask her, but now that I had it felt right.

She eyed me carefully. "Now?"

"Why not? It's not like anyone is giving out actual work. And we're seniors, so we can come and go whenever."

She scrutinized me one more time. "Right. Let's do it, then."

It was just beginning to snow outside. Not a real snow, just the light, fluffy stuff that melted as soon as it hit the ground. A mild flurry. We walked together, enjoying the cool air and the stirring leaves and the branches shaking in the wind. The real snow was coming; if the pale sky was any indication we'd get our first real snowstorm before the end of the month.

"So…are you going to tell me what's wrong?" she asked once we'd settled in at our table.

I held my cup of coffee—three shots of espresso, nothing else—and tapped my foot. She sat across from me, arms crossed, her rice crispy bar untouched on the plate in front of her.

"This is a nice Pair-O'-Moose, isn't it? I know I'm biased, but this is a really nice place."

To be fair, it *was* a nice location. Just a couple blocks from school, in the business block between Jet's Pizza and a Great Clips. I knew some of the managers at this location; they were good people. It had been a long time since I'd actually worked this location.

Mackenzie didn't seem impressed by it. "I come here all the time," she pointed out flatly.

"Ah. Makes sense. You know, I actually did have something to tell you. I think?"

"You think?" Mackenzie said around a grin. She sipped her iced drink through a straw and waited. "I'm all ears."

I took a deep breath. Set my cup down on the table. Picked it up again. Took another deep breath.

"Okay. This is gonna sound super weird. You know how there are people you just click with? Like, it's like you've known each other for a really long time, even when you've only just met?"

She laughed. "Yeah?"

I took a quick sip of my coffee and adjusted the strings of my hoodie. "I've never really experienced that. I mean, it's not like I have that many friends, so there isn't a huge pool to tally from. But it's happened, on rare occasion, and I haven't really thought about it." Another sip of the coffee. "God, this is so good. They really know what they're doing back there. Anyway, I guess, what I'm trying to say…is that, that's how I feel about you."

I chugged about a quarter of my coffee, more out of nervousness than any real desire to continue drinking it.

Mackenzie looked down at the table. "Oh," she said quietly. She looked up at me, and a slow, deliberate smile spread across her face. "That's…that's cool of you to say. Thanks."

"Sure." I nodded because I still wasn't quite sure why I'd said it. Or even if that had been what I was trying to say in the first place.

"You know, Cameron," she began slowly, "arguing with you all the time. I don't do it because I hate you. I guess, it's just how I get on. You know? It's how I… I dunno, make friends?"

"Does that make us friends?"

"I'm not averse to the idea."

"Neither am I. I'm actually into it."

She smiled, and her smile made me smile, and in that moment I felt at peace.

★ ★ ★

The wind picked up as we walked back to school. We walked with our hoods drawn and our hands shoved in our pockets.

"Well. This was…fun," Mackenzie said as we approached the school entrance. She dropped her hood and shook her hair free. I liked when she did that. "Weird as shit, but fun."

"I'm pretty sure *weird* sums up a lot of what we do together."

I had to admit, I felt better. I wasn't sure how, but it was like a weight had been lifted. Being around Mackenzie was refreshing, stress-free.

"True." She smiled. "Speaking of, you guys should come over one of these days. For movie night, or whatever."

"I'm down."

"Good."

We lingered there, at the entrance, me with my hand on the door, her rocking back and forth on the balls of her feet. I pulled the door open, but neither of us moved to enter.

"Thanks, Mackenzie," I said. "You're a good friend."

"I know," she said with one of her cheeky, infectious grins. Even now, I couldn't help smiling.

She walked inside, and I followed. Once we'd passed the foyer we went our separate ways. I had a sudden urge to get away. It was too weird, and my brain was going in a million different directions at once.

"Hey, Cam!"

I stopped, turned around. She had stopped, too, and was looking back at me, grinning. "You're a good friend, too."

I smiled, and I couldn't wipe it off my face.

★ ★ ★

With less than a week left before the debut the cast and crew were kicking it into twelfth gear. Rehearsals were every night now, starting with technical rehearsals, which were when the production crew and the stage crew fine-tuned their act behind the scenes—when to switch props and backdrops in scene transitions, testing the sound and microphones, and making sure the lighting was right and where it needed to be at any given moment during the show. Everyone who was involved in the production was there and at the eye of the storm was Mrs. Vernon, barking directions and waving her arms like she was conducting an orchestra. I supposed in a way she was. There was a music to all this madness, a frenzied rhythm that wasn't unlike a symphony. All I could do was keep out of the way until Karla arrived carrying a stack of five pizza boxes.

"Take a couple of these?" she said as she handed two of them off to me. I followed her up the side steps and behind the stage, where we set the boxes on a random table. "How's it looking?" she asked.

I shrugged. "Everyone is certainly busy. Mrs. Vernon isn't angry-screaming. She's still screaming, just not angrily."

"That's always a good thing." She smiled and kissed me on the cheek.

Dress rehearsals was when things really started to look like the final production. The girls wore light-colored dresses with low necklines and short, puffy sleeves over bodiced petticoats, along with slippers and gloves that extended past their elbows, with ribbons and pearls in their hair. The guys wore dark waistcoats with crisp white cravats on top of pantaloons and riding boots. It all looked incredibly uncomfortable and itchy, but I had to admit, T.J. and Simone had done a great job. Everyone looked like they'd wandered onto the stage straight out of the 1800s. Our Goodwill run seemed to have definitely paid off.

"This is gonna be good," I said as I watched.

Beside me Karla smiled. "You think so?"

I nodded. "I know so."

CHAPTER TWENTY-FIVE

In celebration of the upcoming break, my friends and I decided to do what we always did: movie night.

I headed to D'Anthony's house about an hour after I got home from school. I met Jocelyn as she was coming up the driveway, and my heart fluttered when I saw Mackenzie's car roll up and park across the street. We waited for her to join us. "Hey, guys," she said.

For some stupid reason, I waved, even though she was literally right in front of me. "Hi."

Even though we'd only just gone our separate ways a little more than an hour ago, it felt like it had been ages since I'd last seen Mackenzie, and I felt this weird sense of relief seeing her now.

I could see the look Jocelyn tossed me, but I ignored it, and we went inside. The door was unlocked, as always.

We walked in on him and his older brother Dante having

a shouting match in the living room over a game of *Mortal Kombat*.

"Run that shit back," Dante roared, waving his controller around, "bet I beat that ass."

"Language," their mom shouted from her study. She taught at Metropolitan State University, and was probably up to her elbows in papers to grade.

"Quit your bitching, bitch," D'Anthony fired back.

"Language," their mom shouted, louder this time.

"Sorry," they both yelled in unison.

"Hey, guys," D'Anthony said.

"Is that my two favorite people?" D'Anthony's mom called from her study. I could just make out the edge of her desk from the open door of the study.

"Hi, Mrs. Reed," said Jocelyn and I.

"What's up, y'all?" said Devon, D'Anthony's oldest brother, who was coming down the steps with his girlfriend. For some reason their parents had thought it was a good idea to give all their children names that started with *D*. Mine had done the same with Cassie and me. What was it with parents that made them think that was a good idea? I knew if I ever had kids, I was going to name them as differently as I possibly could. The gimmick wore off fast.

D'Anthony turned the game off, and Dante tossed aside his controller. "Till next time, bitch," he said under his breath. D'Anthony laughed and shoved him. "Sup, Cam. Jocelyn. And…oh." He looked at Mackenzie. "And you're…"

"Mackenzie," she said.

He nodded slowly. "Good to meet you, Mackenzie."

For some reason I didn't like how he said her name.

D'Anthony's home was always chaotic. There were always so many people running around. Devon and his girlfriend left for the mall, and his mom closed the door to her study as D'Anthony popped the DVD into the PS4.

"We skipped *Kiki's Delivery Service*, since we know it's your favorite," he said.

"You're welcome," Jocelyn added as she slipped out of her jacket and tossed it on the couch.

"Kiki is life," Mackenzie said. She sat on the ground in front of the couch and folded her legs.

I looked at her. "Really?"

"Hell, yeah."

I hesitated, reading the terrain. The couch was against the wall, facing the TV. A cedar chest was in front of it. That's where the chips, pop, and popcorn were. Dante had claimed the right side of the couch. Jocelyn was on the floor on the left. D'Anthony was lying down on his back in front of the cedar chest. The only place I had to sit really was next to Mackenzie. But as I carefully settled in beside her I felt weird, like I was too close.

"So, guys," Jocelyn said solemnly as she plucked the bowl of popcorn from the chest, "MangaMinneapolis is in. Two. Weeks. You all ready?"

D'Anthony and I nodded, and for some reason I glanced over to see whether or not Mackenzie had, too.

"I ain't going," said Dante. "I'm not all that into the anime thing."

"It's a good thing nobody asked you, then, isn't it?" D'Anthony said scathingly.

"You do know that's what we're watching, right?" I asked him.

"Yeah, I said I'm not 'all that' into anime, that doesn't mean I hate it. Damn. Besides, y'all have food. Pass the chips."

Mackenzie reached over and handed them to him.

"Thanks. Mackenzie, right?"

"Yeah."

He sat up. "Wait, so you all go to the same school?"

I frowned and glanced over at him. Sure enough, he was directing his question specifically at Mackenzie.

My cheeks flushed.

It took her a second to realize he was talking to her. "Oh. Um, yeah."

"Cool," he said. "So you're a senior, too, right?"

I did not like the way his eyes were lingering on her face. Suddenly, I wasn't paying attention to the movie at all.

"Last time I checked," she answered rigidly.

Next to me, D'Anthony cleared his throat loudly. Dante didn't seem to notice.

"How come I've never seen you around before?" he asked.

My hands balled into fists. Dante needed to back off. I bit my tongue, conflicted, and resisted the urge to try to come to her rescue like some wannabe knight in shining armor. Mackenzie was more than capable of standing up for herself if she needed to. If she wanted to. And besides, I could be reading it all wrong. Maybe she was okay with it. For all I knew she thought he was cute. Maybe they'd add each other on Facebook, exchange numbers, and start dating or something—who could say? Not me. I didn't know anything. Except that the thought of them doing any of that made my chest burn and my stomach twist into tight knots.

"I don't get out much," Mackenzie said without looking away from the TV screen. "Too many creeps around nowadays."

Jocelyn nearly choked on her popcorn, and I could see D'Anthony silently laughing his ass off from my peripheral.

Dante didn't say anything else.

When I got home I sent Mackenzie a text.

Hey. Sorry about what happened tonight.

She didn't respond, which made sense; she was probably still on her way home. It was good to know she didn't text and drive, at least. I took a shower and tried to sort through my jumbled thoughts.

Dante wasn't fundamentally creepy. I'd known him for almost as long as I'd known D'Anthony. He didn't just go hitting on every girl he crossed paths with. Although, yeah, hitting on a high school girl when you've already graduated was gross. But I'd be lying if I said that that was the only reason I'd been so angry. Mackenzie was my friend, and she deserved someone who understood her. Someone who got her. Dante was so not that guy. He was a normie who wasn't "all that into the anime thing." He loved first-person shooters and sports games. He didn't know a thing about Studio Ghibli, or *Dragon Ball*, or any of the stuff that meant so much to Mackenzie. That meant so much to us. That's what had pissed me off.

There was a text alert on my phone when I got out of the shower. It was Mackenzie.

What do you mean?

I sat on the edge of my bed, still in my towel. The thing with D'Anthony's brother. That was weird.

She must have been home by now, because she texted back immediately. Oh that. It's whatever. He's not my type anyway 😊

The smiley face threw me. She'd probably meant it as a re-assurance sort of thing, like one of those, *See? I'm smiling. It's all good* things. And yet, it made my stomach flutter.

He's not my type anyway.

I read it over again, and an odd sense of relief washed over me. But I couldn't shake the question: Who *was* her type?

And was he anything like me?

Thanksgiving was always touch-and-go with my family, what with my parents divorced and my older sister determined to have absolutely nothing to do with our dad. It wasn't quite the family-coming-together holiday it was for most other people. In fact, next to Christmas it was the most awkward time of the year. We used to alternate; one year Cassie and I would celebrate with Mom and her family, the next we'd do it with Dad and his. That stopped once Cassie turned eighteen and refused to play ball, which was literally what she called it. "We're a volleyball you guys are lobbing back and forth, and I'm sick of it," were her exact words that year. I went over Dad's house alone that year.

This year both Cassie and I celebrated with Mom and her side of the family at Grammie's house in Saint Paul. We'd lived here for a couple of months, after the divorce, while Mom struggled to get us stabilized and situated without Dad. Grammie lived a couple blocks away from Summit Avenue, one of the oldest and most beautiful neighborhoods in the entire city. It was home to nearly four hundred Victorian-style mansions and houses, many of which had been pain‑stakingly maintained or restored to look like they did when they'd been built hundreds of years ago. Grammie's house wasn't a mansion, but it had two stories and an attic, and stay-ing there had been cozy but not cramped. It had been rough for my mom, though. I'd never seen her cry before then. I'd never realized she could.

The house was already packed when we got there, and as soon as I stepped through the door I was sucked into a laugh-ing, smiling mass of people who looked just like me. Cassie and I got passed around like heirlooms. Everyone wanted to know "how I got so tall" and "when I got to be so hand-some"—the way older relatives always did. And of course they all liked to remind me that they remembered when I was "barely knee-high with no ankles and the fattest face you ever did see."

When it came to Thanksgiving dinner, Grammie was extra as hell. She handled the turkey, *and* the corn bread, *and* the greens, *and* the pumpkin pie, *and* the sweet potato pie, and heaven help the person foolish enough to try to take over one of those dishes. I didn't complain; no one on this earth could throw down in the kitchen quite like Grammie. It was like she'd made some unholy alliance with the Cuisine Gods to channel their arcane powers.

We were in charge of the honey ham this year. Cassie and

I had made the glaze together, under Mom's watchful eye. I always found it weird that neither Mom nor Grammie had any recipes written down anywhere. They did everything from memory, like culinary savants. I wondered if I would ever get to that point, like maybe one day I'd level up enough for the family traditions and recipes to just manifest inside my head like Neo when he accepted that he was the One.

Probably not.

Grammie was pretty traditional; before we ate, we had to go around the table and say something we were grateful for. Everyone always said the same shit: family, love, the food we were about to get down on, whatever. When it got to be my turn, I said the first thing that popped into my head: "Friends."

Grammie nodded and smiled, like I'd said something profound. I wished my friends were here. As much as I loved my family, it was stressful having to come up with normal things to talk about with them.

I sat between Uncle Rodney and Uncle Reggie. They were my mom's older brothers, and I could count on them asking me the same questions they asked every year.

"Got a girlfriend yet, big man?" Uncle Rodney asked, just like he always did. As always, I said no.

"You're not gay, are you?" Uncle Reggie asked.

"Reginald!" Mom snapped.

He held up his hands. "Not that there's anything wrong with that! I'm just asking."

I couldn't understand my mom's generation sometimes. Toxic masculinity; you weren't a real man unless you had a girl, and if you weren't out there getting laid you were gay, because far be it for a straight male to just not want to screw every girl he came across.

I wondered what would happen if I ever did bring a girl home for Thanksgiving. I couldn't imagine introducing Karla to my uncles or my cousins. What would that even be like?

It was still better than being with my dad's side of the family. To them we were bougie. We weren't Black enough because we talked "white," and because we lived in the suburbs instead of the hood. They would definitely lose their shit if I brought Karla to Thanksgiving. That would go against the unspoken rule, which was to not ever, under any circumstances, bring a Becky home. Granted, Karla wasn't white, technically, but I doubted that technicality would matter to anyone.

After dinner everyone sort of found their own space. After we cleared off the table, Grammie, Mom, and most of my aunts and uncles settled in to play cards, my cousins turned on ESPN in the living room, and because I had nothing better to do, I started cleaning Grammie's kitchen. As I was loading the dishwasher, Uncle Rodney came in.

"Don't let Reggie get to you, man," he said as he took a beer from the fridge and cracked it open. "You do you. Never be someone you aren't proud to be."

"Thanks?" I said. I wasn't sure whether or not that meant he thought I was gay, too, but whatever.

Mackenzie wouldn't take their shit. She didn't take anyone's shit. They'd probably like her. Hell, my dad's side of the family would probably like her, too. Most people did, it seemed.

CHAPTER TWENTY-SIX

I got to school just before seven that Friday for the debut. There was a palpable electricity in the air as I settled into my seat. It was a packed house. I spotted Karla's parents settling in toward the front. They were both dressed up, still looking like Macy's models, but there was something forced about their posture. Now that Karla had told me about the tension between them, it was like I couldn't help but notice it now, too.

I could see feet darting back and forth across the stage beneath the red curtain, and I worried that something might have gone wrong last minute. "Nerves," Mrs. Vernon had warned everyone during their last full dress rehearsal. "We can run through this thing until the cows come home, but it's a whole different ball game when we've got an audience staring at us."

But the lights dimmed, and the curtain rose, from somewhere offstage Wyatt began narrating the opening soliloquy:

"It is a truth universally acknowledged, that a single man in possession of a good fortune must be in want of a wife…"

Something weird happened as I watched Elizabeth and Mr. Darcy go from "you're the last person in the world I'd ever want to marry" to "you're the only person in the world I'd ever dream of marrying." I started to get it. Seeing the play in its entirety, watching all the hard work finally pay off, witnessing the moving pieces come together into one beautifully executed performance, feeling the audience react to what they were watching—it all came together so seamlessly that I wondered if anyone else could really appreciate the hours and hours of work that had gone into the production. I wouldn't have, if I hadn't seen it firsthand. But it made sense now. I was moved, truly moved, and as the lights came on and the cast came out and did that thing where they all held hands and bowed at the same time, I clapped just like everyone else in the audience. They'd earned it, and I understood now. This was their anime, their manga, their *thing*. Maybe we weren't all into the same shit, but we were all geeks about *something*, so maybe we were all idiots for acting like we were so different from each other just because the object of our geekery was different.

The cast and crew spilled from the stage and into the waiting arms of their families and their adoring audience, and I ducked out through the side doors and out onto the loading dock, where I perched against the rails of the stairs. This was nice. Tonight had been nice. I had to hand it to the cast; they kicked ass. Everyone was on point. I was proud of them. I still had to get a few quotes from everyone, but I'd let them celebrate first.

Besides, I needed a moment. I felt this weird emptiness in my stomach, an almost loneliness, and my thoughts inexplicably ran to Mackenzie. I sent her a text asking how her

Thanksgiving went as the door opened behind me, and I turned to see Karla. She joined me at the rails and exhaled, sending a plume of air into the frigid sky. "So," she said, "what'd you think?"

I nodded, putting my phone away. "I was impressed. Seriously. You guys are amazing."

"Aren't we, though?" She smiled. "I can't wait to read your article about us."

"Me, either," I said with a huff. Whenever I actually started it.

Karla poked my arm. "So. What's next for our intrepid reporter?"

I looked up at the gray clouds pulling together in the sky and drew my jacket closed against the chill. "I was thinking about doing an exposé on senior hazing. How to not get stuffed into a locker. I feel like it'll resonate with the freshman crowd."

"Seriously?"

"No," I said, laughing.

"Brat," she said, laughing with me. "Remember when the seniors told us there was a haunted room in the basement where a girl died in the sixties?" she asked.

"Yeah. That actually happened."

She gasped. "You're kidding!"

"I am."

She swatted my arm. "Ohmigod, stop!"

"I can't help it. It's too easy. No, but seriously, I spent three hours going through microfiche at the library trying to debunk it. I read ten years' worth of papers, and nothing mentioned anyone dying here. At least not in the sixties."

"Thank goodness."

"Yeah." I looked up at the sky again, and so did she. We

stared at the stars and the moon together, and I thought, in this moment, we'd never been more in tune. "Really, though. You guys did amazing tonight," I said after a while.

Karla nodded slowly. "Yeah. We did."

She sniffed, and I looked over at her. "Are you crying?"

She wiped her eyes on her sleeve. "No. I yawned."

"You're totally crying."

"Shut up," she said with a laugh. "I'm entitled to cry. This was good. All of it. Just, really good."

"It was, and a lot of that was because of you."

"I just helped Mrs. Vernon yell at people," she said with a shrug.

"You should give yourself more credit. For real." I was being serious now because I suddenly realized that this was her pattern. "You work your ass off and then act like it doesn't amount to anything. You should take a minute. Celebrate. This is your win, too."

"Maybe." She didn't sound like she believed me. "Come on," she said, lacing her fingers in mine, "let's go celebrate."

Backstage was a circus. People in period clothes and black shirts spilled out of every nook and cranny. Ken had somehow weaseled his way backstage and was darting around, snapping pictures. Mrs. Vernon was clutching a huge bouquet of flowers, crying tears of joy in the corner. It was all smiles and squeals and hugs and tears, all of it well-earned. They'd done it. They'd fucking done it. I was still trying to wrap my head around it.

Naomi squealed when she saw Karla and me. "We did it!" she shouted, throwing her arms around Karla. She was still in her gown and bodice, but she'd started taking her hair down. She let go of Karla, then threw herself at me. I was almost too shocked to hug her back.

"Party. My place," Lydia sang. She was smiling, too. It was strange seeing her this happy. It was like she was floating on air. "Somebody bring pizza. Lots of it." She pointed at me. "Cameron, you're coming, right?"

I did a double take. "I'm sorry, what?"

She waved a hand. "You're coming. Karla, make sure he gets there, please?"

"I'm on it." She threw a sidelong smile my way and beckoned with her head for me to follow her. I did, hoping she'd give me the answers to the six hundred questions I had about what the hell was going on.

My text tone went off. Karla wrapped her arm in mine and smiled widely at me. "You did it," she said quietly. "They *like* you now."

"Are you sure? I assumed they were going to make me into a human piñata and beat me with sticks."

"Trust me, getting an invite to Lydia's house is the Holy Grail. She *has* to like you."

Pride swelled inside me. This was it. I'd done what I'd set out to do. I was in the inner circle, or at least circling it. Karla and I were all but dating now. I should have been ecstatic. I should've been over the goddamn moon. A part of me was, I guess. But a part of me, well… I couldn't stop thinking about G.A.N.U., but especially Mackenzie.

Everyone packed into their cars, and we all left for Lydia's house. Karla insisted I ride with her, and I didn't argue. I had no idea where Lydia lived.

"Is, um, Lucas going to be here?" I asked as we left.

Or any of his friends, for that matter. That was one bridge I wasn't quite ready to cross.

"No," she said firmly. "Everybody hates him."

"Ah." That was enough to let me relax. I knew exactly how much sway her friends' opinions held. If they didn't like him anymore, he was as good as dead to her.

"You don't have to worry about him," she said. "Or any of my exes, for that matter."

"Other exes? Do I know them?"

"Why, do you want to be BFFs with them, too?"

Ouch. "I told you about Stella. It's only fair that you tell me about your exes."

We came to a stoplight, and she drummed the steering wheel. "Fine," she said as the light changed to green. "Before Lucas I dated this guy named Scott Foreman. He actually went to our school for a semester in ninth grade."

"I remember him. What happened?" I knew what everyone *thought* happened, but something told me that was more myth than truth.

"His mom got a job in Seattle, so they moved away," she said casually. "Which was fine by me. He was kind of clingy."

"What do you mean?"

"I mean, when he told me they were moving, I said we should break up, and he freaked out. Like, he wanted to do the long-distance thing where we'd visit each other every summer, then we'd go to the same college… I was like, okay, first of all, we're both fourteen. I'm not planning the next ten years of my life around our relationship, and second, we only dated for, like, three weeks."

"Wow."

"Yeah, and when I said all that, he started crying. In the middle of the foyer."

"Sounds awful."

"God, it was *so* embarrassing."

"Seems like you're a magnet for clingy guys."

"God, I hope not. I like to think they're better off after they date me."

"Does that include Lucas?"

Her lips became a thin line. "He is less of an asshole than he used to be. I think you can attest to that."

I could. But it made me wonder if maybe she was trying to do the same thing with me. Trying to change me for the better. I couldn't argue that I had changed, and that those changes were of my own doing, with her encouragement, of course. But was I better off? Had I improved as a person?

"Are you still friends with your exes?" I asked. I wasn't sure why I asked the question, but I felt like I needed to know the answer.

"Hell, no. If we can't make it work as a couple, why would I want to go back to being friends? That seems counterintuitive to me. Besides," she added off-handedly, "most of my exes are fuckboys."

"Fair enough."

"You're not a fuckboy," she said after a few terse moments. "For the record."

"Good to know," I said with a grin.

CHAPTER TWENTY-SEVEN

Summer

"We can't do this anymore," she'd whispered.

It was the beginning of August, a month before senior year started. I hadn't given much thought to what would happen between Karla and me once the school year began. Honestly, I hadn't given much thought to what *we* were, what *this* was, either.

This was probably why. Because I knew that at some point, it had to end.

"What is it that we're doing?" I asked between kisses.

"Being stupid," she said, pausing to grin at me before kissing me again.

"I like being stupid," I mumbled.

The double doors flew open, and we broke apart and retreated to opposite sides of the room, me to the racks, her to the sink as Rebecca blustered in, talking loudly on her phone.

"Straws! Seriously? How the hell do you run out of straws? That's the most nonsensical thing I—"

She slammed the office door. Karla and I looked at each other. We could still hear her muffled voice from the other side of the door.

"I feel really bad for the poor soul who forgot to restock straws," I noted.

"I put in my two weeks' notice."

Her words hit me like a Kamehameha blast, one of Goku's most powerful attacks.

"Why?"

"This was never supposed to be a long-term gig for me." She picked up a platter and twirled it. "And with senior year coming up, I'm gonna be way too busy. Don't look like that."

"Like what?"

"Like I just broke up with you. Look." She set the platter down and stepped over so she could lace her fingers with mine. "*This.* Whatever this is. I like it. I like *you*. But we both know this can't go on forever. Right? Summer is over. It's time for us to go back to our real lives."

"This *isn't* real?"

She scoffed. "You know what I mean. You have your friends… I've got mine."

Ah. That's what this was about. The social order, invisible, unofficial, but unbreakable. Even here, in the real world and not a play, in the twenty-first century, we couldn't escape its grasp.

This, whatever this was, was inevitable.

This was the end.

At least, it was supposed to have been.

CHAPTER TWENTY-EIGHT

Lydia's home was a brick-and-shingle country-style house nestled among the maple and oak trees not far from where I lived. In fact, it was so close that I wondered how I'd never seen her around before. I could walk home from here.

Karla parked behind the rest of the cars in the driveway in front of the two-and-a-half-car garage, and we followed the others up the covered porch and through the French doors and into a sparsely furnished living room with waxed wood floors and cream-colored walls. Lydia tossed her bag on the divan that was opposite the brown brick mantel before opening the sliding panel doors that separated the living room from the dining room. Ken and Wyatt set up the pizza and sodas on the cooktop island while Lydia pulled glasses from the cupboards.

"Alexa, play '80s Mix."

Soft Cell's "Tainted Love" started playing from the speakers. *Sometimes I feel I've got to run away.*

I've got to get away.

From the pain you drive into the heart of me.

"The '80s is my favorite decade," Lydia said. "I wish I'd been around back then."

And just like that I was thinking about Mackenzie, who also loved the '80s. Not that it took much for me to start thinking about her, lately. How could such wildly different people be into the same thing? Was it that the things we were into weren't as important as how they impacted us? Maybe our interests weren't what defined us. If that was the case, what was I even doing here, pretending to be someone I wasn't? Was I even pretending anymore? I'd always admired—and, honestly, been a little jealous of—Mackenzie's ability to exist among so many disparate groups of people and still somehow remain who she was. Could I do the same thing? Was I already doing it? Here I was, a card-carrying member of G.A.N.U., surrounded by theater nerds. But I'd somehow found common ground. Somehow, I could relate to Lydia, of all people, or to Naomi, two people I was absolutely convinced I had nothing in common with.

What the hell was I doing?

Ken started bobbing his head to the tune. "I love this song," he said loudly. I wondered if he actually liked the song or if he was just ass-kissing again.

"What's your favorite decade?" Lydia asked as she texted furiously on her phone. I waited for someone to respond for a full four seconds before realizing she was talking to me.

"Mine's the '90s," Ken interjected. "It's Britney, bitch."

He waited to see if anyone was going to laugh, but it didn't seem like they'd heard him. Not Lydia or Karla, at least.

Once I ran to you.

Now I run from you.

This tainted love you've given.

I give you all a boy could give you.

"I guess mine would be the '50s," I said without being sure it was even true. "Aside from, you know, the institutionalized racism and flagrant sexism."

"Why the '50s?" Lydia asked, and I got the impression she was quizzing me.

"The aesthetic, I guess. I'm a huge James Dean fan, and I like the rockabilly look and feel, with the jukeboxes and the milkshakes. The diners and the poodle skirts and the greasers."

"You like *Grease*?" Naomi asked from the other side of the island. "Lydia, where do your parents keep the liquor?"

"The liquor cabinet, duh." Lydia turned back to me. "Anyway, you were saying?"

"I do like *Grease*, but I like *Hairspray* way better."

"*Hairspray!*" Jackie shrieked. "Ohmigod, Zac Efron was *so* good in that movie."

"Right?" said Naomi as she plucked a wine bottle from the cabinet.

"I saw that on Broadway a couple years ago," Lydia said. "I think the show was better than the movie."

"It always is," I said. I was lying, again. Aside from today's performance, I'd seen, maybe, three plays in my entire life, the most recent being *Hurray for Diffendoofer Day!*, based on the book by Dr. Seuss. I was ten.

But the lies, the half-truths, and the omissions came easier to me now, at least when it came to telling them to other people. It was getting harder for me to believe them myself. As I looked around at all these people I realized that I wasn't enjoying this, and I was finally beginning to understand why.

This wasn't what I wanted. This crowd, this scene—I didn't belong here. I didn't want to be here. I didn't like it, because I didn't like myself right now. Not here. These people weren't my friends. Not really. No, my friends were Jocelyn, D'Anthony, and Mackenzie.

Mackenzie.

I liked who I was when I was with her. I *knew* who I was when I was with her. I didn't need to pretend to be anything other than what I was, and who I was. Yeah, we argued and made fun of each other, but when I was with Mackenzie, I was happy. But this? Whatever this was, it wasn't happiness.

More people showed up with more alcohol and food, and someone turned the music up, and suddenly this was a full-fledged party. I felt like I was back at Lucas's place.

Karla must have sensed that something was wrong, because she came over and plopped down on the sofa I'd sought refuge on. "What's up?" she asked merrily. "Having fun?"

"Are *you* having fun?" I asked, partly to make conversation and partly because I genuinely wanted to know how anyone could possibly be enjoying themselves here without being shit-faced.

"As much as can be expected being the babysitter— Hey! There *is* a garbage can!"

Wyatt picked up the cup he'd tossed on the table and placed it delicately in the waste bin.

"You make a good babysitter," I said as he staggered away.

She sipped from a wineglass. "Somebody has to keep these assholes in line. Are you drunk?"

"Definitely not."

"Good. Come with me."

She set her glass down and took my hand. I followed blindly as she led me back out into the main room, through the foyer and around the corner and up the stairs. She pulled me into the first room we came across.

"Is this Lydia's room?"

It looked like one of those bedrooms people took aesthetic candids in on Instagram, all cream-colored walls, a lavish bed with gossamer curtains, a handsome settee and a ridiculous vanity. I noticed a woodcut loon resting on the nightstand. I couldn't place it at the moment, but I felt like I'd seen it before.

Karla closed the door behind her. "Would you prefer her parents' room?" She shoved me onto the bed.

"Karla!" someone shouted from downstairs. Naomi, from the sound of it.

I started to get up, but she pushed me back down. "Ignore them," she whispered.

We waited in silence for a few seconds. "Karla!" It was Lydia this time. "We need you!"

"Shit," she groaned.

"Maybe we should do this later," I offered. "When there aren't so many people around?"

She sat up and raised an eyebrow. "You thought we were going to have sex? Right now, in *Lydia's* room?" She laughed. "I'm not desperate, Cam. I'd have to be desert levels of thirsty to do something like that."

As we left, I took a last look at the woodcut loon and I suddenly remembered exactly where I'd seen it before.

CHAPTER TWENTY-NINE

End of Summer

The first day of senior year had been like having to watch a mandatory cut scene before playing a level you'd already played. It was like watching the extended edition of a movie you'd already seen a few too many times—some things would happen that hadn't happened before, but all in all the narrative would essentially be the same. Despite all that, I was a nervous wreck walking into homeroom that morning. It would be my first time seeing Karla since the last time we'd hooked up, and even though things were supposed to be the same between us as they'd always been—meaning we didn't exist to one another—I wasn't sure I could just erase the last few weeks from my mind and act like they hadn't happened.

Karla and her friends had swept in a second before the final bell rang. They were all talking and laughing about something. She looked happy, the way she always did. She looked different, too, but I couldn't place exactly how until

I realized that it was me that was looking at her differently. I knew what she felt like, the heat of her skin and the smell of her hair and the taste of her lips, things I'd never known before. The paradigm had shifted. I was seeing her through a different lens now.

I didn't realize I was staring until our eyes met. No, until *my* eyes met *hers*, because it was like she was looking right through me and past me at the same time. No emotion, no recognition passed over her face; she may as well have been looking at a wall. And then she looked away and was swept up in her friends' conversation. My heart had dropped to somewhere in my groin. I'd expected it to hurt, just not like that.

I'd spent the rest of the day trying to forget. About the summer, about Karla, about us—all of it. It shouldn't have happened. *I* shouldn't have let it happen. I'd thought I'd been lucky, that the stars had aligned in my favor—our favor. But now I understood that it had been a curse. I was doomed to live with the memory and nothing more, and the worst part was that, somehow, I'd known that the whole time.

"My god, would you look at them?" Jocelyn said during lunch. She jutted her head in the direction of the theater snobs. One of them was standing on the table, flapping his arms like they were wings while the others applauded. "What the fuck are they even doing?"

"Interpretive dance?" D'Anthony offered.

I didn't look. Karla was most likely there, and I didn't want the added trouble of seeing her in real life. It was bad enough she was all I could think about. Her face was everywhere. Literally. At some point during the day someone had canvased fliers with her and Lydia's smiling faces on them, asking us to vote for them for student council president and vice president. I didn't know what student council was supposed to even do. I felt like I was being haunted, and Karla was my very own poltergeist, and it was worse because she didn't even know it. I wondered if she was having as hard a time forgetting me as I was forgetting her, but the thought was laughable. Of course she wasn't. I was nothing more than a fling, a tiny forgotten blip on her radar.

Jocelyn rolled her eyes. "Anyway, MangaMinneapolis. You both are going, right?"

My phone went off—"Tank!", the jazz opening of *Cowboy Bebop* by Seatbelts. My heart stopped. It was a text from Karla.

Meet me after class? The old library?

I didn't know what she could possibly want, but I did know I could think of a dozen different reasons not to respond to her text. And yet, despite everything, I'd answered.

Be right there.

CHAPTER THIRTY

As the party at Lydia's raged on, everyone was congregating at the bottom of the stairs when we came down. "Come on," Ken said. "Everyone get in."

"What's happening?" I whispered as everyone in the room circled in around him.

"Group selfie, duh," Karla said. "Come on."

She took my hand and pulled me in. Ken held his phone up as high as his long arm would reach. "On three."

Everyone put on their best selfie face. I didn't know what to do, so I just smiled like an idiot. Ken snapped the picture, but his flash wasn't on, and I didn't know he was done until everyone started to scatter.

Karla shook my arm. "Fun, right?"

I nodded weakly. "I guess." When my friends and I took selfies, we made stupid faces or posed like we were doing the fusion dance or like we were the Ginyu Force. Taking selfies with my friends was fun. This was weird.

"Come here." She yanked me toward her and pulled me into a long, slow kiss.

I tore myself away from her. "Hey! What are you doing?"

I looked around nervously. We were surrounded by people.

Karla laughed. "Don't you get it? It's okay now. You're one of us now." She wove her arms around my neck and kissed me again, then rose on her toes to whisper in my ear. "I've been waiting for this."

Her lips brushing against my ear sent shivers through me. "Same," I said quietly.

"Hey," Karla said.

She put a hand on my wrist and looked at me. For some reason it felt like she was looking *at* me for the first time instead of *through* me. She patted the spot next to her on the steps, and I sat back down. There was a strange look on her face, one that worried me. Once I was seated, she turned so she was facing me and our knees were touching. "How are you?" she asked. "Really."

"I'm okay, I guess."

"Nice." She nodded idly, and I knew we were doing the dance, where we talked about things that didn't matter to avoid talking about the thing that did.

"Is everything alright?" I asked. She seemed to be hesitating on the cusp of saying something that she kept changing her mind about. This felt familiar.

She huffed. "Okay. I'm going to be as blunt as possible because I've never done this before, okay? Just, bear with me."

I nodded. "Sure…"

She took a deep breath. I remembered back when she gave the opening speech during homecoming, in front of all those students and teachers, eight thousand eyes all focused on her. She hadn't looked nearly as nervous then as she did now. "I've always told myself that prom wasn't that big of a deal," she began. "Sure it's the last high school dance, and it's supposed to be this grand, perfect, romantic night that you remember forever, but that always sounded so silly to me. It's just a dance, right? It was the same when I was with Lucas. Prom was just something we were expected to do, you know? I didn't really care about any of it. But now?" The question hung potently in the silence between us. "I want you to go to prom with me."

Her words rumbled through me like the shock waves of an earthquake. It was like my brain's processor had shorted, or the disks had fried, and all I had was the blue screen of death.

"You...want *us*...to go to prom *together*?"

"More than that," she said. "I think we should be together. Like, *together*, together, whatever that means. Because I like you. You're thoughtful, you're funny, you're an amazing kisser, and we're about to graduate. I don't know where this is gonna go or if it'll go anywhere, but I don't think it matters. Neither does what anyone else says, or what my friends think. I'm over it. All of it. Call this *my* Mr. Darcy moment."

This was sure to trigger some sort of cataclysm, the rapture, or the apocalypse. This was exactly what I wanted, exactly what I had been trying so hard to make happen. And yet, here it was, actually happening, and I felt...

Empty.

"Karla, I... I don't think I can."

All I could think about was Mackenzie, who loved *Dragon*

Ball and *Little Nemo: Adventures in Slumberland*, who was tall
and lanky, who dressed like she got every piece of her ward-
robe from a different hipster boutique, who wore her curly
hair wild and free, like a lion's mane, who only painted her
nails pink or black, whose lashes were so long I thought they
were fake, until I heard her tell Jocelyn she hated fake lashes,
who didn't sit in chairs so much as lounge in them, and how
I knew I'd said something clever when the scowl on her face
was preceded by this tiny almost-grin.

Karla cocked her head to one side. "Hold on. What?"

I sucked in a deep breath. "I'm never going to be the guy
you want me to be. And I can't keep pretending to be something I'm not. It isn't fair to either of us."

Her lips pressed together. "No one's asking you to pretend
to be anything."

"But I am. It's what I've been doing this entire time. I don't
like Jane Austen, or Shakespeare, and theater is cool, but it's
not my thing. I can't talk about my thing. Not here. Not with
you. And I'm so tired of trying to downplay that side of myself. I… I can't, Karla. I'm so sorry, but I can't."

I started to get up.

"Wait. Before you say anything else." She leaned forward
and kissed me, slowly, lightly, and my head swam the way
it always did. Only this time I couldn't stop thinking how
wrong this was.

I sensed someone watching us and opened an eye. Ken
was standing there, staring at us with his phone in his hands.
His expression ran from fury to shock, and then he screwed
it into something like forced disinterest. "Oh, I'll…leave you
two alone. My bad."

He turned and practically ran away. I stood up. "I should go," I said quietly.

"Are you sure?" Karla asked.

I looked at her. I saw everything I'd gone through to be with her, everything I thought I loved.

"I'm sorry, Karla. I truly am. But this is your world, and I don't belong in it."

It was snowing hard when I left Lydia's house, but instead of the cold, all I felt was numb. I thought I'd at least feel relieved to be rid of the lie I'd created, but I felt like complete shit. I blinked rapidly against the falling snow. I felt completely hollow. My head spun dizzily. All I could see was Karla's face, the hurt and confusion playing out in her big brown eyes. It was better this way, for both of us. I knew that, deep down, but it didn't change the way I felt.

I was grateful when my phone went off. "Where you at?" D'Anthony asked, way too loudly.

"I'm…out," I said.

"Busy?"

"Nah."

"Cool. We're at Jocelyn's," he said. "Get over here."

I stopped. The snow fell gently, building on my shoulders and head. I wasn't far from home, but I wasn't sure that's where I wanted to go. "I'm on my way."

Fifteen minutes later I was in Jocelyn's basement.

"Wow. It's clean in here."

And it was. It didn't look like a cosplay dungeon anymore. The bolts of fabric and the plastic tubs were all stacked neatly against the wall. The workbench was tidy and organized, and

even the glitter that had permeated the carpet had been re-
moved somehow. Mostly.

"Yeah," Jocelyn said with mock humility, as if it hadn't
taken an ungodly amount of time to straighten this place up.
"I'm trying something new. Not sure how I feel about it yet."

"Well, *I* like it."

"How was the show?"

D'Anthony was sitting upside down on the futon watching *Sailor Moon Crystal*.

"Yeah, was it worth the five weeks of your life you're never
getting back?"

"It was decent, guys," I said hollowly. "Seriously, you
should check it out."

D'Anthony chuckled. "Yeah, no, I'll pass."

Jocelyn settled into her chair at the workstation behind the
futon. The twin dress forms next to her were both naked.
"No Mackenzie?"

I looked at her and frowned. "You're asking me? How
should I know?"

"I mean, you usually do."

I stared at her, then glanced at D'Anthony, who nodded
reluctantly. "She's not wrong."

I groaned. I did wish she were here. I took out my phone
and saw that she'd responded to my text from earlier.

Ugggggggh! Jk, it was alright. Sort of

I glanced at my text bubble above her response to remember what I'd asked her to begin with. Thanksgiving. Right.
That seemed like it had been a lifetime ago. I replied.

We're at Jocelyn's. You should come over

Can't, she answered. Doing family shit. Blech.

That sucks. Wish you were here.

I regretted it as soon as I hit Send. *Wish you were here?* What kind of weak shit was that?

I started to add "JK" so I didn't sound so thirsty when the ellipses popped up. She was typing. I waited, and a second later her response bubble popped up.

Wack. Kidding. Wish I was there too ☹

"You're texting her now? That's odd," said Jocelyn. "I don't have her number. Do you, D'Anthony?"

"I do not," he said.

They were both very pointedly looking at me. I glanced up at the ceiling. "Where'd you get that duck, by the way?" I asked Jocelyn. Since we were playing that game.

Jocelyn narrowed her eyes. "It's a loon, and I made it back in seventh grade shop class. Why?"

"No reason."

She eyed me suspiciously.

"You know, I gotta be honest, I don't like *Sailor Moon Crystal* as much as I like the original," D'Anthony said obliviously.

"Why's that, because of the superior animation?" Jocelyn asked dryly. "Or maybe it's the better dub quality that turns you off."

"*Actually*, it's the transformation sequences. I'm so used to the old choreography that came with the Sailor Scouts transforming into their uniforms. The new stuff isn't horrible, just different. Like a remix to a song you know by heart that doesn't ruin the original song but makes it just different enough that you don't quite know the words anymore."

I chuckled to myself. This. This was where I belonged.

CHAPTER THIRTY-ONE

There was something terrifying about waking up to find that you've been tagged in a photo dump on Instagram. Candids rarely turned out flattering, and if you weren't aware of the pictures being taken there were greater chances of being caught in the act of doing something embarrassing, like picking your nose or something.

What was even more horrifying was that the photos had all been uploaded by Ken.

I scrolled through the post captioned: Wrap Partay! He'd tagged me along with about thirty other people.

Halfway through scrolling I stopped, and my stomach dropped to my feet.

Shit.

Front and center, Karla and I, locking lips like no one else was watching. Under the photo was a comment that stood out: love birds??

God-fucking-dammit.

I showed up a couple more times in the post. Every time I was with Karla. Had we really been together that entire time? I scrambled to untag myself as panic bubbled up inside me. Ken knew everyone, not just the Caravan. He'd uploaded these an hour ago so there was no way half the school hadn't seen them by now. The post already had 214 likes.

This was bad. This was really fucking bad.

I didn't know what I was supposed to do: carry on my usual routine, or find some place to bury my head and wait for this all to blow over. I tried to focus on other things. I spent the weekend writing and revising my feature. I texted Stella and asked if they needed any extra help at Pair-O'-Moose. I caught up on some of the manga I'd put off reading. But none of that kept my mind off what I knew was going to happen come Monday. There were people I couldn't hide from forever, and the specter of those coming confrontations hung over me like I was Ebenezer Scrooge.

D'Anthony and Jocelyn were waiting for me at my locker.

"What the fuck?!" Jocelyn said before I could even touch my lock. "How long have you and Karla been secret fuck buddies?"

"We weren't having sex," I explained shamefully. "We were just…hooking up."

"For how long?" D'Anthony asked. "And doesn't 'hooking up' mean having sex?"

"Come on, man."

"No, he's got a point," Jocelyn cut in.

I frowned. "I mean, I don't know for sure what exactly constitutes 'hooking up' but—"

"Not that. How long has this been going on?"

I sighed. They had a right to know. "Since the summer."

They executed a perfectly synced double take.

"But you hate her," said D'Anthony in a voice that was equal parts bewilderment and hurt.

"That was obviously a lie," Jocelyn said in a scathing voice. "A lie he was clearly happy to keep telling us. This is what's been weird about you this whole time, isn't it?"

"I would've told you guys, but I couldn't."

"Oh, because she told you not to, right? Well, it looks like that won't be a problem for anybody, now will it?"

"Come on, guys. This isn't how this was supposed to happen."

"Oh really? Is this not what you wanted? To be popular, for everyone to know who you are? Guess what, you got it, just like *she* did. You're just like *her*."

She stormed off. D'Anthony hesitated. "That's fucked up, man," he said, shaking his head. And then he followed after her.

Karla didn't show up to homeroom. Not that I was surprised.

I could tell by the way everyone looked at me that they'd all seen the picture. It was, just, the *ickiest* feeling. It was like I had something on my face, like a pimple right between my eyes, or a booger dangling from my nose, and no one wanted to tell me directly, but everyone wanted to see it. I was a sideshow freak, the sole exhibit on display in some fucked-up carnival.

It was all the worse because I was alone. Karla was nowhere to be found; she'd dissolved into the ether, or flown right off the face of the earth or something. Lydia was the only one who didn't seem dead set on ignoring me completely. Our eyes met, and the look she gave me was part sympathy, part I-told-you-so. All I could do was groan. But when the dismissal bell rang, and everyone packed up and shuffled out of class, she stood up and cut across the room and stood in front of my desk, where I was still lingering.

"Hey," she said flatly.

I nodded. "Congratulations on the play, again," I said automatically because I couldn't think of another topic to discuss with her.

"Thank you. I read your feature. It was good, so I made everyone else read it, too."

"Thanks, I think?"

She crossed her arms in a surprisingly unsure gesture, and I realized that the look she had on her face was still sympathetic. "I would say I told you so, but… I told you so."

I shrugged. "Can't argue with that."

She nodded, and for a while she just stood there, and I couldn't tell if this was solidarity or something else.

"I figured it out," I said when I couldn't take the silence anymore. "You and Jocelyn. You guys used to date, didn't you?"

Lydia stiffened. "Relax," I told her. "I haven't told Jocelyn. She has the same duck as you have in your room."

"It's a loon, and what were you doing in my room—oh god, never mind."

"Nothing happened. Your room remains unsoiled."

Lydia nodded once, sat down, and folded her arms across her chest. "I'm sorry about you and Karla. She told me some of the real story. Although, I'd already figured out most of it."

"Naturally."

"Jocelyn and I met in middle school. We were both tomboys then. I thought she was the most interesting person I'd ever met. She could do all this cool stuff, make all these amazing things, and she knew exactly who she was, even back then. I came out when I realized I was in love with her."

She stopped talking and smiled.

"What happened with you two?"

She looked down and sighed. "I wanted to grow and change. I wanted friends. Jocelyn wanted to stay exactly the way we were, us against the world, when it didn't need to be that way. We just grew apart, I guess."

She got up to leave.

"She still likes you, you know," I said to her back. "There's still a chance for you two if you would just talk it—"

Lydia slowly turned around. "Have you *met* Jocelyn?" she asked, chuckling bitterly. "Jocelyn doesn't *talk*, and she most definitely doesn't want to talk to me, and anyway it's not as simple as that. Sometimes we can't fix our mistakes. Sometimes we just have to learn to live with them."

"I do know Jocelyn. She's entering the costume contest at con this year. Saturday. You should be there. I know what it will mean to her."

Lydia sighed. "I know. She used to talk my ear off about entering the adult contest as soon as she turned eighteen. She used to literally count down the days. Seeing as her birthday was this past September, I figured she'd be entering."

"Aw, you remember when her birthday is?"

"Shut up," she said without any real anger or annoyance in her voice. "And yes, I do."

Despite every cell in my brain screaming for me not to, I dragged myself to Spanish class, trying to convince myself the whole way that, really, it wasn't that big of a deal.

It wasn't like Mackenzie and I were together.

It wasn't like Mackenzie and I were anything even approaching being together.

What difference did it make if she knew I'd kissed Karla?

She was already at her desk, as usual, hunched over with her face pressed so close to her sketch pad that her nose was nearly touching the paper. She reminded me of a golfer, when they got down on their hands and knees and pressed their faces to the green to analyze their next move. Or maybe a scientist carefully observing a chemical reaction in a beaker.

As soon as I saw her my chest caved.

Who the hell was I fooling?

I trudged to my seat just as the final bell rang. I stared straight ahead, shame and guilt and tepid fear gnawing at my insides. From the corner of my eye I saw her straighten up, but I couldn't tell if she had looked my way, or if she was trying as hard not to look at me as I was.

I couldn't take this. I leaned across our aisle.

"Hi."

"Hi."

She was staring straight ahead when she said it.

I wasn't sure how to interpret that.

I spent the entire class period trying to come up with a way to break through this icky silence between us. I couldn't get a read on where we stood with each other. Maybe she hadn't seen or heard about the photo, after all? The thought made me even more nervous. If she hadn't, I had to tell her, to warn her, before she found out about it on her own.

But how could she not have at least heard about it?

The moment the dismissal bell rang I threw my crap in my bag and caught up with her.

"Hey, can I talk to you about something?"

She stopped and popped one of her earbuds out. I hadn't realized she was wearing them. "You mean the picture of you and Karla?"

My heart froze. "Um…"

"Don't worry about it."

She said it so casually that I almost believed she meant it. "Mackenzie…"

"It's cool. We're cool. I just thought you were someone else." She shouldered her backpack. "See you around, Cameron."

I could only watch her leave. There was really nothing else to say. I fucked up. I fucked up bad.

CHAPTER THIRTY-TWO

I avoided the Caravan like the plague. I avoided my friends. I skipped lunch altogether. I didn't even risk a visit to my locker, just carried what I'd brought with me that morning all day. The irony of it all was definitely *not* lost on me. I had all day to contemplate it, in fact. I'd spun such a complicated web, such an intricate scheme, to embed myself into Karla's circle, her world, that had seemed so much bigger than mine, and now, here I was, more alone than I had ever been. I felt like Vegeta, who had put so much work and dedication into becoming a Super Saiyan like Goku, only to be immediately beaten up by an android. All because I was a grade A dumbass who couldn't appreciate what he already had.

Still, I knew that I wasn't done dealing with the fallout, and that the moment was coming when I'd have to square with the only person I hadn't yet.

"Hey! Cameron!"

I froze in my tracks, knowing the moment had finally arrived. I turned in a slow one-eighty, and the crowd parted to clear the space between us, and I felt the strangest déjà vu, like this had somehow happened before.

Only this time Lucas was definitely mad. "What the fuck, bro," he demanded. "Is it true?"

"What have you heard?" I wasn't trying to be flippant; I really wanted to clarify the particulars to make sure he was at least pissed off about the right things.

He huffed. "That you. And Karla. Have been…hooking up."

His voice was strained, and it was obvious he was fighting a losing battle with his own anger. This was Level One Lucas, nowhere near his final form. Things were definitely going to get worse.

Historically, my tactic for dealing with a Code Lucas was to flee the scene as soon as possible, so as to minimize the damage. A part of me wanted to do it now, but this time, the instinct to run was overridden by the urge to stand my ground. This was a fight-or-flight situation, and my dial had finally toggled to the fight option.

"It's true." True enough, anyway. We technically never actually got as far as sex, but I wasn't about to split hairs here.

The right side of Lucas's lip twitched, and I watched the truth take its toll. His expression ran gymnastics, from shock to anger to shock again, with an infinitesimal pass through hurt, before settling on something between fury and betrayal. "Fuck you, bro. How could you do this? How could you *fucking* do this?"

There was really no way to explain everything that had happened between us, or to begin to justify it. "It's over now," I said instead. "She and I are done."

"I wasn't talking about *Karla*," he spat, and the realization of who he was talking about hit me like a brick, and deflated every ounce of the defiance I had somehow mustered up and left me feeling sick to my stomach.

"This had nothing to do with Mackenzie," I said. "I swear to you."

Lucas's face darkened, and his eyes seemed to turn completely black, like a shark's. Or a possessed person. When he spoke his voice was low and dripping with murderous intent. "I get that you want to get back at *me* for all the bullshit I did to you. But you fucked with my *sister*, too?" He looked at me with the face of absolute disgust. "She fucking *likes* you, bro. And you fucked her over, too."

"It's not like that," I said desperately. "I... I love her."

Lucas stopped, his hands balled into fists.

"I'm in love with her. I'm in love with Mackenzie."

It was a strange sense of surrender, finally saying the words, surrender and acceptance, but most of all relief. I loved her, and I loved everything about her, everything about us.

That relief lasted about as long as it took for Lucas to shove me against the lockers.

"Fuck you!" he bellowed, to the collective gasp of everyone who had gathered to watch.

But if they were here to see Lucas kick my ass, they were about to be sorely disappointed, because I wasn't about to take this on the chin. I was done running, and I was done hiding.

I shoved him back, and then I swung for all I was worth.

Our fight, if it could even be called that—if anything it had been more of a scuffle, or a skirmish—ended the same way every fight at our school ended: with the participants being yanked apart by the hall monitors and promptly marched, separately, straight to the office for swift punishment.

I could count on one hand the number of times I'd been to the principal's office. It was quiet as a crypt, and no one seemed to want to make eye contact with me. The worst part was that they sat me there, in the lobby outside his door while Lucas was inside, probably getting read the riot act, and I had nothing to do but wait, like a convict on death row.

My mom was going to kill me.

I buried my face in my hands and tried not to think about that, or any of the other ways I was utterly and totally screwed. No, all the ways I had utterly and totally screwed myself.

I heard the office door open and close, but it didn't register until someone carefully sat in the chair beside mine. I tilted my head, and my heart dropped to my feet.

It was Mackenzie.

I knew this was coming. I could feel it, creeping toward me, unstoppable, unavoidable, impossible to escape. I knew it was completely, one hundred percent my fault that it was going to happen, and the moment was finally upon me, the weight of just how badly I'd fucked up truly crushed me.

For a while she just sat there, arms and legs crossed. I waited, heart thumping in my ears, until finally she spoke.

"Lucas told me what happened."

I couldn't bring myself to look at her. "Yeah?" I couldn't read her voice, but it sounded like she was outside.

"I wanted to hear it from you." She breathed deeply. She wasn't looking at me, either. "So, is it true? The whole thing, I mean. Is it all true?"

"Yeah."

There was nothing else to really say about it. I'd meant it, more now than before.

I waited, frozen in a bubble of shame and guilt, for her to respond. When she finally did, her voice was flat, devoid of surprise, disgust, or anything else I expected to hear. That made it so much worse.

"Bye, Cameron."

She stood up and left, and it was like I'd been sucked into a black hole and completely pulverized by its inescapable force. The worst part about it was that it was exactly what I deserved, and exactly what she didn't.

Hilltop High had a zero tolerance policy when it came to violence, which meant that even though I was an exemplary student who until now had never been anywhere near a fight, and despite the fact that I hadn't even started this one, *and* that I was only defending myself, I was automatically suspended for a full week. Which was some grade A BS, if you asked me. Not that anyone did. But it wasn't like I wanted to rehash that whole sordid tale anyway, so a week of suspension with no questions asked wasn't the worst way things could have ended up.

Even though I felt as though I'd gotten off relatively easy, Lucas, as it turned out, wasn't so lucky. As I found out later, he'd not only been suspended, but he also got community service, as this was far from his first altercation.

But even though, all things considered, I'd come out relatively unscathed, both literally and metaphorically, the same didn't hold true on the home front.

"You're grounded, obviously," Mom announced after I

explained what had happened, or at least my side of it, since the principal had already called her and filled her in on the official story. "That's your penance."

"What about MangaMinneapolis?"

"What about it?"

I groaned. Cassie shrugged apologetically, but we both knew there was nothing to be done about it. I was about to send a text to Jocelyn and D'Anthony to break the bad news, until I remembered that they had both made it very clear they wanted nothing to do with me right now.

It was going to be a very long, very lonely week.

And the hits kept playing.

Dad called later that night.

"Your mother told me about your school trouble," he said.

"Yeah." If this was the part where I was supposed to explain myself to him, he could forget it. I didn't owe him any explanations. He'd never offered any to me.

"Look, son," he said when it was obvious I wasn't going to elaborate. "I can't say I know all the details of what you're going through, but I was in high school once, too, so I can relate a little bit. I know what it's like."

"Do you? Really?" I was surprised at how harsh the words had come out. There was a poignant silence where neither of us spoke, as the shock of what I'd said settled in, but it only emboldened me, and I couldn't stop.

"What do you know about anything to do with me?" I demanded. "What do you know about what I'm doing or how I'm doing?" I was shouting now, and I didn't care. "You think you can just call me up and, what, drop some fatherly advice on me when I get in trouble? Is that the only time you give a damn about me?"

"Cameron…"

"No. I don't want to hear it. I don't want to hear anything you have to say. I'm done. I'm done pretending any of this is cool. I'm done pretending you might still be a good father. I'm done pretending you actually give a shit about me."

"You do not talk to me like that!" Dad barked.

"No, you don't talk to me. Period." I hung up the phone and threw it across the room. It wasn't until then that I realized that Cassie was standing quietly in the doorway. Without a word she came in and sat down on the bed beside me. She wrapped an arm around my shoulder and stayed with me until I'd finished crying.

CHAPTER THIRTY-THREE

I spent the rest of the week doing every chore Mom could think of to throw at me, which ran the gamut from polishing the china Grammie had passed on to my mom from her mom (the same china we never, ever used, and so had about ten years' worth of dust built up on it), waking up at five in the morning to shovel snow out of the walkways and driveway, to systematically cleaning each room of the house, starting with the living room, then the kitchen, the garage, and finally the den. I took my time in the den. Everything was virtually unchanged since Mackenzie and I had been here together. I wondered what would happen when I went back to school. Were we just never going to speak again? I'd lied to her, and screwed her brother over, on top of everything else. She had more reason than the others to hate me.

I thought I'd wanted to be with Karla, and I'd been so caught up in trying to make that happen that I'd completely screwed up whatever I had with Mackenzie, not to mention my other friends. They had always been there for me when I needed them, and I'd lied to them for months. Hell, I'd lied to just about everyone, including myself.

The shittiest part of being grounded—aside from, you know, the whole being grounded thing—was that even though I couldn't go anywhere or do anything, I still had to go to work. It didn't help that I had to get there in the middle of a snowstorm like I had to that Friday.

As impossible as it was, it felt like everyone there knew I was in trouble. I felt like my regulars weren't as talkative today, like they weren't quite meeting my eyes as I made their drinks, like they were whispering to each other about me behind my back.

On break I checked my messages, even though I knew for a fact that there wouldn't be anything from Mackenzie. I wasn't surprised that there was nothing from Jocelyn or D'Anthony, either. They didn't hate me, at least I didn't think they did, but they were mad, and probably more than a little hurt, and they had every right to be. I'd lied to them. I'd been lying to them for months, but I hoped they wouldn't stay mad for long, not when I needed them. Not when I knew how much I needed them.

When my break was over, I went back out to man the coffee station while Stella worked the drink counter. I could tell she knew something was wrong, but I knew she wasn't going to ask me about it. I was grateful; I didn't feel like rehashing all the ways I'd fucked up.

As I started checking the espresso machines I heard a familiar voice at the register.

"Look who it is," said Oscar. "Long time, no see."

I peeked over and saw Karla, wrapped in a thick scarf and

a peacoat. She looked exactly like someone from out of Abercrombie's winter catalog.

"How are you, Oscar?" Karla asked in a subdued voice. "Hey, Stella."

"Yo." Stella glanced at me and raised a questioning brow. I shrugged. I had no idea why she was here. Until she looked right at me, and I realized it was entirely possible that she was here to see me.

I kept cleaning while she chatted with Stella and Oscar, keeping my back toward the drink counter, but I could feel her watching me, and I couldn't help taking the bait. I turned and moved to the counter and started wiping it down.

"Hi."

"Hey," she said quietly. "Can we talk?"

I shrugged. "It's an hour till my next break."

"That's fine. I have homework to catch up on, anyway."

I looked up at her. "You sure?"

"I am. I'll be over there, I guess." She nodded toward the far corner of the lobby.

"Sure. Yeah."

She took her coffee and left.

"What's up with you two?" Stella asked the second Karla was out of earshot.

"Nothing," I said. "Absolutely nothing."

"Is it weird being back here?" I asked Karla.

We were sitting at the farthest table in the lobby, right next to the window. The irony of us meeting here, where it had all started, now that it was over wasn't lost on me.

"A little bit," Karla said. "I almost want to tie on an apron and start pulling espresso shots."

"They'd love that. Everyone here misses you."

"Including Brunhilda?"

"Especially Brunhilda."

She smiled and took a sip of her drink, something mixed with more chocolate and cream than actual coffee, and cradled her cup in her hands. "How are you holding up?"

I sighed. "Well, my best friends aren't speaking to me, Lucas wants to kill me, and I'm pretty sure Mackenzie hates my guts. Oh, and I'm grounded for getting suspended, and getting grounded is especially shitty when you're technically an adult, as it turns out."

"Sounds shitty."

"It is. How are you?"

She shrugged her shoulders. "Now that the play is over I can breathe. A little. Mrs. Vernon is already talking about the spring production."

"She's intense."

"Absolutely. She's thinking *Much Ado About Nothing* or *A Midsummer Night's Dream*, but I'm trying to convince her to let us do a musical, like *Rent* or *Little Shop of Horrors*. My parents are talking about couple's therapy," she added quickly. "Like, good for them, I guess." She rolled her eyes.

"It could help," I offered.

"Maybe, but I'm not holding my breath. Other than that, business as usual."

"What about what everyone is saying? Everybody knows now, about us. Like, *everybody*."

She shrugged again. "Lucas and I are done. Like, for good. Frankly, that was overdue. You know he actually asked me out again, after what he did? Can you believe that shit?"

I could believe that, actually.

Karla sighed. "Ken tried to hit me up, too. Like he didn't know what he did. Now he's subtweeting about being stuck in the friend zone. Honestly I think I'm over the whole dating thing for now. Trust me, I've had worse rumors spread about me—at least this one is true. Things will simmer back down. They always do."

"That's good, I guess." I supposed that was the difference between us. Whereas my entire world had collapsed into itself like a black hole, she'd emerged from the fallout virtually unscathed. Maybe I should have expected as much. But instead of being bitter or resentful of it, I found myself relieved.

Karla set her coffee on the table and squared her shoulders. "Listen, I wanted to apologize. For everything. I've treated you like shit since, well, forever, but especially over these last few months."

"It's fine."

She reached across the table and squeezed my hand in hers. "No, it's really not. I was selfish, and you deserve better. This whole time I thought you were something to fix. And not just you. Lucas, my parents—I guess I've always felt like it was my job to fix everyone else, and when I realized I couldn't…well, I just wanted to escape. Cut my losses, bide my time until I'd have a fresh start. Because I couldn't accept that I'd failed."

"You didn't fail at anything. And this wasn't all your fault. It's not like I didn't know what I was doing."

She gave a vague shrug. "So, what happens next?"

"Next?"

"Yeah. Like, with everything. With us, with all of it."

"I don't know. I guess we go back to being who we were before, maybe."

"I don't think I want to go back to who I was."

"Me, either."

She took a sip of her drink. I'd never seen anyone nurse a coffee the way she did. "So, while we're clearing the air...you and Mackenzie, huh?" she said. She laughed when I blushed. "She's a nice girl. I've always liked her. She's kind of weird, though. You two would make a good couple."

"Would have, maybe," I said with a sigh. "Pretty sure I torpedoed that possibility. Besides, she's way too cool for me."

"I don't know. You're pretty cool, too."

"I'll have to take your word for it."

"You should."

"Maybe I will."

She smiled, and I smiled back, and for the first time it felt like we were just two people, with no dividers between us, no subtext, no unspoken, invisible rules of etiquette and decorum to adhere to. Just us.

"So," she said, "where does that leave us?"

I was surprised she was asking me. "I honestly assumed you were never going to talk to me again. Seems to be the theme for me lately."

"Cameron." She fixed me with one of her "are you kidding me" faces. "I told you. I like you. You remember that conversation, right? All the stuff I said about not caring what anyone thought or what my friends said, I meant all that, and even if we aren't going out, or hooking up, I still want us to be friends. If that's okay with you, that is."

"Of course it is."

She smiled. "Cool."

I smiled back. "Cool."

CHAPTER THIRTY-FOUR

I went straight to bed when I got home, even though it was barely eight. I still wasn't quite sure what to make of my little chat with Karla. On the one hand, yes, I was glad we were on good, if tepid, terms however that ended up playing out in the real world. At least I didn't have that simmering on my conscience. That only left me with the fact that everyone else I knew hated my guts.

When Saturday rolled around I didn't bother getting out of bed. It was the first day of the con, and while I'd already re-signed myself to not going, the less of the day I was awake for meant less time to sulk about it. I might have slept through the entire day, had Cassie not poked her head in and shouted my name.

"What the hell," I moaned.

"Mom wants you. Downstairs."

I rolled over and checked my phone. It wasn't even ten yet.

"She say why?" What else could she possibly want? How else could she punish me?

"I dunno," Cassie said indifferently. "D'Anthony's here, though."

"What?"

I threw off my comforter, jumped out of bed, and bounded down the stairs. I couldn't think of a reason for him to be here, not when he should have been at Con already.

I entered the kitchen and immediately felt like I'd walked right in the middle of some joke. D'Anthony and Mom were sitting at the table, Mom with coffee, D'Anthony with a glass of milk. He was dressed as Speed Racer, with his blue polo and white slacks and little red ascot around his neck. His shiny helmet with the red *M* painted on the front was resting in his lap. He even had the yellow racing gloves on. I wasn't sure how he was going to get the helmet on over all his hair. He looked at me and clicked his tongue. "Still in pajamas, on a beautiful day like today? For shame."

I frowned, confused, and Mom shook her head with a barely concealed smile.

"What's going on?" I asked, directing the question at both of them, since they both seemed to be in on whatever the hell was so amusing.

"Your friend here ought to become a lawyer," Mom said with a chuckle. "He sure can make a heck of a case."

D'Anthony bowed his head gracefully.

"One day," said Mom, wagging a finger at me. "*One* day. Today only. You can go to MangaMinneapolis."

"Seriously?"

"*Only* because of Jocelyn's costume contest."

I stared, slack-jawed. I couldn't begin to think of something to say to that.

"I'd get dressed if I were you," D'Anthony stage-whispered.

"Oh. Right. Definitely. Thanks, Mom!" I turned around and raced back up the stairs, in complete and utter disbelief.

Twenty minutes later, I was climbing into the passenger seat of D'Anthony's van. Well, his brother's van.

"What the hell did you even say to my mom?" I asked.

He wagged a finger. "A good magician never reveals his secrets."

I buckled in. "Listen, man. I'm really sorry. About everything."

"Let me just ask one question. What was it like to *almost* date Karla Ortega? That's *unreal*, dude! How the hell did that happen?"

"By accident, really."

"Did you guys, y'know, do it?"

"No. We didn't."

He must've known from my tone that I wasn't going to say anything more about it, because he didn't pry for any more details. "I thought Lucas was gonna kill you. He still might."

"Eh, I'm not worried about it."

"Maybe…you should be? A little bit?"

I shrugged. "I sent him a text. He didn't respond, so whatever. Way I see it, if anything, Lucas knows he's done worse shit to me for a much longer time. There's nothing else he can do to me."

"Makes sense," D'Anthony said. He didn't seem quite convinced, but that was okay by me. It was my problem to deal with, and when the time came, I would face it with my head held high, and if he kicked my ass, so be it. It wouldn't be the first time.

"Hey, so, super odd thing happened yesterday," D'Anthony said, and something about his tone set me on edge.

"What happened now?"

"Naomi—you know, Caravan Naomi?"

"Yeah."

"Yeah, well, she came to one of our meetings. A G.A.N.U. meeting."

I couldn't tell from his tone whether that was a good thing or a bad thing.

"It was weird," he continued. "But not *bad*?"

"Huh." I was glad, honestly. "She's got a brother who's into *Dragon Ball*, remember? She's cool. She can be. I think you guys should give her a chance."

"Maybe," D'Anthony said. "I mean, at first I thought she'd come by as a joke, but she seemed nice enough. At least for now. We'll see, I suppose."

I nodded. That was enough for me. For now.

MangaMinneapolis was Minnesota's biggest anime convention. It was held at the Hyatt Regency, right smack in the middle of the city. It was a sight to behold—the streets crowded with colorful weebs, my people, en masse, the one time of the year where we could come together and bask in the power of our collective awesomeness. Being here made me all the more grateful that D'Anthony had somehow swayed my mom into letting me go, if just for one day. I would have hated to miss this.

"Thanks again, man," I said as D'Anthony maneuvered the car into a space in the ramp that I was almost certain was for compact cars. "I really appreciate this, and I'm sorry about all my bullshit."

"Dude." He put the car in Park, turned off the ignition, and looked at me. "If you apologize one more time, I'm going to lose my mind. It's over. I'm over it, you need to get over it. All you need to worry about is enjoying this con. Everything else will fall back in place."

"I hope you're right."

"I am. Let's go."

Stepping through the doors of the hotel into the lobby reminded me of how much I loved this con. The way it smelled: like hot glue and fabric and just a little bit of BO; the sounds: high-pitched shrieks, chortling laughter, and about a hundred different conversations happening at the same time. It was glory, pure, weebie glory, and I couldn't believe how close I'd come to turning my back on all of it. This was my home. This was where I belonged. Never had I appreciated that more than I did now.

We had a whole hour to spare before the costume contest, so we shuffled through the floor, taking it all in.

"Okay, here's something I need to ask you," said D'Anthony as we moved at a snail's pace. "It's extremely important, just so you know."

"Okay…"

He took a deep, dramatic breath. "Here goes. Is Vegeta, the Prince of Saiyans, a kuudere, or a tsundere?"

I rolled my eyes. "That's your extremely important question?"

"Jocelyn and I have been going back and forth on this for days! We *need* to settle this."

I sighed. In the anime world, -dere terms (tsundere, yandere, dandere, and kuudere) were archetypes. A kuudere was a character who was cool and aloof—on the outside. Deep down, though, they were warm, sensitive, and sweet, and typically as their story progressed the icy demeanor melted away to reveal the wholesome interior.

A tsundere was similar, except that instead of a cold, steely exterior, they were hotheaded and brash.

Vegeta had been introduced as a villain, obsessed with obtaining immortality and ultimate power. In his early appearances, he *was* brash and arrogant and hotheaded. But at that point in the series none of us knew about his deeper, better qualities, least of all him. It wasn't until his defeat at Frieza's hands did hints of his interior begin to surface. Each of those traits ticked off a box in the tsundere category.

But...

Once Vegeta sided with Goku and his friends, and made Earth his new home (albeit reluctantly), his hotheadedness simmered down to a slow boil, and his arrogance was less pronounced (though still very much in existence).

"He could be both," I said after taking some time to think about it.

"Oh no, nope, no sitting on the fence this time," D'Anthony said, shaking his head. "It's gotta be one or the other, man."

"Well, which point in the series are we talking about? He's gone through a lot of evolution. If you're talking about the Saiyan through the Frieza saga, I'd say he's a tsundere. But from the Android through the Cell saga, I'd say he was a kuudere. But then, he goes back to being a tsundere in the Buu saga. That's not even taking into account Dragon Ball Super, or *GT*."

"Whoa now, we don't talk about *GT*."

"That's true."

"Dammit, man," he groaned.

The costume contest was held on the third floor in a huge showroom with ugly industrial carpeting and those heavy burgundy drapes hanging from the walls. D'Anthony and I found seats as close to the front as possible, next to the runway. Once it was time, the lights dimmed, the DJ at the back of the room cranked up the hype music, and the announcer—some guy with a scraggly goatee, who couldn't have been much older than us—took the stage. After that, the three judges emerged from somewhere behind a curtain and took their seats along the stage, where they had a clear view of the contestants and their costumes.

There were something like fifteen contestants, and they ran the gamut from minimalist—like the Yoko from *Gurren Lagann*, who was essentially wearing a two-piece swimsuit; to the intricate—*Kill la Kill*'s Satsuki Kiryuin, in her full Kamui Junketsu, with the massive shoulder wings and all; to the massive—the towering Alphonse Elric from *Fullmetal Alchemist*, in his giant metal armor. This was stiff competition, but I was sure Jocelyn would win, or at the very least place in the top three. She'd worked too hard for too long not to.

It was equal parts cringey and hilarious listening to the announcer struggle through all the weird anime names. It was obvious this wasn't his usual crowd, but dammit if he didn't give it his all.

There was some quality craftsmanship on display here, but when Jocelyn took the stage D'Anthony and I whooped and cheered louder than anyone else. Seeing her fully assembled Gundam suit was incredible. It looked even better than I'd thought it would. I understood why she'd sacrificed so much time to complete it.

The only reason she walked away with the second place trophy instead of the first was because of the sheer size of the Alphonse Elric armor, and the wow factor that came with that. Still, she didn't seem upset. If anything, this was the happiest I'd ever seen her.

Once the contest had officially wrapped, the room turned into a madhouse as people climbed and clawed their way over one another to take pictures with the winners. Jocelyn was absolutely swamped. We didn't even bother trying to shove our way through the horde that swarmed around her. Ordinarily being surrounded by this many people would've driven her into a homicidal rage, but here, she was different. Here, she was the picture of collected poise, and I knew why: this was her element, where she belonged. It used to be mine, too, but I wasn't sure I deserved it anymore.

Eventually, the crowd thinned enough for her to move through. D'Anthony waved her over, and she lumbered towards us, using her long sword to clear the path ahead while holding her trophy on her shoulder to keep it out of harm's way.

"Told you it would happen," D'Anthony said when she reached us. "Better batten down the hatches, you're famous now."

"Whatever." She rolled her eyes, but she was smiling.

"Congratulations," I said, looking over her shoulder.

"Well, well, well, if it isn't Mr. Too-Good-For-His-Friends himself? I thought you didn't hang out with people like us anymore."

"I'm sorry. I didn't—"

She held up a hand. "Save it. I'm over it."

"That's what I said, too," chimed D'Anthony.

"Yeah, well, I don't hold grudges."

"I really hope not," I said.

It was too perfect. Jocelyn realized I was looking past her, and shuffled around to see what I was looking at. By the time she'd done that, Lydia was only ten feet away. She and I were almost the only people wearing regular clothes, but at least I had on a *Fist of the North Star* shirt. Lydia looked almost like she did all the time at school, only instead of her usual jewel-tone top, she was wearing a more subdued green. A green that was suspiciously close to the shade of Jocelyn's hair. She stopped, and they stared at each other in portrait stillness.

"Hey, Joss," she said in a voice barely above a whisper. "Your costume looks incredible."

"What's going on?" D'Anthony whispered to me. I shook my head and mouthed, *Tell you later.*

I watched Jocelyn to see what she'd do next. She looked unsteady on her feet, like she might fall over. "What are you doing here?" she asked. She sounded winded, but, thankfully, not angry.

Lydia risked a step closer. "I came to see you. To see your costume…is this okay?"

"Yeah?"

"That's our cue to leave," I told D'Anthony under my breath.

He nodded. "Sounds about right. We'll catch you guys later, then?" he said louder as we backed slowly toward the door and away from them.

Neither of them seemed to have heard him, and they were still staring at each other when we cleared the door.

CHAPTER THIRTY-FIVE

"Long story short, Jocelyn and Lydia used to date," I explained as we walked. "They broke up because Lydia wanted to hang with a different crowd, so I tried to convince her to try to reconcile with Jocelyn. Hopefully it works."

"That's…ironic," D'Anthony said.

"Tell me about it."

"And speaking of ironic…"

He slowed to a stop. The corridor ahead of us was crowded. There was a Princess Mononoke, a Ryu and an M. Bison from *Street Fighter*, and a Ken Kaneki from *Tokyo Ghoul*, with his massive, four-pronged kagune almost as wide as the hallway. A Kiki from *Kiki's Delivery Service* was half-concealed by one of its tentacles, talking to the massive Alphonse Elric from the contest. She turned around, and I gasped, at the same time my heart dropped to my feet.

It was Mackenzie. And now she was looking right at me.

"I'm, um, I'm gonna go…over there," D'Anthony said quietly, and he slipped away, retreating toward the end of the corridor, where he made a show of pretending he wasn't listening or hovering.

I prayed for a quick and sudden death—an aneurysm, or a heart attack, spontaneous combustion, anything—but I should have expected that the one time I wanted something horrible to happen to me, it wouldn't, and I was stuck there, caught like a deer in headlights.

She looked incredible. With her navy sundress, red flats and matching bow, and her straw broom, she was a spot-on Kiki. She looked at me now wearing her trademark indecipherable expression, and it turned my insides into frappé.

"I'm sorry," I blurted without preamble, because it was the most important thing I needed to say, and if she cut me off or didn't want to hear anything else from me—which would have been perfectly justifiable and completely what I deserved—I at least needed her to hear that much. "I'm sorry in the apologetic sense, and the I'm-a-loser sense. And I don't mean that in the endearing, oh-shucks way. I mean the kind of loser where it's really sad and totally embarrassing for everyone."

I knew I was rambling, but I couldn't stop myself now. "And you're just, *so* cool, and by *cool*, I mean in the James Dean as a geek way, and I like you a lot, and I've liked you since we started hanging out, and it took me this long to realize that, or understand what kind of 'I like you' it was, but I know now. Technically I've known for a couple of days now. I like you in the you're–my-best-friend way, and in the I-want-you-to-be-my-girlfriend way, and I get that I screwed things up between us, and I just… I want you to know how truly, deeply, stupidly, ridiculously sorry I am, and…and that's all, I guess."

I was no Mr. Darcy doing the smooth Hand Flex. I felt like I had just run a marathon. I probably would have gone on, but my lungs were completely deflated.

All this time her expression hadn't changed. Now she raised a single eyebrow. "You really think that's gonna work? Like, I'm just supposed to forget everything because you said all those cute things? Like, is this the part where we're supposed to kiss and make up? That's really what you thought was going to happen here?"

Suddenly, of all things, I was thinking about *Pride and Prejudice* again, specifically Mr. Darcy's desperate, heartfelt, and kind of awkward confession of love to Elizabeth Bennet. At least he'd been eloquent. I wasn't even sure what I'd just said to Mackenzie made any sense, considering that I'd just word-vomited at her. Which was probably why she was looking at me like I'd *literally* vomited on her. At least, that was the vibe I was picking up from her now.

I couldn't read her face. Her expression might have been one of annoyance or indignation or even amusement. "To tell you the truth, I didn't expect anything from you. I'm done expecting people to act a certain way, or be a certain thing."

I finished catching my breath. I realized I was doing the thing where I was just standing there past the time I should've bowed out, and that every second I stood here now was only making it weirder. This time, though, I was determined not to let the awkwardness of the situation reach critical mass.

"So…we're gonna go, I guess. It was good seeing you again. You make a great Kiki, by the way."

D'Anthony was still lingering a few feet away, pacing in a circle and acting like he was busy with his phone and pretending not to have been watching the entire time.

Maybe, in the end, things had come full circle. I had D'Anthony and Jocelyn. The status quo was still intact. Except, it didn't matter to me anymore. Maybe that was its power. Maybe the status quo was all in our heads, and only as ironclad as we allowed it to be. In the end, nothing had really changed, except me. Maybe this was what it felt like to level up.

"Hey, Cam."

I stopped and turned back around. Mackenzie was shaking her head, but there was a smile pulling at her lips that she was trying to bite back. "I'm not gonna be your girlfriend," she said. "But I can be your friend."

I stroked my chin and pretended to mull it over. "My best friend?"

She laughed. "You're a dork. Come on. You, too, D'Anthony."

She started walking, and when we caught up she linked her arm with mine. "People are gonna think we're a *Wizard of Oz* group," she said as we walked on side by side by side.

"Hold on, red shoes, red bow, blue dress, *and* a broomstick? Who else could you be but Dorothy?" I grinned.

She tugged at my arm. "God, you're such a dork."

"You're not wrong," I admitted. "I'm okay with it, though."

"I am, too," she said with a smile.

CHAPTER THIRTY-SIX

"If you're not ready to do this, I completely understand," said D'Anthony from the driver seat of his brother's van. He stared at me from the rearview mirror. "And I would not think any less of you."

"I might," Jocelyn said with a smirk from the passenger seat. "Just a little."

We were parked in front of the school with the engine running and the heat cranked as high it would go. "Putting it off will only make it worse," I said. "Besides, skipping school right after being suspended doesn't seem like a great idea."

It was Monday, my first day back since my suspension. The sun was up, but the sky was a flat, cloudless gray, and the ground was covered in six inches of snow from last night's storm. We were here earlier than normal, so there weren't as many cars in the lot yet, but the first buses were starting to roll in. I watched as kids unloaded, huddled in their coats against the cold. I wasn't sure how D'Anthony had convinced his brother to let him borrow the van again, but I was grateful he'd done it, and that he and Jocelyn had insisted on escorting me to school. I knew I didn't deserve it. I hadn't exactly been a great friend lately.

"Hey. Get this." Jocelyn turned in her seat to look back at me. She was wearing thick gloves, but she'd sewn conductive thread onto the fingertips so she could still use her phone without taking them off. "People are calling it 'The Triangle.'"

Jocelyn had taken it upon herself to stay updated on the latest gossip involving me, Karla, and Lucas, and apparently there was a lot to sort through. To those least familiar with the situation—which was most people—I was the home-wrecker, the one responsible for the implosion of Karla and Lucas's picture-perfect love story. Some people thought it was Lucas and I who had been secretly hooking up this whole time ("Kids actually ship you two now," Jocelyn had gleefully reported to me), and there were a surprising amount of people who were convinced that I was hooking up with both Lucas *and* Karla behind the other's back ("That's some fan-fiction waiting to happen," D'Anthony couldn't help but tell me after he was through dying of laughter).

It would have been riveting stuff, had it been about anyone else but me.

D'Anthony frowned. "*The Triangle?* That's unoriginal."

"And not at all accurate," I added.

"What would you prefer they call it?"

"I'd prefer if people didn't talk about it at all. It's over. Not to mention extremely embarrassing."

"You should enjoy your newfound notoriety," Jocelyn said. "Maybe we should make 'Team Cam' shirts to show our support. Oh god, are you the Edward Cullen or the Jacob Black in this scenario?"

"Nah, our boy Cam is definitely the Bella," D'Anthony said, which sent them both into hysterical laughter.

"You two are goddamn hilarious, you know that?" I asked, but I couldn't help grinning. This was nice. And besides, I'd earned a little ribbing. I only wished Mackenzie was here with us.

Jocelyn patted my knee. "Hey. Give it time. Something crazier is bound to happen sooner or later, and then everyone will forget all about this whole thing."

"Yeah," I said with a sigh. "Hopefully sooner."

I knew what it was like to be laughed at by a gym full of people, but this, being gawked at by *everyone* as I entered the foyer, was next level. It almost felt worse because at least when everyone was laughing, I knew where we all stood. I had no idea what anyone was thinking, or what they'd heard, or what they were saying to each other now. Everyone thought they knew something about me, and I couldn't be sure exactly what that something was, or which rumor anyone believed.

When the Caravan swept into homeroom, Karla wasn't with them, and neither was Lydia. I'd assumed that maybe Karla wouldn't be with them, but I was surprised and a little disappointed not to see Lydia. I felt like we'd started to understand one another over these last several weeks, and I'd hoped getting her to talk to Jocelyn again might have led to their patching things up. But, of course, Jocelyn hadn't mentioned her since the con.

I was completely caught off guard when Naomi entered

the room and, instead of taking her usual place at the Caravan table, walked straight over to where D'Anthony and I were already seated.

"I finished the movie," she announced. She was talking to D'Anthony, not me.

"What's the verdict?" he asked.

She reached into her purse and took out a Snickers bar, which she placed on the desk in front of him. "It was *so* good!"

"Yes!" D'Anthony shouted triumphantly. "See? Told you it was dope. Oh, we made a bet," he said to me when he caught the look of confusion on my face.

"Yeah, I told him how *Black Swan* was one of my all-time favorite movies, so he bet me a candy bar that I'd love *Perfect Blue*," Naomi explained. "Which I did."

All I could do was nod. This was surreal.

"By the way," Naomi went on, dropping her voice to just above a whisper and leaning toward me, "I hope you and Karla can work things out."

Very surreal. "I appreciate that, but we're really just friends."

She didn't look like she believed me. "Maybe, but I'm still shipping you two."

The warning bell rang, and Naomi turned and returned to the Caravan table. "What the hell just happened?" I asked in disbelief.

D'Anthony just shrugged as he peeled the wrapper off his newly acquired Snickers. "Brave new world, my friend. Brave new world."

"Well, well, look who it is," said Amanda when I arrived for the *Quill* meeting. "I suppose you don't know how lucky you are that they won't let us have a gossip column."

"You'd be surprised," I said, ignoring the fact that everyone was watching me as I slouched into a chair.

Amanda followed me and leaned against the desk I was sitting at.

"All jokes aside, people really liked your feature. Lots of people. Want to do another one? I just found out that the spring production is *The Importance of Being Earnest*, by Oscar Wilde, and I think you should document it again."

This was unexpected. I mulled it over. *The Importance of Being Earnest*—the irony wasn't lost on me. But to my surprise, I realized that doing another feature sounded...fun.

"What if Ken helps me out this time?" I asked. He was sitting across the room, not far enough to not hear our conversation. I saw his head jerk in my direction without looking at him. "I mean, he's always filming and taking pictures. How about we do a behind-the-scenes sort of thing? We could do live interviews, get footage of rehearsals, and post it to the website."

Amanda nodded. "That could be cool."

"If you think you could handle that, of course," I said with a sidelong glance at Ken.

Amanda looked at Ken, who was staring at me with a wary expression. "I like it," she announced, slapping the desk. "Make it happen."

Ken got up and scurried to me. "What are you doing?" he hissed.

"It's called extending an olive branch. You do know what that means, don't you?"

"Of course I do," he snapped, before backpedaling. "Thanks. Really."

I shrugged. "Don't mention it."

I didn't feel any animosity toward Ken. I wasn't convinced he'd meant any harm when he'd taken the photo of Karla and me. I couldn't even be annoyed that he'd tried to ask Karla out, because sometimes knowing someone failed so spectacularly was enough. Besides, compared to the other olive branch I needed to extend, this one was nothing.

"So, aside from all the gossip, did I miss anything noteworthy while I was suspended?" I asked as Jocelyn, D'Anthony, and I made our way through the hallway during passing time. We didn't have any classes together, but they were both still in escort mode.

"Aside from what I can only imagine is a disgusting amount of homework? Nope."

I really only asked to distract myself from the gawking, which by now was already old, but no less uncomfortable. This day was dragging, and the longer I went without seeing Mackenzie the slower time seemed to move.

"I started playing *Mega Man: Dr. Wily's Revenge*," said D'Anthony. "I heard it's supposed to be really hard, but we'll see."

"Cool. And…how's the rest of G.A.N.U.?"

D'Anthony cocked his head. "That's weird, Mackenzie asked me the same thing."

"That's because they're talking about each other," Jocelyn explained in a dry tone. "But neither of them wants to come out and admit it. And while it's been amusing watching you two flirt with each other all semester, it's getting a little tired."

"We're not…" I started. "I mean, she doesn't—"

"Yes, you do. And yes, she does."

"I don't understand."

"Me, either," D'Anthony added.

Jocelyn looked at us both like we'd just told her we didn't know how to tie our own shoes. "Okay, let me enlighten you, gentlemen. See, Cam, D'Anthony and I haven't seen much of Mackenzie lately. She hasn't really come to any G.A.N.U. meetings since last week, which—wouldn't you know it—coincides with your extended absence, and when she did pop in, it was always to ask about you. Follow me so far?"

D'Anthony and I both said, "Nope" at the same time.

Jocelyn gave a weary sigh. "Look, I know a little bit about carrying a torch for someone. Whatever the exact nature of your relationship with Mackenzie is, it's really obvious that you both really like each other. Eventually, you both are gonna have to deal with it."

"Speaking of…" D'Anthony jerked to a stop, and my heart leaped into my throat. Was it her?

My head swiveled, but when I saw what had made him stop I realized that it was the wrong Briggs sibling. Across the hall, Lucas was posted against the lockers with Lamont, Gerald, and Todd, along with a handful of other meatheads. As soon as they spotted me they started nudging each other and pointing. Lucas pretended not to notice me, but I could tell by the way his jaw was set that he'd seen me. A couple of months ago, this would've been perfect. I would have just walked right on past, grateful to have avoided another encounter with any of them.

But that was then. I'd known this moment would come. Eventually we had to cross paths again. But I wasn't dreading it the way I would have before. I was looking forward to it.

"I'll catch up with you guys," I told Jocelyn and D'Anthony.

They exchanged an uncertain glance, and I gave them what I hoped was a reassuring smile. "For real. I'll be fine. I have to do this."

Jocelyn looked at me like I'd lost my mind, but she nodded. "Good luck, Cam," she said before steering D'Anthony down the hall. I watched them go, then sucked in a deep breath and turned to face my destiny.

This was what Goku would do.

A hush fell over the entire group as I approached. Lucas still had his nose up in the air, refusing to so much as turn his head until I was standing right in front of him.

"Oh. You," he snorted, finally acknowledging me. "The hell do you want?"

"I want to apologize."

The others snickered and muttered to each other, but I tuned them out. This wasn't about them. "I'm serious," I insisted. "I'm sorry."

The others snickered louder. Lucas's expression hadn't changed. He stared down at me with his nose turned up, like I was an insect. But then he huffed, and stood up straight. Instantly, the whispers and the snickering stopped. Everyone stared at Lucas and me, waiting to see what would happen next.

"Gimme a second, y'all," he grunted.

The others passed disappointed looks among themselves, but they obeyed and slowly shuffled away, glancing over their shoulders in case something popped off.

When they were out of earshot Lucas crossed his arms. "You got something to say to me?"

He sounded annoyed instead of angry, which I took as a

good sign. "Look, man, what I did was messed up. Seriously. But it wasn't personal."

Lucas scoffed. "Oh yeah? You're saying this wasn't just you getting back at me?"

"No, because contrary to what you seem to think, my life does not revolve around you."

He cocked his head, like he was surprised at my audacity. I swallowed my temper. "Look, I'm sorry about Karla, alright? And I'm sorry about how I made Mackenzie feel. But I meant what I said about your sister."

Lucas uncrossed his arms and ran a palm across his waves. "You done?"

"Yeah. I'm done."

"Good." He shouldered his backpack. "Listen. We're not friends. Get that? But Kenzie says she's cool with you, so for her sake, I am, too. But I swear to you, if you fuck with her, I will end you. Do you get that?"

He was in my face, trying to intimidate me. I held my ground. "Fair is fair."

Lucas glared at me for a moment longer, but then he stepped back. "I guess you aren't the pushover I always thought you were."

As far as compliments went, that was pretty backhanded. But all things considered, this could have gone a lot worse.

By lunchtime I was either so used to people gawking at me that I wasn't noticing it anymore, or they'd already gotten bored with me and stopped doing it.

The cheerleaders and the band geeks, the debate crew and Robotics Club—they were all here, just like they'd always been. Everything was the same as it had been before. Except, it wasn't. It all felt different. New. Something about all of this had changed. Unless it was just me. Yeah, it was probably just me. Leveled-Up me. Cam 2.0. All New and Improved.

Okay, that was doing a *little* too much. But I did have a new perspective now. Looking at the theater snobs, I realized that they weren't just "the theater snobs" to me anymore. There was Naomi and Jackie and Kevin—people I'd spent weeks interviewing, observing, and, in some cases, even befriending. If I wanted to, I could probably go over there right now and eat lunch with them, and everyone there would be totally cool with it. That didn't mean I *was* a theater snob. It just meant that being one or not being one wasn't as important anymore, at least not to me. I had friends at that table, and I wondered how many other friends I could have at other tables.

And why one friend in particular wasn't at our table now.

A familiar commotion erupted at the entrance of the cafeteria as the student body council ushered in, with Karla in the lead, followed closely by Lydia. Maybe neither of them had been in homeroom this morning because they were prepping for this, and not because they were both avoiding me. There was a sharp inhale next to me, and I glanced over to see that Jocelyn was suddenly staring intently at her tray like it held the secrets of the universe or something.

Meanwhile they had gathered at the head of the cafeteria, and Karla had the microphone. "Hey, everyone, happy Monday," she said with her trademark cheer. I knew she was no stranger to rumors being spread about her, but it was still impressive how little the latest gossip seemed to have affected her.

"Just a couple quick things, and I'll be out of your hair, I promise," she began. "First, prom is coming up fast, and tickets go on sale tomorrow. We're taking a dollar off the total for every canned food item you bring in. As a reminder, please, *please*, make sure the food you bring in isn't expired."

Some people laughed, but I did not see which part of that was supposed to have been funny.

"Hey, do you think Karla is gonna start coming to G.A.N.U. meetings?" D'Anthony asked.

"Nah, probably not."

Despite everything we'd gone through together, and despite the fact that we were friends now, I couldn't picture Karla hanging out with us. But that was okay. We could be friends without being best friends, without hanging out with the same people or being into the same things. I understood that now.

Once she was finished making her announcements, Karla gave one last smile before handing off the microphone and crossing to the exit. As she passed our table her eyes met mine. She smiled and raised her hand, like she was about to wave, but instead her fingers formed a Vulcan salute.

I did a double take, unsure of what I'd just seen, and she was already gone.

I guess this really was a brave new world.

"Okay, so answer me this," said D'Anthony as he ran his pick through his hair. "Is it better to watch anime, or read manga? And yes, there is a right answer."

From the other side of the tech lab Jocelyn groaned. "That question makes no sense. None."

I'd been looking forward to this. My first G.A.N.U. meeting since I'd been suspended, but instead of waiting until

Friday Jocelyn and D'Anthony insisted that we should meet today, in celebration of my "triumphant return." Whatever that was supposed to mean. Things were a little different from how I'd imagined they'd be. For one thing, Jocelyn wasn't working on anything with the 3D printer. Now that the con was over and the next one wasn't for another six months, she was taking this time to recover. D'Anthony's Game Boy was suspiciously absent, too. *Sailor Moon Crystal* was playing on the wall-mounted TV. I recalled that he didn't like that version as much as the original, so I would have been confused as to why he was watching it so intently, if not for the fact that Naomi was sitting right next to him. She raised her hand like we were in class. "Isn't that like asking if you prefer the movie or the book the movie is based on?"

"Kind of," D'Anthony allowed.

"And the book is always better," Jocelyn declared.

"Yeah, if you feel like waiting an eternity for new manga to be released, or translated. Meanwhile the anime adaptation is already finished with multiple seasons."

"Yeah, seasons with plots that completely deviate from the source material."

"They do this all the time," I stage-whispered to Naomi. "Sometimes it's best to ignore them."

The door opened, and I bolted upright in anticipation. But it was Lydia who stepped quietly into the room.

"Hi, everyone," she said in the ensuing hush. She hesitated in the doorway for a second before shuffling over to where Jocelyn was and plopping down on the stool next to her beanbag. I glanced at D'Anthony, who was already staring at me with a "What's going on?" expression on his face.

Naomi leaned over and mouthed *What's up with this?* to him, and when he shrugged, she turned to me. I pretended not to notice.

The door burst open again. My heart jumped in my chest as Mackenzie sauntered in, and my face flushed with embarrassment. She paused in the doorway, her eyes falling on Lydia and Jocelyn in their corner, then to D'Anthony and Naomi on their beanbags, and then she cut across the room and slouched into the chair across from mine and pulled out a plastic bag full of apple slices. "What's up, everybody? Welcome back, dork."

That last part was directed specifically at me.

"Look who's talking," I replied.

It was absolutely ridiculous how happy I was to see her, and it dawned on me then that maybe I'd always felt like this. I'd always told myself how much I didn't like Mackenzie, but I think that might have been me trying to convince myself of something I knew wasn't true. I'd been trying so hard to dislike her because I thought I was supposed to. But I was done caring about how things were *supposed* to be.

Suddenly, Jocelyn sprang to her feet. "I'll catch up with you all later. Movie night tonight? My place?"

"Where are you going?" I asked as she ushered Lydia, who looked just as confused as I was, toward the door.

"I gotta take a shit," Jocelyn fired back.

"Gross," Lydia said with a grimace.

"I think that might be code for 'hanging out with my new girlfriend,'" Mackenzie said with a sly grin.

Jocelyn and Lydia both blushed. "Actually, we're going to work on some preproduction stuff for the play," Lydia stammered.

"Just ignore them," Jocelyn muttered as she hooked her arm in Lydia's and hauled her quickly out of the room.

Damn, they were totally cute together.

The room was quiet again, except for the sound of the movie playing and Mackenzie's crunching.

"You like apples?" I asked her. As far as conversation starters went, it was a definite swing and a miss.

"Sure," Mackenzie answered. "My mom used to take me apple picking at this orchard in Saint Paul. We'd go on hayrides and drink hot cider. It was dope. My favorite kind is Honeycrisp. Did you know they were developed by the University of Minnesota?"

"I did not."

"Yep. They were."

"Apple picking and hayrides in an orchard sounds amazing."

"Have you ever been?"

"Nah."

"We should go."

I did a double take. Had I heard her right? "Yeah?"

She nodded. "I'll take you. The season's over, though, so it'd have to be next year. If you're still around, I mean," she added quietly.

"I'll probably be around. I mean, if all goes according to plan, I'll be going to the University of Minnesota myself. Maybe I'll end up engineering a new kind of apple."

Mom couldn't afford to pay my tuition. Cassie and I had always known that. Cassie was doing fine with her scholarships, grants, and working part-time and living at home, so I figured I'd be okay going that route if I wanted to.

Mackenzie smiled at me, and it made my stomach flutter.

"What about you?" I asked, clearing my throat. D'Anthony and Naomi were too wrapped up in the movie to pay any attention to either of us. "Are you planning on being around?"

"Most likely. I'm trying to get into the Art Institute. I've looked at other places, but honestly I think I like the city too much to want to leave just yet."

"Sounds like graduation won't be the last we see of each other."

"Sounds like it," she said with a nod. "Hey, Cam?"

"What's up?"

"Try not to get into any more trouble, because prom is coming up, and I'm gonna need a date."

I grinned. "I'll do my best."

Karla had once said that everyone was weird. I hadn't believed her at the time, but I did now.

And you know what?

There's nothing wrong with that.

★ ★ ★ ★ ★

ACKNOWLEDGMENTS

I don't think it's possible for me to put into words the gratitude and appreciation I have for the people who helped bring this book to life, but putting things into words is something I'm supposed to be good at, so here goes:

To everyone at Inkyard Press for taking a chance on me and believing in this book, these characters, and this story.

To Stephanie Cohen, my amazing editor. This book wouldn't be what it is without your encouragement, insight, and enthusiasm.

To Emily Forney, my agent, who is quite literally the most awesome person on the planet. You are literally my hero.

Frank Ocean, Miss Lauryn Hill, the Notorious B.I.G., and so many other artists that helped shape this novel.

To Akira Toriyama. If it weren't for Dragon Ball I don't know what type of person I'd be today. The same goes for

Hayao Miyazaki and everyone at Studio Ghibli, and so many others.

To my agent siblings. You all are not only some of my favorite people, but some of the most brilliant writers I've ever known. I love you all.

To all of the cosplayers I've had the honor of calling my friends. Your passion and creativity and dedication to your craft are awe-inspiring.

To Jane Austen, who still influences everything I write.

And finally, to the Geeks and the Nerds and the Dorks out there.

Thank you. Each and every one of you. Sincerely, truly, and deeply. Thank you.